ONE

"Are you sure you're ready for this?" Kate Conrad asked from the edge of the bed, a tentative smile forming on her cupid's bow lips.

"I'm so ready," Christine George said, leaning back against the headboard, eyes closing, right hand reaching forward.

"It's kind of a big deal," Kate pressed, that smile that had been waiting emerging. "I mean, I know it's been a long time since you've done this with someone."

"Just give me the damn coffee!" Christine retrieved the mug from Kate's hands—black coffee, one sugar. The menswear poplin shirt she'd worn the night before draped her figure, unbuttoned to the third button, sleeves rolled up to her elbows. Her hair had grown over the summer, the tousled bob she'd sported months prior becoming ponytail worthy, its grey-flecked cinnamon a sign of wisdom, she told herself. And willingness to age gracefully.

Raindrops tapped on the bedroom window, puffy grey clouds reminding them it was the day after Labor Day. Fall would be there soon, and the rain would settle in like an old friend who'd come to visit for the weekend and neglected to leave.

Just like that, with the delivery of a mug, things were how Kate thought they should be. Rain tapped the window. Hunter and Dallas were sprawled on the floor, their black and yellow Lab noses sniffing the air for overdue breakfasts. She was cuddled with the charming woman she'd pined for all summer, covers pulled to their waists, leaning against the headboard. They were participating in a simple morning ritual that takes place around the globe: Having coffee. Kate had wanted for so long for coffee in bed with someone she *wanted* in her bed. All the anxiety and worry about what to do with her life and with whom she should spend it evaporated with the first sip of her daily French roast out of one of the many mugs acquired on trips to ski towns, beach towns, and big cities. This one boasted, "Moonlight Basin—Your Side of the Mountain." There must've been two dozen mugs from her travels in the cupboard, maybe more.

"I'm so glad you took the day off with me. I've been looking forward to this moment with you." Kate sunk deeper into the pillows, a hand finding short blonde locks for the first time that day—if her fingers were correct, her hair was a disaster. And she didn't care. The nervousness in her stomach that had followed her when Christine was around had been replaced with a sense of calm, of comfort.

"Me, too. You only get one first time with someone." Christine winked, raising her mug in acknowledgement. "It's nice to just be 'Chris' today, not 'Dr. George.'"

"Who said you have the day off from playing doctor?"

"Kate!" Christine laughed.

LONG DISTANCE RELATIONSHIPS

A.K. ROSE

ISBN: 9798528928524

Cover design: Angela Curran

Printed in the United States of America

For my mother,
who taught me how to be strong,
kind, and unstoppable.

"What? Maybe I need a cardiologist. I have a bad heart. It's been broken too many times, and it needs to be patched back up." Kate grinned—that was clever, she thought. And true.

"Yeah?"

"Yeah. And then, this woman I met over the summer did a number on it. It was really broken, only to be saved by a sexy doctor who tripped me on a hiking trail. So really, she tried to kill me before she saved me!"

"Ouch." Christine mimed a dagger to her own heart, head falling back against the headboard from the impact. "But I deserved that. I'm sorry I sent you so many mixed signals. I wasn't ready and—"

"Don't apologize! I'm only kidding! As my mom always told me, it works out in the end. And I'm so happy you stayed last night."

"Me, too."

"What do you say, wanna play doctor with me?" Kate wouldn't let that idea go so soon—it was just too easy.

"I get to be the doctor," Christine put her coffee mug on the nightstand, the little chuckle that punctuated so many of her sentences appearing again.

"And what do I get?"

"You'll see."

"I like where this is going—" Kate pulled Christine in for a kiss that brought back the nerves in her stomach and sent electricity through her veins. What was a summer in the scheme of a lifetime? In that moment, the mixed signals, the trying to be friends, the bad dates with others all disappeared. In that moment, the pause button in Kate's mind took over, and she forgot everything—except the one thing that mattered: Christine liked her, too.

# # #

Across town, Liza Barrett had been up for hours, spinning her way through the boredom of riding a bike inside on the trainer she'd already brought to Nathan Stapleton's house, her impending move just around the corner. The race of her lifetime—the Ironman World Championships—was in six short weeks, and rain or no rain, she needed a ride that day. Her competitors didn't care that the rainy season was starting in Seattle, or that she needed to move before the race, or that her boyfriend was about to leave for California to try and be a rock star.

So, in Nathan's basement she pedaled with her phone mounted to her bike, an old Ironman race video playing to motivate her. She liked to pretend she was in the race, adjusting her gearing to match what she might use for the terrain being shown.

As she pedaled, she thought about the future. She and Nathan had a few more days together before he headed to San Francisco to spend time with his new agent to begin his transformation into Nate Staples. Perhaps it was good that they were both occupied—she could focus on training, he on his music. They'd meet up in Kona and stay for a week to unwind and relax. It seemed like they'd been going nonstop since they'd gotten together—they'd gone from old friends to *together* in one night, to the mania of her race schedule and his band schedule, not taking time to date or have a honeymoon period.

Sweat dripped from Liza's body onto the mat below the bike, her defined muscles accentuated by the glisten, her head of fiery red hair bowed as she concentrated. The 3-hour session was almost over—time to give it everything. When she looked up, a text popped on top of the race video:

We're going on a date tonight. I'll pick you up at 6. It would be okay to dress a little fancy. ❤

# # #

The first day of school was a blur, year in and year out. As Emily Hall rushed around the kitchen in her old Craftsman style home, she thought about what lay ahead: new students, new names to remember, new books to teach. Though she got older every year, the kids stayed the same. Names changed, hairstyles changed, teenage slang changed, but every year her students were age-locked copies of those before them. Those she'd taught her very first year were in their mid-30s, and thinking about that fact opened a rabbit hole she didn't want to dig. As her own son aged, time passed at warp speed. Angus would be driving soon, which meant he'd be graduating soon, which meant—she didn't want to think about it.

Her first day of school outfit showed off her sewing skills. Over the summer, she'd made a new forest green skirt with deep pockets to hold dry erase markers, phone, work badge, and her notoriously nervous hands. She'd pulled her russet brown hair into an updo, applied some modest makeup—a little neutral eyeshadow, some mascara. Dabs of concealer covered the hints that she'd stayed up too late the night before at Kate's Labor Day party. Pouring coffee into her travel mug, Emily yelled upstairs to her son. "Come on, buddy! Let's go! I can't be late and it's raining—traffic is bad!"

Angus wasn't alone in his tardiness. Even the birds were slow to get their days started. The active Townsend's warblers who liked to sing outside her windows were either sleeping in or had begun their migration out of the impending rainy season. It seemed even they understood the rule, as with Labor Day, so went summer. Without saying a word, Angus appeared in the kitchen, looking dapper in khaki pants, button-up shirt, and a blue sport coat. His normally wild mahogany hair was combed flat, with a defined part to one side. He'd skipped the jeans and polo his mom had set out the night before.

"Wow, you look so handsome! What's the occasion?"

"Nothing," Angus said, hands tucked into his pockets with thumbs draped outside.

"Okay, if you say so." Emily reached to smooth the shoulders of his blazer; the scrawny little boy she'd known was becoming a muscular man.

"Mom! Don't wrinkle me!"

"Sorry! So, what's her name?" That had to be the reason for the snappy first day outfit.

"Mom." He wasn't going to talk about it.

"You used to tell me things."

"There's nothing to tell." Angus shrugged and grabbed the brown sack that held his lunch from the edge of the kitchen counter. "Let's go."

No amount of badgering would get more information out of her son; it was pointless. Thinking that he'd set the stage for her day, Emily grabbed her handbag, flipped off the kitchen lights, and followed Angus out the front door, travel mug in hand. Teenage angst was the theme of the day, and it would be the theme of the quarter. She'd decided to teach *The Catcher in the Rye* that semester, its angsty first-person narrative a favorite amongst her classes. After teaching *The Great Gatsby* the year before, it was high time to move on from unrequited love to general teenage anxiety. *Gatsby* had hit a little too close to home, her own struggles with unrequited love running in parallel with Jay Gatsby's. And while his story had worked itself out, hers was still in progress. It didn't matter; she was done with that, anyway. The unrequited love. The pining over someone who didn't know she existed. The fantasies and "what ifs." Instead, she'd stumbled into love on the inside—for herself. Without the drama of dating, she'd found space to write her first novel; she was already starting to think about and work on her second. Without worrying about dating—getting to know someone enough to meet for drinks, reading and mis-reading signs, determining if she wanted to see them again—she had so much more time to think about writing. Which was what she told people she wanted to do. She was an English teacher studying to be a writer, she said.

With Angus dropped at the curb near his school, Emily travelled over the floating bridge that connects Seattle to its sister city and looked south. Mt. Rainier was absent from the day's commute, hidden by puffy grey clouds. In bumper-to-bumper traffic she sat, thinking about her lesson for the day, which had been planned out months prior. She didn't expect much of the first day—it was a "getting to know you" day. So, she'd planned an ice breaker activity for the students—a disguised attempt to help herself remember their names. Their assignment was straightforward, but not simple: write at least two paragraphs about their summers in the form of a story narrative, wherein they were the protagonist.

Emily had issued this assignment every school year for the past several, but realized she'd yet to complete it herself. With time to think in the car, she worked through the assignment in her head. If the students had to do it, she should, too.

Emily Hall was torn. No, torn doesn't begin to describe it. She was borderline distraught, her mind and heart at war over a woman who didn't know she existed. She tried to push it down. The yearning. The desire. The fantasizing. But she wasn't strong enough to beat back the thoughts that worked their way into her mind, leaking through pinholes in the dam she'd built around her feelings for Liza Barrett.

Her rational mind told her she had a life to lead and a son to raise and students to teach—she should focus on those things. But her hopeful heart told her she should try to get closer to Liza and see what happened.

So she did.

And what happened was . . . nothing. And everything.

She spent the summer finding ways to run into Liza. She held her cards close. She dated others. But her heart wasn't in it. Emily was certain there was one person for her. And that one person happened to find her one person that same summer. Surprise: It wasn't Emily!

Filled with emotions she couldn't parse, Emily did what felt natural: She wrote. And wrote some more. And before long, she had a finished novel, a publisher, and a plan for more. Which goes to show you, things don't always work out like you hope. Sometimes they work out better.

"Sometimes they work out better," she said aloud to an empty car, reiterating the point of her story. So things didn't work out with Liza. That false start led her to something much more important: herself.

# # #

"San Francisco, huh?" Tyler asked as he fished wire through the hole in the floor joist Nathan had drilled for him. They'd been at it for an hour, drilling holes and pulling wire for a whole house re-wire in the posh Madison Valley. The old Prairie-style home still had knob-and-tube wiring from its original construction in the 1920s and it was being completely replaced.

"Yep," Nathan said, crawling forward to the next joist. The low space overhead allowed for an Army crawl, and either drill lying on his stomach or back—nothing more. "For a few weeks. Then, we'll see."

"Are you going to cut a record?"

"Not yet, but I hope so."

"Dude, that is so awesome." Tyler grunted as he pulled the wire through one more hole. One more bay down, only two dozen to go. He could do the job by himself, but it was more efficient to have help, especially in the tight quarters in which they were working. "I wish I could sing. Singers always get the ladies."

"I don't know if that's true."

"It's true. Come on, man. Look at any lead singer—and then look at the hot chick they have on their arm. Singer equals babe magnet."

"Okay," Nathan said as he drilled, the whir of the blade cutting through wood reducing his obligation to continue the conversation.

"I mean, I'm sure you have women beating your door down, don'tcha? You have that rock star look thing and you're all pretty and shit. I bet you have a new chick every weekend. And two on Sunday."

"Nah, it's not like that."

"Why not? You're missin' out!"

"I have a girlfriend," Nathan said, matter of fact, scooting forward to the next joist. Drill, scoot, repeat. Focus on the work, he reminded himself.

"So?" Tyler pressed. "Have a girlfriend. And a groupie or three."

"I don't want to. Liza's my person. Period."

"Sorry, man. Didn't realize it was like that. I was just daydreaming through you. It's been a while's all. Liza have any friends who like dudes who are good with their hands?" Tyler laughed at his own joke, baritone voice surrounding them, his hands showing the effects of crawling around in the dirt under someone's house. Regardless of how good he was with them, they were filthy.

"Liza's friends are probably not your type." Nathan smiled to himself as he drilled the last joist, aided by the light of his headlamp. Liza's friends were *definitely* not Tyler's type, unless Tyler's type were lesbians. "Why don't you just hit the apps? I'm sure there are plenty of women who like a dude who's good with his hands."

Working his way back across the crawlspace, Nathan was drawn to the entry hatch like a moth to a flame. He saw daylight again, the opening to the outside an invitation to freedom from the damp, dark bowels of the old house that was standing between him and time away. He and Tyler would be there two more days, and then it was time to head to California to work with Julian DeMarco, his new agent. Julian had told him they'd work on his image, meet with some potential band members, maybe cut a couple demos. They'd hone his sound, build marketing materials, and get ready to find him a label.

"I'm gonna head on up and start on the walls, okay?" Nathan shouted back to Tyler, his lanky body already halfway out of the crawlspace, senses ready to escape the smell of soil and sawdust. He'd planned a special evening with Liza that night, and the faster they finished for the day, the faster he could set the wheels in motion.

Looking at the electrical plan, Nathan pulled his ballcap down tighter over shaggy chestnut hair—no place for rockstar hair on a job—and located the areas he needed to drill holes to pull wires. As he drilled, he thought about what was next with Liza. She was moving in soon—in fact, she'd be moved in when he got back from California. But after all the buildup that got them together—the years of wondering and hoping and not knowing—to move in together after a summer of dating with no fanfare to mark the occasion just didn't seem right. He felt they'd been robbed of a mutual decision that, *yes*, they'd like to live together. Yes, they felt secure enough in their relationship to co-mingle their books and bowls, to share a bathroom, to give up the autonomy that comes with living separately. Kate's impending Montana move threw a spanner in the works—Liza was out of a home and his only made sense.

Drilling into an old plaster wall in an old house, superfine dust filling the air around his body, he realized he needed to formally ask Liza to live with him. It was a big milestone, and it should be treated that way. He'd do it that night. When they'd gotten together, she'd done the asking. It was his turn.

TWO

"Is this fancy enough?" Liza asked as she turned in a full circle in Nathan's kitchen, the sleeveless little black dress she was wearing hugging her muscular physique and showing off her defined shoulders and triceps, knee-length cut highlighting her calves. She'd taken him seriously when he said to get a little fancy for their date, a rare opportunity to dress up when it wasn't for work, for photographing someone else's wedding. Her short red locks were elegantly styled and parted, simple diamond studs sparkling in her ears.

"Wow," Nathan said, instantly feeling underdressed, the dust of a hard day's work still on the worn knees and shoulders of his work clothes. "You look amazing!"

"Aw, thank you." Liza flashed her perfect, all-American smile—she was even wearing lipstick. "If you play your cards right, you may be able to convince me to take it all off later . . ."

"That's good to know, because I'm an excellent card player," he said, bringing forward the right arm he'd been hiding behind his back to reveal a single red rose. "Give me 15 minutes and I'll pick you up for our date."

"It's a deal. You won't have to go far! I'll be here. Perk of living together," Liza said, pursing her lips and placing a kiss on his cheek. "But hurry! I'm hungry."

Liza was always hungry.

# # #

Nathan returned in a slim-fit navy-blue suit, tie almost exactly color-matched to his steel blue eyes, the blue-on-blue outfit a vast departure from his favored plaid and Levi's look. He'd also done something he hadn't expected: shaved. His beard was as reliable as his buffalo plaid—a signal to himself and the world that that he was living his truth—and he'd let go of both for the evening.

"So handsome," Liza said, "Your face! Come here and kiss me with that smooth chin."

Not wasting time, Nathan held his head high, normally shaggy mop of hair well under control thanks to hair product and strolled across the kitchen with one hand in his pocket, as if he were in a fashion show. Slipping his hands around her waist, he pulled her close, lips meeting with the warmth of a desert sunrise.

"Mm," she sighed, and he drew her closer, the aromatic cedar scent of his aftershave enveloping her completely.

By now, they'd kissed hundreds of times; there wasn't a surprise waiting, the tension of the early days had evaporated and transformed itself into a reliable electricity. A steady source of power. A comfortable connection. But there was something different in this kiss. A newness. Like seeing an alpine lake in the height of wildflower season, vivid and bright, colors bursting from all angles, Liza saw Nathan in a new light. It wasn't the suit and tie. It wasn't the smooth face. There was something *new* about him. Was it confidence?

"I'm going to miss you while you're gone."

"Me, too. I wish you could come with me."

"I know. But we'll have a whole week in Kona after the race, just us. Thinking of that'll get me through. And, we have tonight. Why are we dressed up, anyway?"

"You'll see," Nathan smiled.

# # #

"Alright, what can I help with?" Christine asked, pretending to roll up the sleeves on the T-shirt she'd borrowed, her little dog, Sadie cuddled on the couch beside her.

They'd spent most of the day in bed, but evening was looming. Rain tapped on the roof and windows as filtered grey daylight faded to darkness, providing a romantic soundtrack to their so-far lazy day. A big pot of chili was simmering on the stove—they'd made it together, laughing and joking and stopping every so often to make out. Kate always said the beginning of a relationship was the most fun, and this one had been so much fun. They had a few more precious hours together to not think about work.

"I don't even know where to start," Kate said with a sigh, petting Sadie's fluffy apricot coat, her own Labs curled up on the floor near her feet.

"We'll start at the start. You've probably got to clear out all the personal things first, make it more neutral so buyers can envision themselves living here."

"You sound like a realtor!"

"Oh, I could be a realtor. I love old homes. If medicine doesn't work out . . ." There was that signature chuckle that punctuated Christine's sentences again. A reminder that she had a serious job, but she didn't take herself seriously.

"Okay, I think you're right. We can box up some books and records."

"Great! I can't wait to sift through your books." Christine rubbed her hands together in anticipation. "You can learn a lot about a person by the books they've read. Or pretend they've read."

"Oh yeah?"

"Yeah," Christine said, standing and pulling Kate up from the couch with both hands. "So much. Now, go get me some boxes. This is going to be fun!"

The last thing Kate wanted to do was box books, but that's what she needed to do. She had three days before the townhouse went on the market, so she went to retrieve boxes from the garage, three dogs at her feet. It was Hunter and Dallas's standard practice to follow their mom when she changed rooms—you never knew when food might drop—but Sadie was a fresh addition to the room-changing parade.

"Aw, Sadie loves you," Christine yelled as she dragged a couple of dining room chairs to the built-in bookcase that held Kate's collection, its floor-to-ceiling frame displaying hundreds of titles. As she pulled books off the shelf, one-by-one, she narrated. "Romance. Romance. Hm . . .

very suggestive romance. 'Effective Java.' 'CSS and beyond.' 'Coding with Python.' You have quite an eclectic book collection. Romance and computers."

"So, I'm a sucker for love and geeks," Kate said as she returned with a pile of copy paper boxes and dropped them at Christine's feet. "Keep looking—there's more to me than just romance and work. I'm gonna make some coffee."

From her kitchen, Kate watched as the woman who'd been in her head all summer wore her T-shirt and sifted through her too-big book collection. As happy as she was to have a new beginning—the start of a life she was making for herself, on her own terms—these casual, unplanned moments were fleeting. The easy togetherness they'd experienced all day would soon require Facetime and flights—the anticipation of time spent together longer than the actual time spent together.

"This one's so good."

"Which?" Kate asked, wondering if maybe she wasn't the only romance novel fan.

"'Rising Strong.'"

"Ah, you found the self-help section."

"I did. Lots of Brené here. I approve. And what's this one? 'When Love Leaves?'"

"Oh yes. My post-divorce instruction manual."

"Ah. You know, I don't know her, but I can say with certainty that you're better off without Jen. The woman I'm getting to know is strong and sexy, and more than a little loveable. I don't wish the pain of loss on anyone. But I'm not unhappy it didn't work out."

"Well, thank you," Kate said, offering a steaming mug and sitting in the chair next to Christine, the little butterflies that had been living in her body for months taking flight again, her stomach full of nerves. "There've been times I haven't felt like any of those things—a lot of times—but, I do when I'm with you."

"That's sweet—you're sweet, you know that? You come off all hard-nosed and driven, but there's softness to you, too, and not just when your accent comes out." Christine continued to stack books in the copy paper box at her feet, stopping to push her red tortoise shell readers up into her hair. "Though I do love that accent . . ."

And with that statement about her southern roots that only showed up when too much booze did too, Kate was again swept away in the warmth of a kiss. For a moment, they were back on Christine's couch, lips meeting for the first time, water rushing over the edge of a cliff and filling up all her senses. This woman's touch lit her skin on fire, her kiss the spark that started the wildfire that raged in Kate's heart. She had it bad, alright.

"So, what have you figured out about me from my book collection?" she asked when they parted, patting down the little hairs on her arms that were on full alert.

"Oh, this is easy. You're a hopeless romantic who believes in self-help. You have a pile of biographies about soccer players—so you're definitely a lesbian, if all the girl-on-girl love stories didn't give it away. You're a not-so-secret computer geek, and you love to hike. With all those hiking guides, I'd think you *were* a hiking guide. Am I close?"

"Yep, that's me in a nutshell. We don't need to do the records now—you've written my unofficial biography!"

"Oh, I think we need to do the records!"

Under the dim light of a floor lamp they worked, filling boxes, laughing, draining their cups of coffee. All the while, the playlist Kate had created for her Labor Day party the day before piped through the whole-house speaker system, filling the air with local music and those who'd made it beyond the Northwest music scene, mixed in with Kate's favorite country songs. She loved her country, but her playlist revealed a wide variety of music. As they boxed records, one of her favorite Maplewood songs played.

"Dance with me," Kate insisted as Nathan's former band's biggest song played and reminded her how different her life had become since their show at the Tractor Tavern. It was only two months before, but felt like an eternity. All she'd wanted was to find her person—the one sent for her, just like in the song.

"Oh, I don't know, I don't really—"

"Please? Dance with me."

As the wind blows through the canyon,
As the sea washes over sand
As the mountains rise-up and stand there,
I look at you and know there is a plan

As they swayed in place, socks gliding across hardwoods, mere millimeters separating their bodies, stacked boxes and sleeping dogs the only observers, Kate's head fell to rest on Christine's shoulder. Hands interlaced as comfortably now as the first time they'd touched, Kate breathed in the smell of bodywash from their earlier shower together, the familiar scent of linden filling her with each breath. This song got to her every time. And she wondered, had she found her canyon? Her haven from the wind, her mountain-top view? Was this going somewhere? Could it stand the time and space of . . . time and space? Or was it destined to run its course as so many others before?

"I could get used to this," Kate whispered.

"Me, too. Thank you for the dance. And the amazing 24 hours. I meant what I said about thinking you're strong and sweet—and sexy as hell. Just so you know."

# # #

Nathan parked his truck in a garage on 3rd Avenue in the heart of Downtown Seattle. Full of office towers and close to Pike Place Market, it wasn't an area of town either of them frequented; he was confident his surprise was still a surprise, though Liza had been grilling him since they'd left home. Where were they going? What were they doing? Were they meeting people?

"Seriously, you can tell me now," Liza said as she slid off the truck seat, high heels hitting concrete with a soft thud. Even with four-inch heels, she was a good half-foot shorter than her date. "I really have no idea."

"Just wait, it's a surprise," he insisted, offering a bent arm to escort her out of the dimly lit garage.

As they walked under an umbrella to preserve their outfits—unheard of for locals; Locals don't use umbrellas!—they talked about the logistics of the next few days: him, finishing that job in the Madison Valley; her, packing her belongings at Kate's.

"Here we are," Nathan said as they stood on the corner of 2nd and Union, streetlights illuminating a fine mist raining down on the sidewalk.

"We're going to Target?" Liza stared at the bright red bullseye sign she was facing. Certainly, she hadn't dressed up for a Target run.

"No! We're going here—" Nathan turned her trenchcoated shoulders to reveal the backside of Benaroya Hall, home to the Seattle Symphony.

"Oh my God, really?"

"Yep. We're having a proper date," he said, guiding them around the block to the building's glass-clad front, to the rows of double doors that awaited. Nathan opened a door for her with one hand and closing the umbrella, following her in. "I hope this is okay—it's Vivaldi concertos."

Nathan knew it was okay.

It was one of the best surprise dates he could've planned. One of Liza's moms was a classically trained violinist and played with the Boise Symphony for most of her childhood. She herself had been in her high school orchestra but gave up music when she went to college on a cross country running scholarship. Liza couldn't do both at a top-level and had chosen sport. She was a deep well of classical music knowledge, though few knew it. Nathan knew.

"It's more than okay." Liza smiled as she grabbed his hand and squeezed. "I haven't been to the symphony in . . . I don't even know."

Liza did, in fact, know the last time she went to the symphony. In an instant, her brain took her back to a young woman in the lobby of Benaroya Hall, alone, crying, and defeated.

The last time she'd been in that spot was the night she and her most significant girlfriend had broken up. The night she realized long distance wasn't working, and the end of something that had needed to end for a long time. Set to Mozart, their five-year relationship came to a dramatic end, with Jackie leaving the symphony hall in her rental car and Liza having to call a cab—a reminder of just how long ago that really was; it was pre-Lyft.

They'd met in college in Seattle—both cross-country runners and had lived together for several years when Jackie moved home to Minnesota to care for her ailing mother, to whom she was not out.

Liza was initially supportive of the move—she understood an only child moving home to care for a sick parent. Who was she to deny someone the right to care for their mother? But trying to have a long-distance relationship with a person four states away who was living with her mother and in the closet proved problematic. Visits were few. "I just can't explain it to Mom," Jackie would say when Liza wanted to visit, and something similar when Liza asked her to come to Seattle. They'd gone from living a life together—sharing daily struggles, celebrating little victories, having dinner together—to very much separate. She tried to be patient, understanding, but Liza hated it. It wasn't what she wanted, and that night at the symphony, she realized she no longer loved Jackie—how could she? They didn't even know each other anymore. In that lobby, she ended it.

Years later, she'd come full circle. The same place under different circumstances.

She was back in the lobby of Benaroya Hall, socialites dressed to the nines milling about, standing in line at the bar with someone new.

Someone who was about to embark on a career move that would most likely put them in a long-distance relationship. Though her face may not have said it, on the inside, she was scared. She didn't need her sports watch to know her heart was in her zone five—almost freaking out zone. She coached herself with something Kate had told her, "Nathan's not Jackie; You're not the Liza who was with Jackie," and forced a smile. Took a sip of the red wine that had somehow landed in her hand. Looked around.

"Should we go find our seats?" Nathan took her hand in his. His hand felt good holding hers—strong, comforting.

Walking towards the doors that led to the actual hall, Liza heard her name called. And then, again. As she turned to look, a former wedding client revealed herself.

"Liza, hi!"

"Oh, Deidre! So good to see you," Liza kept smiling, offering a half hug—they weren't friends worthy of a full-contact greeting. "Where's Anna?"

"Oh, she's in the bathroom. She has pee anxiety—has to go several times before anything where she's pinned into a row of people," Deidre laughed, her curly brown hair shifting on her shoulders as she did. Certainly, this was understandable. Certainly, she hadn't shared far too personal information about her wife with the person who'd photographed their wedding.

"I totally get it," Liza smiled. "I do that before races. This is my boyfriend, Nathan."

"Oh!" Deidre said, extending her hand to shake. "I'm so sorry. I thought you were—"

Liza stood, squeezing Nathan's hand just a little tighter as Deidre tried to walk back what she almost said. The pink presenting itself on her cheeks said enough, as she struggled to find words that wouldn't make this situation more awkward than it already was, her body beginning to lean the opposite direction in search of an escape route.

"Family?" Liza finished Deidre's thought. "I am. Nathan is *too*."

"Oh, right. Geez, I'm so sorry. It's not my business. I shouldn't have interrupted your evening. You look gorgeous, by the way."

As fast as she appeared, Deidre and her thoughts vanished.

"*That* was awkward," Liza said as they walked into the auditorium.

"Well, she was right about something," Nathan said, bending to kiss her cheek. "You do look gorgeous. I can't wait to get you home."

THREE

Friday night at Prospect drew a large crowd, its prime location off Greenlake Drive making it a social hotspot. Nevertheless, the universe provided Kate and Liza their regular booth right when they wanted it, the people just beyond the window playing their roles in the friends' ongoing story. Walkers and their dogs, runners and their goal paces, cyclists and their flashing lights existed in harmony, circling the 3-mile perimeter trail with a comforting familiarity.

"I'm gonna miss this," Kate said, looking outside to the show unfolding. Same story, different day.

"For sure," Liza said. "This, and having the pool so close. Can't beat walking across the street for my swim workouts."

"You can't. Would you believe—eight years here and I've never swam in that pool?

"I'd be surprised if you had!"

"True."

"So," Liza said as she scanned the room for their server. She'd run 14 miles that day—she needed food. And soon. "The house is on the market. It's getting really real. How ya doin'?"

"I don't know—"

"Hey, ladies, know what you want?" The server appeared, pencil behind his ear, tight white t-shirt's sleeves folded precisely twice, gum-smacking in time with the beat of the Nirvana song filling the air.

Aside from the overall feeling of accomplishment from swimming, biking, and running, one of Liza's most favorite side effects from her sheer volume of exercise was she got to eat (mostly) whatever she wanted. She didn't believe in wasted calories. But she did believe in burgers. And, on days like this, fries. One glass of wine at the symphony and a burger here wouldn't kill her, or her Kona splits.

"I'll get that right in," the Ken doll look-a-like offered as he strutted off.

"Thanks," Liza said over her shoulder to his back; he really was getting it right in. "Okay, let's try that again, I'll be a much better listener now. Why don't know you know?"

Kate took a deep breath and let it out slowly. "I do know, I guess. It's kinda mixed. I'm doing it. I know I *want* to do it. I'm aware of the privilege that's letting me do it. But damn. For once, I wish I could have it all, all at the same time."

"That's the rub, isn't it?"

"Yep. I had a good job and a good house, but not a lover. Now, I'm quitting the job and selling the house, and I got the lover. I mean . . . what does it take to have them all, all at once? In the same location?"

"You're asking the wrong person." Liza raised her voice to compete with the overhead music and crowd, the steady din of conversation escalating. "If I knew, I'd have it all, too."

"But you kinda do have it all. Solid relationship. You work for yourself. You landed on your feet with a place to live."

"Yeah, but—it's not *my* place. I'm moving from your house to Nathan's house. I've never had my own place. I've always lived with someone, except when I lived alone in my and Jackie's place. You can't have all three. Who do we know that has it all? I don't think it's possible. It's like the Triad of Impossibility."

As Liza outlined her theory, Kate got it—maybe it *was* the Triad of Impossibility.

"Are you okay moving to his place? I didn't even ask."

"Oh, yeah. Totally okay with it. In fact, he was so sweet. He took me on a surprise date to the symphony a couple nights ago."

"Symphony? How was that?"

"Well . . . he doesn't know the whole Jackie thing, so that's good. It was weird to be there. My stomach was nervous the whole time, just remembering, you know? Muscle memory. But it was Vivaldi," Liza closed her eyes as she thought through the music, taking a beat to remember the concertos that took the audience through all four seasons via violin. "It was so lovely. After, we went for a nightcap and he asked me to move in with him, officially."

"Wow, you went for a nightcap?"

"Come on!"

"Oh, I'm just kidding. That *is* sweet. I didn't realize it was in question though," Kate said, mouthing "thank you" to the server who'd just placed a salad in front of her.

"It wasn't, but I thought it was adorable that we got all dressed up and went to the symphony, and then he got all serious, and was like, 'I have something I want to ask you.' His hands were shaking when he asked, as if I would say anything other than yes. I mean, of course I was going to say yes!"

"He loves you, Liz."

"He does," Liza said, taking a bite of the much-anticipated burger. It was everything she'd hoped it would be.

"You still worried about the distance thing?"

"Oh, hell yeah. Going back to Benaroya brought all that back one hundred percent, but I kept reminding myself he's not Jackie. I'm not me from back then. But, yeah, I'm nervous."

"And you're not going to tell him about her?"

"I don't think it matters."

"Okay, but you're nervous, and that's a big reason why. Don't you think it might help to talk about it?"

"I don't know. I mean, he knows about Jackie—not everything, but it's not like we haven't talked about it. It's more like, you know when you have something you've wanted for a long time—and it's real—all you can think about is not losing it?"

"I know that one," Kate said, as she watched a woman with a cute yellow Lab walk in front of the window, holding its leash in its mouth. Almost as cute as her yellow Lab, Hunter, she thought. "I know that feeling exactly. I'm in it right now."

"And?"

"I'm terrified. But trying to enjoy it."

"I wonder how many relationships we've fucked up by getting too in our heads?" Liza asked.

"More than I care to admit."

"Yeah, me too. It's going okay with Christine?"

"It's going better than okay. Which is maybe why I'm scared to leave, I don't know. Out of sight, out of mind . . ."

"Oh, crap," Liza said as Kate finished her thought.

"I know, but that's where my mind goes."

"No, not you!" Liza whispered, for no reason. It was plenty loud in there—no one was going to overhear her. The sound system and '90s grunge music made sure of it.

"I'm not following. What?" Kate asked, looking over each shoulder.

"Twice in one week—I can't believe it."

"Liz, you're doing that thing again. Where you think I'm in your head. I need more."

Liza tried to make herself as small as possible, hiding behind her glass of iced tea as she told the story of running into Deidre at the symphony, her confusion around why Liza was with a man, the whole awkward mess of it. And while she had nothing against Deidre, she didn't really need to engage with her again—so soon, or really, ever.

"Too late," Kate observed as she watched the brunette make a beeline in their direction.

"Perfect," Liza said, her head bowing toward the table momentarily so she could gather her thoughts. "Deidre! Fancy seeing you here!"

# # #

She sat in the tiny speakeasy, pot lights in the ceiling illuminating a half-dozen bar-height tables—not a window to be found. Its décor purposely trying to look old, its clientele the same. A quick scan of the techies and yuppies revealed Emily Hall was by far the oldest in the joint, her martini simple compared to the custom concoctions being created at the mahogany bar beside her. She shifted on her stool—crossing her legs left over right; right over left—trying to look casual. She'd let her shoulder-length hair down, leaving the "I'm an English teacher" updo behind for the evening. It was Friday, and the first week of school was officially in the books.

"Hi!" Jen said as she whooshed in from behind, satchel over her shoulder, big smile on her face, designer jeans on point. "So glad you found it!"

"Oh, it wasn't that hard. I only walked past here three or four times!"

As opposed to their first meeting location—a well-signed and well-known cat café, Washboard and Vodka was neither signed nor widely known. On purpose.

"Sorry about that—they're trying to be all 1920s secretive. Let me get a drink and we can go through the edit." In minutes, Jen held a classic—dirty martini, extra olives. "Before we start, congratulations are in order. Cheers to you and your first novel!"

"Cheers to that! And to the simplicity of ordering a martini in a speakeasy. I like your style." Emily smiled as they clinked glasses.

"For sure . . . we're a little old school for this place, but who cares? So, I talked to the editor this morning," Jen started, all business. "This'll seem like a lot. But try not to get overwhelmed—it's mostly easy fixes. Typos, style, that sort of thing. There's only one major item, and that's about building up Sam's motivations earlier. We agree you need a couple more chapters that let us get to know her and her relationship with Jasmine more before the rising action of the accident."

"Fair enough." Emily attempted to project confidence while mentally digging the arrow out of her heart. She hadn't planned on writing *new* content.

"Alright, so—" Jen clicked and swiped the tablet that had appeared out of her bag, "here we are. You'll see he's marked up typos and style directly in the document. Easy. And here," she said, continuing to swipe, "he's left comments where you need to expound more. And here—he's marked through extraneous content that either doesn't add value to the story or muddles the readability."

"Wow," Emily said, noticing that her pages were extensively marked up, even more than she corrected most student papers. "That does seem like a lot."

"It does, but trust me, it isn't. It's just part of the process."

"Right."

"And that's about it. Pretty straightforward, really. And—the look on your face is exactly why I like to meet with writers in person for their first edit, when I can. Tell me what you're thinking."

"Oh, sorry." Emily's martini was drained. She'd drank her way through the feedback. "It's just—it's fine. It's a lot, but it makes sense."

"Yeah, exactly," Jen said, "but trust me when I say the book is going to be better. This really isn't bad feedback. I could tell you stories . . . but I won't. This is a good book. It's solid. For a debut novel, you knocked it out of the park. Most authors only have one book in them, but I don't think that's the case. I think you're at the beginning of something big. So, enjoy this time. You're unknown. No one's waiting on the book—we have time to get it right. Let's get it right."

In this scenario, the roles were flipped. Jen was the teacher, Emily the student. All she could do was nod along and smile, and cross and re-cross her legs, looking for that place on the stool that conveyed casualness and comfort when she was feeling neither.

"All good?"

Emily noticed the blue of Jen's eyes dancing in the overhead light, the glasses she'd been wearing were now pushed into locks of board-straight auburn hair. Her eyes were gentle, kind. The soft smile on her face and the little dimple in her left cheek helped sell the message—it was really going to be okay.

"All good."

"Great," Jen said, placing her hand on top of Emily's. "Get me the edits back in two weeks, and we'll keep moving forward. I'm sure you have other plans tonight, so I don't want to keep you."

"Oh, you're my only plans tonight. Besides patching my slightly bruised ego," Emily laughed a little too hard.

"Well then, I know the best recipe for fixing bruised egos—even if they shouldn't be. Another drink?"

Over fresh martinis—gin, not vodka, they agreed—Emily and Jen talked. About day jobs and dream jobs and what it might be like to not need a job. About Angus's increasing moodiness and how it fit in with the novel Emily was teaching that semester, her own little Holden Caulfield becoming more and more distant. They discussed Jen's dream of having a family, the fits and starts of fertility treatments and IVF. The years she'd wasted looking for the "one." And, about whom they knew in common. The community was small—certainly, they had mutual friends.

And there it was.

It was going to come up eventually.

"It" being the fact that Emily and Jen's ex-wife were friends. Which shouldn't matter. Why would it matter? From what Emily understood, their relationship was a distant memory. Kate had confirmed as much—they were married once, but she harbored no ill feelings towards her ex. Certainly, as the one who'd left, Jen must have felt the same.

Emily wouldn't let on that Kate was still searching for the "one," or that she'd carried a lot of pain from the direct way in which Jen had ended their marriage. But she needed to tell her, right?

"I think we do know one person in common." Emily turned the base of her martini glass, the energy buzzing in her hands finding its way into the conversation. Her mind couldn't overrule her nervous system.

"Really?"

"I'm friends with Kate." No going back now.

"Kate?"

"Conrad."

"Oh! *That* Kate!"

"Yeah, that Kate."

"Wow."

"I didn't know how to tell you—or if it was important to tell you. She knows about my book, so she kind of knows about you, but not really. I haven't said anything beyond publishing." All the sudden, the pot light above seemed to be a high-powered spotlight, and the heat was on Emily's ears and cheeks.

"Oh."

"I mean, I assumed it would be okay to talk about the book with her—"

"It is, it is," Jen dismissed with the wave of a hand. "You caught me off guard with that one. I haven't come across Kate in—it's been years. How's she doing?"

Sitting in the awkwardness of telling her publisher that she was friends with said publisher's ex-wife, Emily couldn't help but wonder what went wrong in their relationship. They were both good people. Smart, engaging, considerate. What had driven them apart? She knew what ended her marriage: she was married to a man and undeniably gay. But what drove apart two people who had at one point loved each other enough to fight for the right to get married? To leave the state to actually get married when it was legal? There had to be more to it than the temptation of a hot firefighter.

"She's good. Busy."

"That's all you're going to give me after *that* news? 'Good' and 'busy'? Come on, how *is* she?" Jen insisted.

"Well . . . she really is good. She just bought a ranch in Montana. She's leaving Seattle."

"*Kate* is leaving Seattle?"

"She is. Leaving her job and taking some time away . . ."

"Wow. I can't believe that, but good for her."

"I'm a little jealous, if I'm totally honest. I'd love to run away to Montana for a while," Emily said, the freedom of full days to write without other obligations a mere dream. "You're not upset?"

"About?"

"That I'm friends with your ex-wife? It's a little weird."

"Oh God, no. I'm glad she has friends like you. You're exactly the kind of friend I wish for her. And I'm glad she's finally taking a risk."

There was something in Jen's tone—was it longing? Reminiscing?—that told Emily she really was happy for Kate. And there was something in Emily's head that wondered—and then scolded herself for wondering—if she was imagining something in Jen's gaze. Was there something more than a business bond forming? Jen's hand landed on top of Emily's several times while they'd talked. Maybe she was just a touchy person? Maybe, it was her way of offering comfort? Or was there more?

FOUR

It was his first time in San Francisco. And California, for that matter.

His mind held images of what to expect—pastel colored row houses, hills upon hills that put Seattle's to shame, that famous bay and its more famous bridges. Beautiful sunsets and beautiful people. Television and movies had programmed his brain with scenes and snapshots. Songs directed him how to arrive ("be sure to wear some flowers in your hair"). Social media provided smiling photos of strangers standing on the lip of a streetcar, holding the little pole, perhaps a rogue foot dangling off the edge. He'd envisioned a place of culture and wealth and overt queerness, but so far only seen camera-laden tourists and the all-too-familiar tech bros that were commonplace back home.

Standing in front of the rental his agent secured, Nathan Stapleton breathed deeply. Enveloped in gasoline and salt air, he faced a Queen Anne style walk-up mere inches from its neighbor, which was mere inches from *its* neighbor. The building had potential, but the years hadn't been kind. It could use a good pressure washing and fresh coat of paint. In a past life, it had been a pale green color, but was now presenting grey, like the sky. Perhaps, it was foreshadowing. Perhaps, the sky was a reflection of the uncertainty he felt deep inside.

His gut was giving him advice to turn on his heel, get back in a Lyft, and fly home. If he left right then, he'd be in Seattle in time to snuggle into bed with Liza, a full weekend ahead of them, governed only by her workout schedule and where they could secure brunch reservations.

And yet.

He stood in the discomfort. He waited.

Nathan watched as a twenty-something woman in Lululemon pushed a baby jogger up the hill, unfazed. Sitting on the no-longer-white marble stoop, he pretended he lived there. Because—for the next six weeks—he did.

I made it, he texted Liza, along with a selfie of himself sitting on that grubby old stoop, guitar case leaned against the wrought iron hand railing. *Home for now. I miss you already! XOXO*

He didn't tell her he hadn't summoned the courage to go inside, or that every fiber of his being told him to come home before he'd even started. Instead, he called his brother-from-another-mother. Charles Martinez would be the help he needed to get past this blip. Certainly.

"Hey, Nate," Charles answered, his gravelly voice unmistakable.

"Hey!"

"You make it to San Fran?"

"I did. I'm sitting on the stoop outside my apartment," Nathan said, kicking fallen leaves that were gathering around his feet, red Chuck Taylors otherwise spotless. He'd polished the white toe boxes and soles that morning.

"And?"

"Oh, it's—" his voice trailed to nothingness, words escaping him.

"What's wrong?"

"Nothing."

"Okay? Then what's up?"

Nathan hesitated. And then, "I guess I'm wondering if I'm doing the right thing."

Silence. Hushed Spanish. Breathing.

"Did I lose you?"

"No, still here. I was coaching myself to not chew your ass out! You broke up the band to do this, so you'd better fuckin' do it!"

"I know," Nathan said, head bowed as he stared at his leaf collection. The wind was whipping in the canyon created by the row houses on either side of the street.

"Dude, I can't even! This is the opportunity of a lifetime—do it. Plus, I'm counting on you—I'm still your drummer, you know."

"I know," he repeated. "I guess I'm just nervous. I'm sitting outside this old—like really, really old—house, and nothing looks familiar. And it kinda smells like pee and dirty diapers. I'm feeling alone, that's all."

"Well, only one thing to do, right? Hang on a sec."

Charles was talking to someone in the background, but Nathan couldn't make out what he was saying.

"Okay, I'm back. Anyway—"

"Did I interrupt something?"

"No. Yes. But, no. I met this guy and—"

"Uh huh. Got it," Nathan laughed.

Charles was doing what Charles did. "You know how it goes."

"I do. So, you were saying—only one thing to do?"

"Yeah, dig deep in that lonely little head of yours and write a new song. Everything lately has been all lovey-dovey. We get it. You love Liza. And that's great. But it's time to find the angst, bro."

Just then, one of Nathan's new neighbors walked over him on the stoop, the obstacle course of luggage and a guitar case not a deterrent. Without a word, he put his key in the front door dock, turned it, and slammed the door behind him.

"Wow. That was rude," Nathan said. "Oh, the neighbor, not you. This guy literally stepped *over* me, like I wasn't even here. Geez. And yeah, that's a good idea."

"It's not rocket science. You're a songwriter in a new situation. Write a song! But really. Try to enjoy yourself. Get settled. Have a drink. Go to the Castro—there's a bar—*Brazen*. The bartenders are friendly. Go hang out. Where's your place?"

"Umm, The Mission. Close to Julian's office. It's—not what I was expecting."

"Okay, well remember it's a place to sleep. You're in one of the best cities in the world. Get out and see it. Talk to strangers! Get some culture! You'll live, I promise. You'll probably write some damn good songs, too."

"I'll try."

"Dude, no. Just like Yoda said, 'there is no try.' Do! I gotta go. Emory wants to go to dinner, but seriously. This is a gift. Don't fuckin' blow it, okay? I'll see you in a couple weeks—get some songs ready for our demo session."

"Heard," Nathan said. "Thanks. Go have your dinner. Tell Emory it was nice to not meet him."

"Fuck you."

"Nah, that's okay. But talk to you later. Love you, brother."

"Love you, too."

Nathan stood, dusted himself off, and slipped the key into the lock.

# # #

Alone in the near-dark, only the dim glow of the Tiffany light on the end table guiding her, Christine George flipped pages in a tattered photo album.

Sadie tucked in a tight ball at her side, cushy leather couch hugging her body, she nursed a glass of Merlot, and talked to Meg.

And cried.

It was a ritual they'd done for years. Workweek complete, responsibilities covered, they had a standing date to talk about the things they always talked about. New developments in their worlds. The serious and silly, significant and sordid. For twenty years, no matter where they were in the world, they came together on Fridays. When other days fell through, when medical emergencies interrupted or national security intervened, whether in the same state or different, they found a way to talk on Fridays.

Now, four years after Meg's death, Christine still held her Friday night date with the love of her life. In the beginning, Meg was easier to summon. Christine felt her presence in the conversation—and in the room—even if it was one-directional.

Lately, it seemed she was losing Meg. She still talked to her. Still told her everything. But the signs that Meg was there were fading. Christine had draped Meg's flight suit on the cushion next to her, but its scent—sweat and baby powder—had all but disappeared; the warmth of her spirit sucked from the air.

"I miss you so much," Christine said, blinking back tears, looking at a photo of the two of them from the early days—just babies. Babies so clearly in love. "I miss our life together. I miss hearing you bounding through the back door, knowing you were running to get to me. I miss hearing you call me 'Chris' and the way you made my coffee just right, every time. I miss holding your hand and hearing you laugh. God, I miss that laugh."

Right about then was when something would happen to show Christine she was heard. A floorboard would creak, the furnace would turn on, the record would need to be flipped. But this night, Meg was quiet.

"I suppose you know I've met someone. We never talked about what we'd do if one of us outlived the other. It seemed implausible. Remember how we were going to die together, Thelma and Louise style? You had me convinced that jumping out of an airplane without a parachute was how we should go, holding hands all the way down. And you went and jumped out of an airplane alone? What the hell, babe?

"I will always love you, deep in my heart. In a place no one else can access. But my love, are you mad about Kate? Please don't be. She's good. She's kind. She's helping me find something close to 'happy' again. I haven't been in a happy place since the day Rog called me with your news. We're taking it slow. In fact, she's moving to Montana soon— maybe that's a sign that you approve? The whole long-distance wrinkle?"

Sadie's apricot fluff was soft and comforting. Christine petted her and waited, turning the page every so often. She steadied her eyes on a photo from Christmastime: her, Meg, and Meg's sister, Jess, all sitting in Santa's lap at a mall in San Diego. The Palm trees behind Santa were lit up like Christmas trees, California warmth radiating through the celluloid. All three were cracking up in the photo, and the look on the Santa's face was priceless. He obviously wasn't sure how much longer he could hold three adult women in his lap; his eyes big, smile forced.

The whir of the garage door broke her trance, and seconds later, Jess was standing in their living room, knee-high leather boots, skinny jeans, and slouchy knit purse slung over her shoulder. Long strawberry blonde hair hitting her mid-back, she looked like she was going out, not getting in. Even if you saw them side-by-side, you'd never guess she and Meg were sisters. She'd moved in when Meg died—togetherness helped them both.

"Hey, you okay?" Jess flipped on the overhead light, illuminating a cross-legged Christine on the couch.

Jess showing up at the precise time she'd asked for permission to date Kate had to be the sign. She hadn't seen her in at least a week, their opposing schedules rarely aligning.

"Yeah, I'm okay."

"Need to talk?"

"Maybe. I'm trying to talk to Meg, and dammit, she's not answering."

"She gets like that," Jess said, sitting on the couch and putting her arm around Christine's back. "What's up?"

As they sat, Christine explained everything. She'd become close with Kate, the woman they'd met camping over the summer. Much as she'd fought it, there was something there, and she wanted to explore it. She didn't want to live her life alone. She'd met someone with whom she enjoyed spending time, who was fun and smart and totally different from Meg. Kate was moving to Montana in short order, which made things feel normal—if a little rushed—and in the midst of it, she thought she was losing her connection to Meg.

"You'll never lose your connection to Meg," Jess said. "She'd want you to be happy. I know it."

"I know . . . I just don't know how to be happy and honor her impact on my life."

"Chris! You honor her every single day. She was lucky to spend her life with you—you've done your time. You have my blessing to see where it goes with Kate. I know you already are, but trust me, it's okay. No one's going to be mad at you or think you loved her less. Mom and Dad would agree. We all know how much you loved her. It's time."

"Thank you," Christine said, her head falling to Jess's shoulder. "You showed up at exactly the right time. I was starting to think I'd lost her. And you've proven she's still listening."

"It's so hard," Jess said. "I miss her every day. But her free spirit is in me. It's in you, too."

"It is."

"And for what it's worth, I really like Kate. She's her own person. I can tell she's smart enough to keep up with you."

"She is."

"Then, see where it goes. And if she hurts you, she'll have to answer to me. I may not look as tough as Meg, but I grew up fighting her—I had to be scrappy!" Jess hugged her sister-in-law and stood to leave. You want the lights back off?"

"Nah, I think it's time to live in the light." Christine wiped the tears from her eyes. It *was* time.

# # #

When Kate awoke Saturday morning, she had two priorities: coffee—and a second cup of coffee. The filtered light sneaking through the bedroom window told her it was morning; the clock on the bedside table revealed three hours to spare before she had to be elsewhere for the first of two open houses that weekend.

She'd been awake into the early hours of the morning packing, stacking boxes, and checking items off the action list she'd created for her move. Based on the schedule, she had three weeks to get everything she wanted to take to Montana into a container scheduled for delivery the following Monday. Not wanting to wait until the last minute, she'd started queuing boxes in the garage. With Tetris-like precision, she stacked. At the same time, Liza'd been stacking her things on her side of the garage. Her movers were coming Sunday morning—so though she mirrored her friend, she did it at Liza-speed—fast, and faster. If Kate's pile was Tetris, Liza's was Leaning Tower of Pisa.

Mindlessly flipping through her phone as the coffee brewed, Kate leaned on her kitchen counter and caught up—if one could ever catch up—on the comings and goings of people she knew on social media. Knowing someone on social media didn't necessarily mean "knowing" them. Truth be told, she didn't care who was out with whom, who had the best selfie, or whose dog was the most adorable. Okay, maybe she did care about that last one. She'd hesitated to post her own life updates until she was sure they were happening. But now, garage full of boxes, townhouse on the market, ranch set to close in less than a month, she was confident. Her realtor had sent a photo of the "For Sale" sign in front of her future ranch with the big, bold red-lettered "SOLD" flag nailed to it. Maybe it was time to tell the world she was on the precipice of big changes?

Posting before coffee was ill-advised, but she did it anyway. She'd resigned from her job the day before—what did she have to lose now? Engineer humor on full display, she posted the photo:

I bought the ranch. Not that ranch. #theregoestheneighborhood #montanabound

Then, she texted Christine good morning, just as she'd done every day since they'd gotten together. She liked having someone to say "good morning" to, enjoyed the rituals of waking up and going to sleep, knowing the person she was thinking of was thinking of her.

Good morning, good doctor. Speaking of doctors, I have a check-up at 2. See you for dinner tonight! XO

She'd left only a few mugs unpacked to get her by until the move—her favorite three. That day's was from back home in Tennessee. She'd gotten it on a day trip to Dollywood in her early 20s and still loved it. It had a silhouette of Dolly Parton on a cream background and the quote, "Find out who you are, and do it on purpose."

She was trying to do just that.

FIVE

In the packed University Medical Center waiting room,
she—well, waited. For almost an hour. When a gruff voice from the back repeatedly called for "Katie," she looked around the room for the source of the summons. No one else had stopped their scrolling—it had to be her.

Please, God, let it be her.

"Kate?"

"Oh, yeah, sorry. Kate," he said, stepping out from behind the swinging door where he'd been standing, revealing a tall goateed man with powder blue scrubs. "Come with me."

As instructed, she followed Goatee to the exam room, answered a litany of questions about her medications (none), alcohol consumption (um . . . some), and current relationship status (unknown, but hopeful)—probably not what he was looking for with the question. She was weighed and blood pressured and temperatured and given a reflex test, then left to change into a gown. Which put her back on her phone, scrolling, bare feet dangling off the edge of the exam table. Her morning post had twenty-five likes and a handful of "congratulations" and "what?!" comments from friends, and a novella from her mother about how she proud she was of her only daughter.

Finally, for the second time that day, she heard her name.

"Kate?" the voice asked as a white-coated, dark-haired, middle-aged man entered. This one, goatee-less.

The start of her appointment notwithstanding, the first few minutes she spent with the doctor—not *her* doctor, the first available—were as expected: *No, she didn't need birth control. Yes, she was sure. Yes, she understood that meant she could get pregnant. No, she wasn't worried. Why? Because she was gay. Yep, that does make sense.*

The great birth control debate concluded, her height/weight ratio was a concern, the doctor said as he looked at his clipboard, single page folded over top; she could stand to lose 10-15 pounds. Twenty would be better.

As he lectured about eating less and moving more, she sat engulfed in the generous hospital gown and remembered why she rarely took the "first available" physician. This doctor was the worst kind: pleasant while delivering judgement. His tone was upbeat—he could've been wishing someone a happy birthday as much as lecturing them about their BMI. His message was judgey and unnecessary—she knew she could spare a few pounds. Regardless, this was an extenuating circumstance. She wanted peace of mind that her health was at least reasonably good before moving to Montana.

"Montana, huh?" Dr. Lawrence looked up from the clipboard. If his white lab coat hadn't held a nametag, she would've already forgotten his name. "I grew up in Bozeman. My sister still lives there. Doesn't understand why I moved to Seattle. Why I'd put up with the crowds and the traffic. But I love it here. I need a big city."

"Yeah, I get it," Kate said, happy to talk about anything but her hip-to-waist ratio or how many servings of alcohol she consumed in a week. "That's exactly why I'm leaving. I need away from the city for a while. What's your sister do? In Bozeman?"

"Oh, she's some sort of marketing type. I don't really know, I'm ashamed to say. We're not terribly close. We stick to common ground—horses and cowgirls. She doesn't need birth control, either." His laugh was familiar. And, he thought he was funnier than he was.

"Horses?"

"Yeah, she's big into the dressage circuit. I have a horse in a stable out in Woodinville. Just ride for relaxation, though. We grew up riding." Dr. Lawrence was writing something on the top sheet of his clipboard, a signal that her appointment was ending.

"Jennifer?"

"Wow, that's weird," he said, eyes suddenly disinterested in the clipboard and focused on hers. "How'd you know?"

"Believe it or not, we met on the plane when I was coming home from house shopping. She was kind and listened as I talked way too much about whether I should move."

"She was in Seattle?"

Apparently, the Lawrence siblings *really* weren't that close.

"Yep. A couple weeks ago."

"Wow again," Dr. Lawrence cleared his throat, the "mm-mmm," serving as his segue. "Well, Kate, it was nice chatting with you, and I hope you have a great move. Aside from working on the weight, everything else checks out A-OK. I'd like you to do a blood panel just to be sure, though. You can schedule that with the receptionist. I'm going to email you a referral to a GP in Bozeman. Med school buddy. She's top notch."

And with that, she was told to dress and leave when ready. Left to navigate the maze of hallways that led back to the lobby, Kate made two left turns, and then questioned those turns. Had she turned right twice, or just once, on the way in? All the hallways looked the same—bright white walls, bright white lights, bright white floor. It was like an intelligence test for mice—find your way back to the cheese!

"Oh, sorry," the woman said as she brushed Kate's shoulder with hers, her closing speed too fast to re-route before bumping the stranger in her way.

"No worries." Kate looked in the woman's direction, getting why anyone would be in a hurry to get out of that place. As she looked, her eyes focused on the blur of a woman in designer jeans and a bright red button up top, black leather boots, shoulder length tawny hair combed straight.

Was that? It couldn't be.

But was it?

"Jen?"

"Yeah?" the woman turned over her shoulder, body still moving forward. Until it wasn't. "Kate?"

Two coincidences involving Jens in the span of five minutes. What were the odds? First, Cher-a-like's brother was her doctor. A woman she'd momentarily thought could be her future—and who lived two states away—showed up out of the blue through a sibling. Then, her past bookended the story when her ex-wife literally bumped into her in a hallway. The universe was sending a message—but, what?

# # #

It was mid-day when Liza arrived at Nathan's—soon to be her—house. She'd packed all her remaining things the night before, loaded those she could into Kate's garage, and then set out for her bike-run workout that Saturday morning. The Kona countdown clock read T-35 days. Soon, she'd be in the Hawaiian Islands racing the race of her life. There wasn't time to let up now.

In search of new scenery, she'd biked out of the city, taking the Burke-Gilman trail to the north end of the lake before weaving her way through the suburbs that lead to the country roads in Snohomish County. The Burke Gilman wasn't new; she was on that trail going *somewhere* several times a week, its semicircle path bordering Lake Washington reliable. The speed bumps created by tree roots under the asphalt trail predictable. The northern burbs, however, were new to her, their spacious lots painted with large homes and larger trees, their wide streets peppered with drive-thrus and strip malls. Lonely country roads found at the turnaround point of her ride were a respite from the city crowds. Tall Douglas firs filled the landscape, the occasional stop sign drawing her attention to the sheer amount of space available to those who lived outside the city. It was a different universe than the one she knew so well, and the unfamiliar sights and sounds helped the time pass. In no time, she'd clocked 100 miles and was out on her run, a quick 6-miler—

twice around Greenlake—to remind her legs they still had work to do. They delivered with an excellent split—a 41-minute 10K.

She parked her car in the driveway, and like a border collie happiest when exercised, almost skipped to the front door with the groceries she'd picked up on the way. It had been a good day—she'd hit her watts on the bike and pace on the run—and she had a Facetime date with Nathan planned for later that evening. They were having dinner together, him in California, her at home. She'd thought about the date on her bike—how to close the distance between them over the airwaves—and had a plan.

It seemed he did, too, as there was a bouquet waiting for her at the front door. White lilies. Her favorite. The florist had tucked the card into the middle of the bouquet, its simple line classic Nathan.

Who cares if roses are red and violets are blue? There was only one choice to send my love to you.

First, the symphony. Now, flowers. He'd turned up the charm. So different from what happened when Jackie left. Nathan was becoming *more* engaged in their relationship with distance. Liza couldn't help but smile as she looked for a vase in the kitchen. Cabinet after cabinet revealed pots and pans, plates and bowls, twelve different cereals, even a new-looking juicer that she made a note to figure out how to use.

In the last drawer of the last cabinet, she saw it.

Not the vase.

The drawer held a stack of unopened envelopes. All different shapes and sizes saved and tucked away. She closed the drawer and wondered. What had been so important to save, but not open?

Liza told herself it was okay to just have a little peek at the return addresses. If they were private, why were they stored in a kitchen drawer? Which begged a bigger question—why hadn't he opened them? She pulled the drawer back open, its hinged handle squeaking a warning. There had to be a hundred letters in that drawer. Maybe more.

Stretching her hand into the drawer as if she were a detective in a B-Movie, Liza grabbed the stack. She started to flip through the pile when her phone buzzed—a text message. Though she knew the alert tone, it startled her, and she jumped back, dropping the pile all over the slate floor.

"Shit!" she shouted to an empty room, bending to pick them up. "I shouldn't be doing this."

Stacking them to re-bundle, she noticed it. They all had the same return address in Maple Valley, Washington with no sender name; they all seemed to be addressed to Natalie Stapleton. The most recent was postmarked less than a month before.

"What the hell?"

Liza's mind ran away with the possibilities, but the letters indicated someone in Nathan's family was still reaching out. Someone wanted to connect with him. It seemed they didn't know of his transition, but they hadn't stopped mailing him. They even knew his proper mailing address.

Nathan told her he'd been disowned and hadn't heard from anyone in his family since he was sixteen. He was sparse with details, beyond that defining moment. He'd said nothing about the letters. Liza sank down to the kitchen floor and leaned against the maple Shaker cabinet, knees pulled tight to her chest. Her family was accepting and supportive when she'd told them she was gay. There was nothing shocking about coming out to people who'd had to come out themselves, as her mothers had. She'd grown up with exposure to a variety of people and had an example of a healthy, queer relationship to guide her.

But Nathan had come out to a religious mother with no experience in receiving such information, in a time when gender non-conformity wasn't a mainstream topic. Had she regretted her reaction? Had she been trying to make up for her mistake all these years, only to receive silence? It sure seemed that way.

This discovery meant Liza had her own decision to make. Pretend like she hadn't seen the letters. Or tell the truth. Two binary options in a non-binary world. If not that day, she'd surely have found the letters when unpacking her things.

Decision made, she checked her phone for the missed text. It was Nathan, telling her he couldn't wait to talk later, and he had something exciting to tell her.

# # #

"It's so good to see you," Nathan said to the camera in his phone, steel-blue eyes shimmering in the late afternoon light. "I miss your face."

"I miss yours, too," Liza said. "It's so weird to be in your house without you."

"It's your house now, too. Our house."

"You know what I mean. So, how's San Francisco?" She wouldn't call it her house yet, regardless of what he thought.

This was new for both. The pleasantries and catching up, finding their rhythm. Trying to simulate 3-D intimacy in a 2-D environment. Nathan on the futon in his rental in the Mission district, Liza at the dining room table at his house in Beacon Hill. Eight-hundred seven miles separating them. Eight-hundred seven too many.

"Different." Nathan shifted in his seat, dragging a bent knee under his body, the slip-covered cushion flat underneath him. He wouldn't think about the sources of its voluminous and varied stains. "Beautiful, I mean. I get why people like it here. But it's different. Not what I expected. But not bad."

"That's pretty vague, babe. You okay?"

"Yeah, fine. But I don't want to talk about me. How are you? How's the move going?"

It was odd he didn't want to share San Francisco stories with her, but Liza let it go. Instead, she brought him up to speed on her move, noting the movers were coming the next day. It was almost done; she just had to unpack and get settled. It'd been two weeks since Kate told her she was moving to being packed and ready to go—in the race of moving across town, Liza was winning.

"Which brings up something I want to ask you," she said, not wanting to let it simmer. This wasn't simmering material.

"Sure."

"I was putting some things away in the kitchen—"

"Oh, crap," Nathan stopped her before she finished, right hand holding his fallen head.

"I'm sorry, I didn't mean to find them."

"No, no. It's not your fault. I forgot to move them before I left." His words said it wasn't her fault, but his tone said otherwise.

"Why haven't you opened them?"

Silence.

"Babe. It seems like they've tried really hard to reach you. Why haven't you—" Liza pressed, leaning in closer to the laptop screen. Maybe she shouldn't have gone there. Her cheeks were on fire and her stomach in knots—the romantic dinner wasn't going at all as planned.

"I don't want to, okay?"

"But don't you think—"

"No! I don't," Nathan stopped her.

"All right. But—"

"Look, Liz. I'm not mad you found the letters. It's my fault for leaving them there. But you don't understand this. And I don't want to talk about it. Not right now. Can we please drop it?"

"Yeah," Liza sighed. She didn't know this side of her boyfriend. And didn't know if she wanted to. "Why don't we just have dinner?"

Liza changed the topic to the stuffed squash she'd made, its protein-fat-carb ratio ideal for recovering from her long ride and run earlier that day. She told of the country roads and her fast clip around Greenlake on foot. Of working out her pace charts for Kona in her head. The new bike shoes she'd ordered that promised to save minutes on an Ironman course with their superior aerodynamics. She could've been talking to one of her running buddies.

"That's great," he smiled every so often, his equivalent of "mm-hm," and "uh-huh."

"Anyway, that's enough about racing. I was hoping," Liza said, "that we could take this into the bedroom. Maybe get a little romantic? But if you're not up for it—"

Nathan's face, with its furrowed brow and borderline frown, said it all.

"Maybe next time?" he shrugged.

"Yeah, of course," Liza agreed, unsure what to say next. She'd tried to connect. She'd turned the ignition, but the spark plugs just wouldn't ignite. "Thanks for the flowers—they're beautiful. And smell amazing."

"I'm glad you like them. When I see lilies, I think of our first night together."

"You do?"

"Yeah. There was a vase of white lilies on the table beside the front door. I could smell them when we kissed."

"I don't remember that!"

"Yeah, and you were wearing those tortoise-shell glasses, looking so hot, in a sporty librarian way. I was scared out of my mind, but you took my hand and told me it was going to be okay."

"I remember that part," Liza smiled her winning smile. "I wish I could kiss you right now to let you know it's going to be okay. Because it is."

"Thanks," Nathan said. "I'm sorry our date didn't go how you wanted it."

"It's okay, we'll get better at this. Spending time together is what's important. You said you had something important you wanted to tell me?"

"Yeah, but it can wait," Nathan said. "It's not that important."

"You sure?"

"Yeah, next time."

SIX

Their table overlooked Lake Union, the restaurant encasing it perched on the edge of the city. A cloudless September day gave way to a clear night, houseboats and fishing boats illuminating the water, lights of shore doing the same. Downtown Seattle presided—as always—its skyscrapers and tower cranes a reminder of a vibrant and growing metropolis.

"We're finally at Haven," Christine smiled, holding a glass of red wine just off the white-clothed table. "Cheers to a night out in this beautiful city with beautiful company."

"Cheers," Kate said, a micro-quiver in overtaking her hand as she lifted her glass, "to us." Still shaken from the collision with her ex-wife earlier in the day, she told the voices in her head to drop it.

"I'm embarrassed to say, I missed you."

"Why's that embarrassing?"

"It's only been a day since we've seen each other," Christine said, the glow of the candle in the middle of the table lighting her eyes, the color of pine. She was wearing a black cashmere sweater with a strand of pearls laying across the collar. "I have more restraint than that!"

"I'm happy to hear you missed me and you have no restraint." Kate lowered her voice. They were in a classy restaurant. "And later, I'd like you to show me just how little you have. A few times."

"I plan to."

With Christine's hand now on her thigh under the table, Kate regretted she'd made reservations for a five-course, fine dining meal. All she wanted was to pay the check, go home, and practice lack of restraint. But there was something to suspense—the stacks of romance novels she'd read had taught her this—and they had hours to let it build.

"Good evening," the server said, and then explained their dinner options, asked about their food restrictions, and filled their wine glasses. Her black tie was fashioned into a textbook Windsor knot, dark hair slicked back with intention into a taught bun.

"She came just in time," Kate said. "I was about to tell you we were bailing! How was your day?"

"I would've gone!" Christine's chuckle was as sweet as ever. She used it as a punctuation mark and transition, its presence as automatic as breathing. "But I'm glad we're staying. I took Sadie on a long walk in the neighborhood this morning. Talked to my dad for a while in the afternoon. I told him about you."

"You did?"

"Yeah, he's happy for me. For us. He knows about finding happiness for a second time. Mom left differently than Meg, but we were both left against our wills."

"Wow! That's a big deal. I'm honored. And you look stunning in this light. I mean—you look stunning, always, but—"

"I didn't take it wrong! Thank you." Christine adjusted the pearls. "You do, too. I didn't know you were into dresses."

"I'm full of surprises." The sleeveless black dress Kate picked for the evening was her singular special occasion outfit which only came out to go to the theater, weddings, and funerals. It was making its restaurant debut. She'd even tamed her spunky blonde locks into tidy part, a rare occurrence.

"You really are. What do you have for me tonight? It's kind of hard to top moving to Montana, but I'm learning not to put anything past you."

As she thought about telling Christine her surprise encounter earlier that day, she changed the topic to the crowd. Around them, couples dined with varying degrees of intensity. Kate proposed you could tell who was in a new romance versus a steady romance versus a failing romance by the distance from each other they sat, the angles of their upper bodies. New romances held very little space between them. They leaned close to their companions. Maybe they sat side-by-side. Perhaps held hands under the table when they weren't eating. Established lovers sat comfortably with each other, making eye contact from time to time, but also free to take in the atmosphere, enjoy the setting. Failing love— those trying, but not finding their way back to each other—looked as uncomfortable as they must have felt. Couples in the third category sat quiet, rarely speaking, looking out the windows or scanning the room— but not at each other.

"Which category are we in?" Christine asked.

"Oh, new romance. Naturally. But one I hope will become a steady romance."

"Me, too."

Steady romances bared everything, with kindness.

"I don't know what it is about this year, but it's been a doozie," Kate said without a segue. "When I was at the doctor today, I ran into Jen. Literally ran into her, in the hallway."

"Jen? Your ex-wife, Jen?"

"The one and only."

"Wow."

"Yeah, I said the same thing. Twice in a matter of months. Well, only once that she knows about, but still. She asked me to have drinks next week. I said I'd think about it."

"Do you *want* to?"

"I don't know."

"Maybe the universe is finally giving you the opportunity to get some closure. Twice in a couple months after not seeing each other in years seems like a pretty big sign to me."

"Would you be upset?" Kate asked, the nerves in her stomach escaping through a heartfelt question.

"Why would I? You spent over a decade of your life together. You've wondered for years what went wrong. Maybe you'll get what you need out of it. I figured seeing her at the drag show probably shook you a bit—maybe this is what you need."

"You don't think it's weird?"

"I still talk to Meg."

"Really?"

61

"Every Friday night. We're not twenty, Kate. We have pasts. The past made us. It's important to honor that. Do yourself a favor and see what she wants. Maybe it's nothing. Maybe it's something. You won't know unless you go."

Just then, their food arrived, the server's timing impeccable. "And will you need anything else?"

"Nothing at all," Kate said, "everything's perfect."

# # #

When Jen Scott clocked in for the night shift that Saturday—working nights and weekends was standard practice since she'd started her publishing company—she did something uncharacteristic. Before checking her emails, before checking book sales numbers, before anything else, she Googled her ex-wife.

Someone she hadn't considered beyond a passing thought in years.

The hallway encounter at the medical center had thrown her. But, why? She was the one who left. It was she who wanted out.

They'd met when they were both young. So young. They'd weathered the storm of a decade-plus relationship. A three-year marriage. They'd had some wonderful times. And horrible ones. But that was all in the past. A sepia-colored filmstrip played in her mind as she scanned for information on how Kate had spent the past eight years. Their first date at a restaurant in Pike Place Market, overlooking Puget Sound as the green and white ferries chugged to and fro. Holding hands as the fish guys threw fish, laughing, the unknown what 'could be' filling her with joy. Ski vacations. Beach vacations. Adopting a dog. Losing the same dog to cancer. Legally marrying at San Francisco City Hall. Disagreements. Doubt. Temptation. Infidelity. Divorce.

The memories came flooding back, breaching the concrete dam that had held them in the recesses of Jen's mind.

Kate looked good. She'd aged well. Better than well. She must've had Botox injections, Jen reasoned. Her perfectly blonde hair was believable—Jen knew Kate had a standing date with a colorist once a month. But there was no way a 42-year-old could be that smooth-skinned. Had to be Botox. And maybe some fillers. Probably fillers.

As she scrolled, she found little.

Kate Conrad, of Seattle, Washington, kept a low profile. She had an Instagram account, but it was locked. Her LinkedIn showed, but Jen didn't dare click—Kate would be able to see she'd looked at her profile. The only other notable information the internet provided was Kate's address. Another search revealed it was a townhome in Greenlake. Figured. Kate had lived in a studio near the lake when they'd met. She'd returned home.

Reminding herself that she'd left Kate, and her life was where she wanted it, Jen closed the browser screen with a forceful click.

Work wasn't going to happen that evening. She needed to get out of the house. A distraction. A drink. A hook up wouldn't be horrible, but that was asking a lot, considering the way her day had gone.

"Hey," Jen said when her sister, Maggie, answered. "Got any plans tonight? I need to get out."

"What's wrong?"

"Why does something have to be wrong for me to want to see my sister?"

"Because it does. I know you. You're happy to stay in that basement of yours tabulating royalties all weekend. What's the matter?"

Silence.

Then, "I ran into Kate today after my doctor's appointment."

"Really?!"

"Yeah. Like, I *ran* into her. Bumped her in a hallway."

"And?"

"And it was awkward. We fumbled over our words. I looked at my feet. Asked her to go for drinks, but I don't know why. We hugged. Sort of. And then went our separate ways."

As Jen replayed the encounter, she heard herself speak. She sounded weak and wounded, not the other way around. It should be the other way around.

"Okay, that doesn't sound horrible," Maggie said. "It was bound to happen. It's a freaking small world. I ran into Matt at Whole Foods a few months ago, in the paper goods aisle. Same thing. We didn't know what to say to each other. What do you say to someone when too much time has passed for it to feel comfortable? You don't."

"You think?"

"I *know*. Are you going to have drinks?"

"I don't know. She said she'd get back to me. Maybe it's a bad idea, but since I asked, I'll go if she wants."

Why did Jen ask? Knee-jerk reaction? Guilt? A hidden curiosity of what was going on in Kate's life? Perhaps, all three. Emily told her Kate was moving to Montana. That was a big deal. The Kate Jen knew wouldn't quit her job and buy a ranch. Hell, if the Kate Jen knew would've done that, they'd probably still be together.

"And there's one other thing," Jen said. "My new author—the teacher—is friends with her. Apparently, Kate just quit her job and bought a ranch. In Montana."

"Woah. That's a big deal."

"I know."

"She hated the idea of not having a steady paycheck. And health insurance."

"I know."

"She was so upset with you for wanting to start your own shop."

"I know."

"She really didn't want you to quit *your* job."

"I know."

All these things were true. Maggie rattled them off from memory because she'd heard about them, over and over, until Jen decided that Kate's fear was holding her back. That she couldn't chase her dreams with the weight of her wife's disapproval on her shoulders. Daily disapproval got old, and she couldn't fight her dreams—they popped up and retreated. Popped up. Retreated. They could be shooed, but not silenced. In the ether, they waited for Jen to do something.

So, she did.

Enter the firefighter. The hot firefighter. The two seem to go hand-in-hand, don't they? Regardless, she was a convenient—and short-lived—cover. The real reason Jen left—the lover who'd stolen her heart—wasn't another person. It was herself. Her dreams. Her wants for the future.

"Well, I guess people change."

"I guess so. Anyway, are you up for a drink?"

"Aren't you in a hormone cycle right now?"

"You're right. I just started today—that's why I was at the doctor. Okay, so no drink. Maybe a movie? There's a new adaptation of a book I'd like to see."

"Not tonight, sweetie. I have a blind date later—it's probably nothing, but I should go make sure."

"Okay, thanks for listening."

"Anytime. Have the drink. It'll do you good to get some closure—you don't have to keep bearing the guilt burden because you made a decision to put yourself first. Just make it virgin, okay? Don't blow your plans because of a backslide to the past. Promise?"

"Pinky swear." Jen raised her pinky to a tradition she'd had with her sister since they were kids. "Have a good date. I hope he's Mr. Right. Or at least, Mr. Right Now."

# # #

"He did what?" Emily asked, pinching her phone between her shoulder and ear as she put down the spatula she was using to sauté dinner for one. "Are you sure?"

"I'm sure," Kevin Hall said, confirming their son had been caught with marijuana edibles. "I found them myself."

"Well, have you talked to him?" Emily asked.

"Not yet. I think we should do it together."

"So I can be the bad cop?"

"No, so he knows we're both serious about this. How do you want to punish him?"

Emily hadn't seen this coming. Angus was a good student—not a *great* student—but he was doing well enough in his classes. And he excelled in sports. The football team had elected him co-captain during summer practice. Unheard of for a sophomore. He had high hopes of getting into the pitching rotation for baseball in the spring.

"It's a tough one," Emily said.

"I know. How do we punish him for doing something we did at his age? When it was illegal?"

"It *is* illegal. For him."

"Yeah, but again, we did it too. A lot."

Kevin had a point. When they were in high school, they bought pot from a hippie kid from Ballard with dreadlocks. They'd meet him on Shilshole beach, his hair visible for hundreds of yards, his VW van with the '70s-style multicolor paint job visible from farther. When the occasion arose, they'd page him—page him!—with a request to meet, hang out for a while, pretend to be friends, and exchange cash for a tiny bit of weed tucked into an M&Ms bag. The kid was ahead of his time—he left some of the M&Ms in the bag before resealing with a glue stick. To the naked eye, it looked unopened. And the candy was handy when the munchies came around.

How could they punish their son for experimenting, just as they'd done twenty-five years before him?

"You remember that kid? Jimmie?" Emily asked.

"Yeah, he thought he was the white Jimmy Hendrix. I don't think he could even play the guitar."

"He did. And he couldn't. I saw on Facebook a while back he's clean cut now. Dad bod. Square haircut. Drives a Mercedes G-Wagen and lives on Clyde Hill. Figures."

Kevin laughed. "It makes sense. He was in tune with supply and demand at an early age. We must've bought enough dime bags to fund at least a tire on that SUV. Maybe the rim, too."

"Yeah," Emily sighed, leaning back on her kitchen counter, the red curry she was preparing wafting through the house, asking her to get off the phone and finish cooking. "Okay, let's talk to him tomorrow when you drop him off. Maybe just a warning this time?"

"I think so. Maybe he'll be more careful. Anyway, if he's like me, he won't like the paranoia feeling and he'll stop."

"Or he'll be like me. Giggle a lot and go to sleep."

"I hope he's more like you," Kevin said. "This one time. Hey, listen, what happened with your book? You never said."

Emily 'hadn't said' on purpose. Kevin's advice about publishing—while ultimately landing her a publisher, sent her on a goose chase. She wasn't mad at him—she'd asked for the advice—but she didn't need any more of his opinions about how to market her work. She was learning to trust her gut and follow her own advice.

"Well—I signed with a local publisher. A two-book deal. I just got *Always Be You* back from the editor and have a pitch developed for another."

"Wow! Congratulations. I'm proud of you!" Was that sincerity in Kevin's tone?

"Thanks. I'm proud of me, too. I didn't know I had it in me. Now we'll see if I can do it again. My publisher said the second book is harder, because you've had your whole life to write the first one, and only a few months or a year to follow it up."

"Ha."

"Ha?"

"You're getting a small glimpse of my life. My first few—dozen, even—articles were easy. Hell, the first year was a breeze. Writing was new and fun, and we got to travel. Twenty years in, it's hard to find fresh places to go and new things to say. I'm over adverbs."

This side of Kevin—the side she'd seen since telling him about her first book—was new. He was more open with her. More vulnerable.

"Well—don't let this go to your head—but I think I get it now. I've gotta run—my dinner's ready. See you tomorrow."

"Okay, see you then. And Em?"

"Yeah?"

"I really am proud of you."

As she hung up the phone—for a split second—Emily missed the ease of her old life. Knowing who she was going to bed with each night. Having someone to work with her through problems. A sympathetic ear. Someone who knew her past. No one else would ever know her past the way Kevin did, because he'd lived it with her. She could tell others. She could write about it. But only one other person knew it the way she did.

Their trip down memory lane made her crave M&Ms, so she left the pan on the stove and took a walk to the mini market near her house. This time, it would just be an unaltered bag of M&Ms. But she had to give credit to Jimmie. He'd been a savvy entrepreneur, even at seventeen.

SEVEN

He walked from the Mission to the Castro, taking in his home for the next six weeks. Pretending he belonged. Summoning courage. Talking himself out of it as much as into it. He had a mile of pavement underfoot to debate—more than enough time to clear his mind. And more than enough to change it. Nathan Stapleton looked on as people went about their normal Saturday night routines. Restaurants lining the sidewalks on Valencia Street were full, patios bursting with chatter and laughter. People milled outside the laundromat. Bars with were string-lit and hopping, music piping through outside speakers into his receptive ears. The September air was still warm, but there was a hint of coolness to it. A suggestion of change to come.

In no time, he was there. The sign outside said, "Karaoke Tonight."

The crowd inside said queer hipsters.

His head said, "do it." His gut said, "DON'T."

Nathan told himself to chill. He was in San Francisco to sing. What did he have to lose by going to Karaoke night at Brazen, the bar Charles had recommended, to sing? Nothing. There was nothing to lose. But without the safety net of his band, without the protective shield of his guitar, his stomach churned. The band gave him wings.

In front of this bar, alone, he was just Nathan, some random guy.

He was also, Nathan, a random guy whose girlfriend had found the secret stash of letters he didn't want anyone to know about. All evening, he'd beaten himself up for not moving the letters. For storing them in the kitchen. They'd had a rough Facetime call, and he'd chided himself for that, too. It wasn't Liza's fault for finding the letters. But he didn't want to talk about them. He wanted them to go away. Now that she knew, they weren't going away.

Leaning on the poured concrete bar, he caught the eye of a shirtless bartender, dark, skin-tight denim on his bottom half, bowtie around his neck, clear plastic eyeglasses frames likely for effect, not necessity. More abs than natural, for the same reason.

"Hey," the bartender said, sliding a cardstock coaster across the smooth top. "What'll it be?"

"Whiskey. And an Anchor Steam," Nathan said. "And can I get on the list for Karaoke?"

"You bet. What's your name?

"Nate. Staples."

"Okay, Nate. Whatcha singin'?"

"'Lights,' by Journey."

"Nice choice. Tough crowd for that one, but nice choice."

Tough crowd?

"How so?"

"Oh, you know, every guy who steps off the bus from Des Moines or Denver or Dallas, lives here a second, thinks it's his city now. Thinks he's

Steve Perry. Just a fair warning. They've heard it." He gave everyone who picked that song the same tip. Because—they'd heard it.

"Thanks for the heads up." Nathan downed the shot and returned the glass to the bar with a thud. He didn't think San Francisco was his home. Or that he was Steve Perry.

"You bet. We've got five in front of you."

With nowhere to go, Nathan maintained his solid bar lean, arm draped over the edge. He'd traded his signature cutoff buffalo plaid for a black V-neck but kept the vintage 501s and Chuck Taylors. His face sported five-day stubble, chestnut beard well on its way back. He waited through an off-key rendition of "Cabaret" by an Alan Cumming wannabe wearing the full-on suspender getup. A butch guy with a lumberjack beard delivered a beautiful cover of Adele's "Hello." As strangers sang, he sipped his beer and watched. Singles coupled. Then, disappeared. Friends laughed. A guy in a black Polo shirt with giant biceps appeared to hustle pool. When a woman with caramel-smooth skin took the stage in a three-piece tuxedo, he tallied the singer count—she was his opener. The first note out of her mouth was angelic. She'd chosen "The Sound of Silence." He was floored. Sure, there'd been the one off-key musical theater fan, but otherwise, everyone who'd taken the stage could *sing*. Who chose Simon and Garfunkel for an open mic night? If the obsidian hair and purple tips didn't give it away, if the suit didn't scream, "Janelle Monae meets Brandi Carlile," her song selection did. This chick had balls.

Looking up at the flat screen TV over the stage, he saw his name. For the first time in print: Nate Staples. He leaned forward in slow motion, righting himself from the angle where he'd melted into the bar and jogged through the crowd to take the stage. Tux woman was holding the microphone and handed it to him with a bow.

"Thanks," he said, walking the mic to the center of the small stage and placing it in the stainless-steel stand. "That's gonna be hard to follow."

The view from the stage was different. Better. From above, he was at home. Where he should be. Entertaining the crowd, not observing it. The high-top tables were so close together they practically touched. A sea of twenty and thirty-somethings was buoyed by the occasional long timer. Drinks were half-drunk, and so was the crowd.

"I've been told this one's a risk, but I hope you like it."

On cue, the music started. And on cue, Nathan eased into the opening line, his smooth alto bringing a new dimension to the classic. When he hit the bridge—mic now cupped between his hands, eyes closed—he wasn't singing about San Francisco anymore.

He was singing about Seattle.

And Liza.

"Thank you," Nathan said to a roomful of applause when he finished. "I'm Nate and I'll see you around."

Relieved he hadn't been ignored—or worse, booed—Nathan held his head high as he bounced off the stage with the same energy he'd used to climb it. His stage presence was returning. His confidence, too.

"Hey," the bartender said again as Nathan leaned on the bar, again. "Gotta give it to you. That was one of the best covers I've heard. And I've heard that song *a lot*. Another Anchor?"

Nathan nodded. "Thanks."

"You gonna come back next week?"

"Yeah. I think I will."

"You should. This one's on the house. I'm Jason, by the way. No place to put a name tag on this outfit." When Jason smiled, the deep-set crow's feet near his dark eyes appeared. He must've laughed a lot in his life.

Nathan raised his glass to the barkeep, feeling better already.

# # #

The Lyft dropped him off close to—but not in front of—his place. He'd walked a half block to the granite stoop, put the key in the lock, and— nothing. He fumbled with the key; it wouldn't turn. A second and third try produced the same results. He was locked out.

Sinking to sit against the door, knees pulled close to his body, Nathan closed his eyes. It worked earlier. He'd had no trouble coming and going since he arrived. His pulse was beating in his fingertips as he thought. What to do? It was after two. He didn't have a friend on whose couch he could crash. Couldn't call his agent, Julian, at that hour. Wouldn't wake Liza.

Blinking his eyes open, he reached for the phone in his back pocket, and a folded piece of paper landed on the stoop beside him.

415-233-6569

Text me.

Jason

That was a surprise. The bartender had put his number in Nathan's back pocket.

Aside from the obvious questions—How? When?—he also wondered, Why? He hadn't had the full high school experience, having dropped out at sixteen. But in those sixteen years, he'd gone without the knowing glances of passing secret notes with friends, without a "Do you like me? Check yes or no," survey from a nervous classmate, without a teacher looking over his shoulder to see what he was reading and asking him to share it with the class.

With a quick shake of the head, he folded the note and stuffed it back in his pocket when he realized the railing to the left of his legs wasn't quite right. His place had a black wrought iron rail—didn't it? In the dark of night, he'd neglected to notice the finer details. This rail was stucco.

"You idiot," Nathan said to himself, stood, brushed himself off, and looked at the address number: 575. He lived at 579.

It was 20 steps to *his* apartment. Nathan smiled and walked. He'd just gotten someone's number without trying. Never mind that he wasn't interested. Being noticed felt good. No harm in being noticed.

This time, when he put the key in the door, he made mental notes of his surroundings: Mint green door; one small window. Black wrought iron rail. A tarnished round doorknob.

This time, the key worked.

# # #

"I got an offer," Kate said when Liza showed up to direct her movers, who'd be there any minute.

"That's awesome! Are you taking it?"

"Already signed it. $50K over ask and no inspection. I'd be a fool not to."

"Wow!" Liza settled into the barstool where she'd spent so much of her life the past eight years and grabbed the mug Kate handed her. Her favorite, from one of Kate's Hawaiian vacations: "Kona: More than coffee," with a stick figure cyclist smiling as he pedaled. "That's really great."

"So, when will you leave for Montana?"

"October 15. In time to get there, settle a little, and get ready for winter. I want to get over the pass before the big snow. I haven't really thought about winter. I mean, how do you even prepare for a Montana winter? Stockpile canned goods? Freeze a lot of chili? Buy half a deer?" Kate spun her mug on the counter as she wondered. Where did one even procure half a deer?

"You'll figure it out. And if not, I'm sure there's a homesteading channel on YouTube."

Kate didn't acknowledge the snark. "I'll figure it out. Right now, I'm worried about all the things I need to do here first. Including have drinks with Jen."

"Jen? Which Jen? Jen Scott?!"

Clarifying last names of people named "Jen" was important. In their age group, every third person was named Jen.

"Yeah, she popped up again. At my doctor's appointment yesterday. The universe is obviously sending me a message. It's fine. I'll go have a drink. Christine said it would probably be good to get some closure."

"She doesn't care if you have drinks with your ex?"

"She doesn't."

"I like her so much," Liza smiled, twisting her wrist to look at her watch. "You found a grown up."

"I did. And it's incredible. I can talk to her about everything, not just things I think she'll approve—"

As Kate talked, Liza looked at her watch. Again.

"You okay?"

"Yeah, I want to get a run in this afternoon and these guys are thirty minutes late."

"Why don't you go run? I can direct them for you."

Liza rattled off reasons she *couldn't* go on the run, including a potential blister she sensed was forming, but couldn't prove.

"This isn't about a run, huh?"

"Hm?"

"You just gave me six reasons you can't run—none of which make any sense. A phantom blister? What's up?"

Kate waited as Liza stared into the kitchen, Dallas and Hunter at their feet, black and yellow fur blending into one oversized dog rug. It was early afternoon—their siesta time.

"You're right. I should go. I just—"

"Wait. Last night was your Facetime date, right? Trying out a little distance . . . learning?"

"Yeah."

"And it didn't—"

"It's not that. Well, it sort of is. I found a huge stack of unopened letters in Nathan's kitchen. Like, a hundred."

"Okay?" Kate moved her stool closer to the bar. She was looking forward to the space of her new ranch, but she'd miss these moments with her best friend. Even when she felt alone in the world, she always had Liza. They'd talked about everything imaginable in that spot. They weren't fancy—simple round maple-topped stools with white legs—but they held secrets and laughs and tears that spanned years.

"I'm pretty sure they're from his mom. And he hasn't opened any. I brought it up last night, and he didn't want to talk about it. Maybe I shouldn't have said anything. But I didn't want to hide it from him. I've felt bad all day. Like I did something wrong." Liza worried, her forehead frown on display, emerald eyes cloudy.

Dallas poked his head up from her feet, his periodic check for dropped snacks, and let out a sigh when there were none.

"Were you snooping?"

"Kinda. Not really. I was in the kitchen looking for a vase—he sent me the most beautiful lilies—and I accidently found them and closed the drawer. But then, I opened it again and looked to see who they were from."

"Nothing wrong with that," Kate said. "It's your house too. And if he didn't want you to find them, he shouldn't have left them in the kitchen when you were moving in."

"Right? He said it wasn't my fault. But I'm worried he's mad."

When the doorbell rang, Dallas re-raised his head, let out a guttural "woof," and plopped back to the floor.

"Ooh, aren't you a tough guy?" Kate crossed the living room to open the door. It rang at the most inopportune time.

"Hi," a butch woman said, trucker cap turned backwards, wisps of short mahogany hair escaping around the ears, which held three tiny silver studs each, blue coveralls zipped to her neck.

"Hi," Kate smiled.

"We're here for the move?"

"Come on in. You're here for Liza."

"Thanks," the mover said, wiping her work boots on the mat. "I swear I've been here before."

"Don't think so."

"No, I definitely think we've met." The woman snapped her fingers as she followed Kate to the kitchen. "Yeah, Halloween a couple years ago. I was Captain America—you were Wonder Woman, right?"

"Yes, but—"

"And, you have—yep! Two Labs!" She bent and offered a limp hand to Dallas and Hunter, who were uninterested. If she'd had cookies, they would've feigned interest, at least.

Kate had no memory of an encounter with Captain America, or why this woman knew Dallas and Hunter.

"Hey," Liza stood from her stool, raising her hand to her shoulder as if she were a shy student in a classroom. "You're getting us confused. I also went as Wonder Woman for Halloween—the year after Kate. Remember, I borrowed your costume? And you were mad, because I had it taken in," Liza directed that last part at her former roommate.

"Oh! Yes, I thought she was too tall, but I've been here." The mover said, standing and looking around the room for confirmation.

"It seems you have," Liza smiled sheepishly. "Anyway, the stuff's in the garage. Not much—some boxes and my bedroom furniture. It should be easy. Here, I'll show you."

When Liza returned from the garage, Kate was sitting on her stool, waiting expectantly. "What? I like a superhero."

"No judgment here," Kate said, sinking to the floor to pet Hunter's golden coat. Her dogs were nothing if not conversation starters. "But seriously. What's up with the letters?"

"I don't know. There are years' worth. But he said he didn't want to talk about it, and I respect that. It's confusing. I mean, they're clearly trying to reach him. Wouldn't you want to know what all those letters said?"

"I'm not sure. They kicked him out—when he was a kid. What could possibly make up for that? So, no. I don't know if I'd want to. And his life is going pretty great right now. He probably doesn't want to fuck up his head with the contents of a long-lost parent with a guilty conscience."

"I hadn't thought of it that way," Liza tugged on the black running hat, bits of angle-cut red sideburns the only sign of hair. "You're right. He probably really *doesn't* want to know what they say. So, what should I do? Leave it alone?"

"Leave it alone. If he wants to talk to you about it, he will."

"Fair enough. Hey—if I leave now, I can get my run and meet them at the house. I'll run back for my car once they start unloading. Okay with you if I leave it here till then?"

"Sure."

"You're really moving to Montana?"

"I'm really moving to Montana," Kate said, standing to hug her friend. "You're just going to have to make room for me in your Facetime calendar."

EIGHT

Between selling her house and tending to a new relationship, Kate Conrad lost track of time. The work week flew by as she'd wrapped up projects, written briefs, had coffee dates with colleagues, and repeatedly explained why she was leaving a cushy job with killer benefits to move to Montana and run a ranch.

"It's just something I want to do," she'd begun saying for simplicity. "I'm burned out and I hate this job and the city is getting to me and I just need away from it all," was too much of a mouthful.

It was true.

But a mouthful.

"I'm jealous," or some variant often followed, with its owner smiling a fake smile that confirmed they were indeed, jealous.

The sun shone with the glow of fall on Greenlake, its golden orb lower in the sky, a noticeable crispness in the air foreshadowing a fact of life: winter was coming. Kate walked the dogs with purpose. There was no time to dawdle, though Dallas lunged at squirrels and Hunter stopped to sniff every lamppost and trash can. She'd agreed to drinks with her ex-wife in the early afternoon, and she and Christine were going to a show at the Tractor that evening. Seeing her past and present in back-to-back fashion was unnerving, but her gut said Christine was right—it would be okay to see Jen. It would be helpful, even, to gain some perspective on a chapter in her life that had closed without answers so many years before. She'd be lying if she said she wasn't nervous.

"Okay boys, had enough?" Kate asked as they rounded the last bend, the kayak rental in plain view. Those colorful boats would soon be put away for another year.

Hunter grunted as he saw the boats. He wanted the cookie that was earned at the end of their walk. A whim that had started years before when he was learning to sit on command had become routine.

"Okay, but you know what you have to do." Kate snapped her fingers and both dogs sat to receive biscuits, which they devoured in an instant. Just as they were ready to leave, Kate's phone rang.

"Hi Mom. We're almost home from our walk."

"Good," Glenda Conrad said, "Then you have time to talk. Are you getting excited?"

"I am! And, I'm relieved that the house sold so fast."

"Yes, that is really lucky. Not that I'm surprised—it's such a nice house and you decorated it so well."

"Aw, thanks Mom. How've you been?"

"I'm good! I've been thinking about you. I was thinking I could come visit you when you get moved. Help you unpack? I already asked Sissy to cover for me at Sunday School." Glenda Conrad said "Sundee" and "tomatuh" and "winduh," her pronunciations endearing—reminiscent of Kate's childhood in Tennessee.

"I'd like that. But—"

"But?"

Kate sighed, readying herself. "I'm seeing someone. She's helping me drive out and is planning to stay a while. I need to ask her, too, but are you ready to meet someone new in my life?"

Kate sat on a bench alongside the trail, stretching her feet in front of her, left crossed over right.

"Of course, darlin'. Why would you ask?"

"Well, you were upset when Jen and I got divorced. I know you loved her. I didn't know if—"

"Don't be silly, daughter of mine. I'm happy for you. See! I told you, it just takes time. Now tell me about this woman. She must be special if you're keeping her from me."

Glenda asked, so Kate told.

She was a cardiologist (big points for finding a doctor); had a dog (wonderful, a sign of a kind person); was partnered for 20 years with an Air Force pilot who died tragically in a training accident (how horrible). Kate told of meeting on the trail and not knowing where she stood. Of camping at the coast. Putting the pieces together after she'd bought the ranch. Of uncertainty and hope.

"It feels different this time, but I'm worried about the distance," Kate said, trying the same message on a new audience. Liza had told her to roll with it. Christine had promised she was good at long distance. Kate kept floating the worry to new people.

"If it's meant to be, it'll be. Love will find a way." Glenda said, platitudes on point.

From the bench, Kate watched the Saturday crowd buzz by, the familiarity of her weekend routine passing with lattes in hand and dogs on leashes and bicycle bells dinging. "I know, Mom. I don't know if it's love, yet. It could be, but—"

"Are you scared?"

"Yes."

"Are you worried she's going to up and disappear and you won't know how the story ends?"

"Well—yes."

"Then it's love."

"You're saying fear is love? I don't think so, Mom." Glenda had some wild opinions, but this one took the cake.

"No, darlin'. I'm sayin' if you've found someone you can't imagine your life without, you've found love. I'm not sayin' it'll be easy. Even love takes work. *Especially* love takes work. But if you've found someone who sees you for you and supports you chasing your dreams while they chase theirs, without either of them having to trump the other, well dear, you got yourself a keeper."

Glenda had a point. Was Kate scared because she wasn't sure it would work, or scared because it might? She didn't bring up the fact that she was seeing Jen later that afternoon. No sense in stirring up her mother over *that*.

# # #

They hadn't seen each other—at least on purpose—in eight years. Two-thousand, nine-hundred, and twenty-one days to be exact, accounting for one leap year. Kate wondered if they would have anything to say after almost three thousand days of not knowing each other. If a date with her ex-wife was a good idea, considering she was—finally!—in a relationship she wanted to tell people about. If dredging up the past would provide the answers she'd wanted since Jen left, or if she was opening a door to pain. Again.

She'd put more thought into her outfit for this meeting than she had in ages, settling on dark-washed denim with a little give. Nothing worse than being uncomfortably squeezed at the waist while being uncomfortably squeezed emotionally. Paired with a black long-sleeved T, plaid scarf, and ankle-high black leather boots, Kate was sure her outfit said, "confident, casual," and in-season. Jen's notorious fashion sense had added extra weight to her wardrobe decision.

"Hi," Jennifer Scott said, hands laced together behind her back, bright red glasses highlighting her eyes—piercing blue. Her auburn hair sat neatly on her shoulders, not a hint of grey to be found. Kate wasn't the only one who kept up the hair dye continuum.

Kate smiled, standing for a quick, sterile hug, and motioned for Jen to sit. She was one martini in—she figured a head start in the gin department would help with this conversation. "Fancy meeting you here."

Though they were at The Orchid, a bar in the gayborhood—Capitol Hill—nowhere near the site of their first date, Kate pushed down a Deja vu feeling. That day, she'd sat across a table from a woman who looked an awful lot like the one in front of her now, but younger. Feistier. Much like on their first date, Kate didn't know where to begin. So, she waited, resisting the urge to fill the empty airspace with chatter. Jen invited her. Jen owed the answers. Kate was under no obligation to fill the void.

"So," Jen said, nodding her head for no apparent reason. "It's been a long time."

"It has."

"I heard you're leaving Seattle. I'm surprised!"

"You heard right. News travels fast."

"That, and it's a small community. Congratulations, I'm glad you're trying something new."

Kate smiled. What was that supposed to mean? "Yeah, me too. I'm ready to get out of the city for a while. It's time. Can you believe I worked for the evil empire for 20 years? I just got my 20-year crystal last month."

"I *can* believe that. I thought you'd retire there." Jen took a drink from the ice water in front of her, a clue to important aspects of her current life—though she'd suggested a bar, she wasn't drinking.

It was early afternoon, but the bar was filling up, the relief of other people's conversations softening the space between them.

"Funny how we've gone all these years apart and then bump into each other at the doctor. Maybe it was time for us to re-connect." Kate pivoted, leading the conversation where she wanted it to go.

She set it up—now, it was up to Jen to spike the ball. If she didn't, Kate wouldn't get what she wanted out of the conversation. Maybe not getting what she wanted was as good as getting it.

"About that—" Jen said, pausing. "I've thought about this for years, and there's no other way to say this. I'm really sorry I hurt you. I've had a long time to regret the way I ended things. It was the right thing to do, but I did it the wrong way. And for that, I apologize."

Kate closed her eyes as she heard the words she'd dreamed of hearing. Her head bowed ever-so as she listened, recognizing the shade rolled up in the apology: *It was the right thing to do.*

Of course the, *I'm sorry,* came with a side of, *but not really.*

It was better than nothing.

"Kate?"

Silence.

"Yeah," Kate said, her body righting itself, eyes again alert and focused. "I just needed a moment. I've imagined this so many times over the years—I'm kinda taken aback that it's happening. Thank you. For saying that."

"Sure. I mean it."

"I know you do. And I'm sorry, too. I didn't get it then, but I do now. Present me understands things that past me didn't."

"Older and wiser," Jen said, tipping her glass in acknowledgement. "But wouldn't it be nice to be younger and wiser?"

"Nah. I like this age. I'm not decrepit yet, and I have a lot of good things going on."

"I'm glad."

"And you? How've you been?" Kate asked.

"Can't complain. I, too, have a lot of good things going on."

Jen told Kate that she was a few months and a few more steps away from trying to get pregnant. That she'd downsized to Phinney Ridge—to a family neighborhood, she reinforced—and she was ready to start the next chapter of her life: being a mom.

As her ex-wife talked about the realities of creating a family without a partner, the twinge in Kate's stomach was familiar. They'd had this conversation many times in the past, its tone different, but its intent the same: Jen wanted kids. Kate didn't.

"Jen?" Kate interrupted as she heard about hormones and shots and mock pregnancies. The ice water told a story of its own, but she wanted more.

"If I'd wanted kids—"

"You didn't."

"Yes, but if I'd wanted kids, do you think we'd be sitting here today? Familiar strangers? I forgave you a long time ago for leaving—I had to—but I never pieced together exactly what went wrong. I thought you were happy."

Jen stared at the wall behind Kate's head, posters of local bands tacked over every square inch. "Again, I'm sorry. I was. Happy. Until I wasn't. But I did—I do—want kids. And I wanted to start my own shop. I guess I just got tired of hearing 'no' all the time."

As people laughed around them, and someone started a new song on the jukebox, Kate sat with the silence in her head. The glass and metal front door flapped in the wind, its stopper doing an insufficient job of keeping it in place. People milled about, drinks in hand. A cacophony of noise surrounded her, but she didn't hear any of it.

Her mom had always said, "Don't ask questions you don't want the answers to." Perhaps she hadn't needed this answer, after all.

"Wow," Kate mustered.

"I know. That's hard to admit. It must be harder to hear. But you deserve a 'why.' The 'why' is, I felt defeated all the time."

Noise and silence intermingled as Kate processed.

Question asked. Question answered.

After not knowing for almost a quarter of her life, she now knew. "Meet me in Portland," played on the jukebox, that damn Grasshoppers song the soundtrack to her year. It played when she'd broken up with one of her short-lived summer romances, and it played while her ex told her the truth about their past life together.

"Thank you for telling me. Like I said, younger me didn't understand. I get it now. And I hope you get the kid you want. I always thought you'd be a great mom."

"Thanks," Jen said, glancing at her watch, a white gold bracelet-style Coach.

"Yeah, it's probably time to get going, huh?" Kate saw the watch move. Some things never changed. Just like Liza, she had a tell.

"Yeah, I need to head out. I'm having dinner with Maggie tonight."

"Tell her I said 'hi'," Kate said, standing to conclude the meeting with the same brevity it had begun. "And Jen?"

"Mm?"

"Thanks again. It took a lot to come here and say that, and I appreciate it. Good luck with your in vitro."

"Thanks," Jen smiled, hugging the woman she'd once promised to love for the rest of her life. "Good luck with your ranch."

# # #

"So, how was your date with Jen?" Christine asked, leaning on the front wall of the Tractor Tavern, darkness enveloping her, maroon raincoat blending into the red brick of the façade. It wasn't raining yet, but the odds were good. Along with almost two hours of daylight and warm temperatures, September had stolen reliably dry weather and replaced it with a constant chance of showers.

"Good," Kate sighed loudly, leaning harder against the brick. They still had a few minutes before the doors opened for the Dysfunctional Kittens show, a band neither had seen. Her boss's daughter was the lead singer—he'd gifted her tickets as a going away present. It was up in the air whether this was a good present. "It was really good," she repeated.

"Are you sure?"

"Yeah, I'm sure. It was weird, but good."

"Are you silver lining me?" Christine asked.

"Hm?"

"You've said it was 'good' three different ways, which isn't really saying anything. So, it was either a completely vapid meeting—which seems unlikely—or you're silver lining me. Telling me it's fine even though everything's not fine and you really need to talk about it?"

"Damn. You know me already." Kate looked at the sidewalk under her feet, its splattered and stained canvas a story of the thousands of people who'd waited for a show in her very place. The last time she'd stood there, it was summer and she and someone she'd dated briefly were waiting to see Nathan's band play—it was only two months before, but felt like years. "Okay, it *was* good—easier than I thought it would be—but also, I learned some things I didn't know."

"Like?" Christine stretched her hand and encouraged Kate's chin upward, looking for answers in her light green eyes. The answers weren't on the sidewalk.

"We don't need to rehash it, but I understood what she said. And I see her perspective differently now. So, thank you for encouraging me to go."

"Of course. I'm glad you got what you needed. Are you okay?"

"Yeah, I'm better than okay. I'm here with you, about to hear live music—one of my favorite things with one of my favorite people. I couldn't be better," Kate stuffed her hands in her overcoat, a surprise tube of Chapstick finding her fingers. The day just kept on giving. "Maybe I wasn't supposed to know her side until now? She found me again when I was happy; when I could hear her. When there was nothing I could do but listen, acknowledge, and move on."

"That's a good way to look at it," Christine said.

"Yeah, I really believe that. Serendipity at work, no question. So, why do you think they're called 'Dysfunctional Kittens?' They don't like to chase string? They like baths? They only eat vegetarian?"

Christine laughed. "They stay awake 23 hours a day and only sleep for one, is my guess."

"Naturally."

As they considered other reasons the band may have chosen its name, the front door cracked open, and the line-dwellers filed into the warmth of the tavern.

"Ah, smell that cheap beer," Kate said, taking a deep breath. "Doesn't matter how long it's been. One whiff and I know exactly where I am. Can I get you a drink?"

"Rainier," Christine smiled, shrugging her shoulders as she turned and walked towards the bathroom in the back of the bar. "When in Rome, drink as the Romans do."

Waiting in line for their beers, Kate found it fitting that Dolly Parton's "Here You Come Again," was playing through the bar's speaker system. Dolly seemed to follow them around. It was "I Will Always Love You," at the drag show over the summer, "Nine-to-Five" when they'd been in the car driving to Haven, and now, this. In the past, she'd have thought "Here You Come Again" was a negative story of a lover who came back at all the wrong times to remind her of the past. This time, she'd turned a lyric in her head and only heard positive.

Her mom was right. Without even meeting Christine, Glenda knew. Kate had it bad. She was a grown up, like Liza'd said. She was charming. Nurturing. Funny. The way her eyes crinkled when she laughed melted Kate's heart. The growl in her voice when she was frisky sent her to the moon. Her up-for-anything energy made her so easy to be around. Kate didn't walk on eggshells as she had with so many in the past. No worries about saying the wrong thing or doing the wrong thing or choosing the wrong restaurant. As she thought through all the different ways she'd bent parts of herself to fit into someone else's mold, she realized she didn't have to bend for Christine.

"Two Rainiers, please," Kate said when her turn came, burnished bar smooth under her jacketed forearms, which she'd crossed as she leaned in.

"Here you go, that'll be eight." The bartender cracked the pop top, the distinctive pt-zz of pressure releasing as familiar as the smell of stale beer surrounding them, the hum of chatter reminding her of the excitement that came with seeing bands live.

"Thanks." Kate dropped a ten on the bar and shook the daydream out of her head. She'd been in a far-off land wherein she and Christine were in Montana, living a life of adventure, together. Grabbing the cans, she set off to secure a spot and find out just why the band was named as it was, the natural buzz in her head eliminating the need for beer. She took a swig anyway—it was, after all, perfectly good Rainier.

NINE

"Mom!" Angus Hall yelled from the top of the stairs to no avail. So, he tried again. "Mom!!"

"Yes?" Emily answered this time, backing from under the kitchen sink on all fours, tattered purple University of Washington sweatshirt draping her upper body, yoga pants barely protecting her knees from the chill of slate tiles.

"I can't find my new Jordans!"

"What?" Emily continued to extract herself from the deep cleaning she'd just started, peeling off elbow-high rubber gloves and tossing them on the counter. "Come down here if you want to talk to me."

Like a pack of wild horses, Angus thudded and thumped down the stairs, his energy not waning in the search for the precious sneakers. "My new Jordans. That Dad bought me. I can't find them."

"Okay?"

"Do you know where they are?"

"Haven't seen them, sorry," Emily said, leaning against the counter, mentally preparing her to do list for the evening. She wanted to clean both bathrooms, get all the laundry done, and empty and re-arrange the fridge. Right after she cleared out the under-sink gunk that had been accumulating thanks to the trash can. "Now, if you'll excuse me, there's a head of lettuce in the fridge just screaming to be put to rest."

"Mom!"

"Sweetie, what's the big deal? Wear a different pair of shoes. Where are you going, anyway?"

Angus shifted in his stance, socked feet arranged in a near-perfect third position. "I have a date."

"A date?" Emily smiled.

"Yeah. It's not a big deal."

"Then what's up with the frantic shoe search? Did you check your closet?"

"No big deal, Mom. Just a girl from school," Angus said over his shoulder. He was halfway up the stairs in no time. "I'll find some other shoes."

As Emily returned to the task at hand—determining what the yellow stains were on the bottom of the cabinet, and therefore how to remove them, she smiled. Angus had a date. It was cute. And terrifying. First, edibles in his work apron. Now, secret girl crushes and dates. He used to tell her things. But then again, he used to not be a teenager.

"Mom!"

How could such a simple word be used in so many ways? Angus used it as a name, descriptor, question, and exclamation mark. And who knows what else? He created entire sentences' worth of meaning with the tone and urgency in his voice.

"Angus!" Emily answered, and again dragged herself out from underneath the kitchen sink to find her son, hovering behind her, feet now shod with a pair of basketball sneakers. "Oh, you found the shoes."

"No, these are just my normal Jordans. I couldn't find the new ones. Whatever. Anyway, can I borrow fifty bucks?"

"I'm sorry?" Emily stood back to look at the handsome young man in front of her. He'd combed his hair to one side, and she swore his eyebrows looked different. Had he plucked them? He had! And he'd put together a pair of flat-fronted khaki pants with a white shirt and blazer, finished with the basketball sneakers. All the fuss was about the sneakers—which had no part in that outfit. She wouldn't mention it.

"Can I borrow some cash? I'm taking Becky to dinner and I'm worried I don't have enough."

"What about your grocery store money? Didn't you just get paid?"

"Yeah, but I had to buy some things."

"What things?"

"Just some football stuff."

Emily raised an eyebrow. "Let's go sit on the couch for a minute."

"Mom."

"It'll just be a minute. Sit."

"Okay, fine." Angus complied, sinking into the cushy leather seat, arms crossed.

"Thanks. Listen, honey, it's great that you have a date. But we need to talk about a few things, first."

"Mom, Dad already—"

"No, not that," Emily said. "I know you and your dad had *the talk*. I want to talk about your responsibilities. To Becky, and to me."

Emily did her best to relate to her son, not lecture. She lectured enough in class. This was about expectations. Just like with her students, she believed the best way to be disappointed was to not explain the rules.

So, she'd spell out the rules. When it came to dating, she wanted to know in advance where he was going and when he'd be back. With whom he'd be, and if her parents knew. He was to keep his cell phone ringer on, and answer if she called. And she expected him to comply with his curfew—home by 10 p.m. Also, for the record, she knew that the things he bought weren't football related. They'd talk about the edibles another time.

"Okay," Angus nodded. "I will be. Home by 10. What are you doing tonight?"

It was Saturday, the best night of the week to go into the world and socialize. But she'd spent the day making edits to her manuscript, putting off working on the new novel she owed soon. She was wiped—no creativity was in the picture. "Just cleaning."

"I figured you'd go out, too," Angus shrugged. Was she being called out for her lack of a dating life by her kid?

"What do you mean?"

"Mom, you haven't been out in ages. Since before school started."

"You're keeping tabs on me?" She was totally being called out for her lack of a dating life by her kid. But going out seemed like way too much work. The bar scene was trying. Rousing a friend to see a movie, the same. When the whole Liza/Mallory implosion happened, she'd taken a break from dating. What was the point of going out?

"No, but I notice things. You haven't had a date in a really long time. Maybe it's time?"

"Thanks, but no thanks," Emily said. "Don't worry about me. Go have fun tonight. There's some cash in the junk drawer. And I expect to be paid back."

"Suit yourself," Angus said, bounding towards the junk drawer. "I'm taking $50. I'll pay you back next week. My Lyft's here—later."

"Later. Angus!"

"Yeah?" Angus pivoted, hand on the front door. Steps from freedom.

"I love you."

"Love you, too, Mom."

# # #

"I need to get an assistant," Liza Barrett said to no one in particular, hoisting the last of her equipment cases out of the back of her Subaru, which she'd crammed into the only available spot she'd found on the street.

"Say again?" a man asked, stopping in his path.

"Oh, nothing," Liza closed the back hatch to her wagon. "Just talking to myself. Thanks."

"Need some help?"

"No—you know what, yes. That would be great. Could you grab that tripod and this tube? I'll meet you over there." Liza tilted her head towards the old cream-colored brick school building across the street, its entrance flanked by four stately Roman columns and lush greenery. What once had been Queen Anne High School was now a ritzy condominium building with an incredible view of the city, and her office for the evening.

She was practiced in this; it was as routine as pumping up her bicycle tires. And still, Liza was pushing the limits of her heart rate zones. Her watch said zone three, and she hadn't left the parking spot.

Photographing a wedding was a special kind of stress that only the closing miles of a tight race could rival. Though she'd asked for more, they had scheduled an hour for pre-wedding photos. Not enough time. There were always additions. Always, "just one more" takes. Cousins and friends and aunts who were left out of the shot list by accident. Someone who closed their eyes for every shot. The person who felt they should make a funny face during a serious pose. For all these reasons, and more, it wasn't enough time. But, as she always did, she'd make it work.

"Thanks," Liza said as she caught up to her helper at the top of the short staircase, bending to place a rolled backdrop on the marble landing.

"No worries," he said. "Is this where you're going? Just the front door here?"

"Well, no. I need to get up to the roof, but you don't have to do that."

"It's no trouble. I'll help. I don't have anywhere else to be."

Liza looked at the mystery man. He appeared to be in his mid-40s and was dressed in a navy-blue suit with brown leather wingtips. A bright pink tie provided a pop of color, and his left lapel showcased a blue and yellow equal symbol pin. His head was shaved close—hinting at light brown locks, but she couldn't be sure. His smile was broad; honey-colored eyes friendly.

"It sure looks otherwise," Liza said, "but I'll take the help. What brings you here?"

"My brother's getting married."

"Ah, so you knew this wasn't my destination. Gregg or James?"

"I had a hunch," he said. "I'm Gray, Gregg's older brother."

"Liza."

When she shook his hand, she saw it. Gregg's smile. Of course this was his brother. One of the more heartwarming side effects of photographing weddings was piecing together the family trees. Putting people together in photographs and seeing it—the family resemblance. The same smiles or eyes or turned up noses. Other than funerals, there wasn't another time when so many members of the same family showed up for each other. When they got together and supported those who shared their ancestry, their history, their troubles and triumphs. She was usually good at spotting family resemblance but had missed it with Gray.

"Gregg's told me about you," Gray said, turning toward the double-front doors and leading the way inside with his assigned equipment. "Kona, huh? Congratulations!"

"Yeah, three weeks and ticking," Liza said, "You race?"

As they carried gear up four flights of stairs to the roof, they discussed triathlon strategies—he was a short-course specialist; the hair made sense—the differences between sprint and Iron-distance races and the characteristics of people who favored the different lengths. Turned out they had more than Gregg in common. Gray once dated Liza's arch-nemesis, Nancy Callahan. In four flights of stairs, Liza found out more about Nancy Callahan than she'd learned in a decade of racing her. Gray'd heard the doping rumors, and was surprised. Liza said she was too, but grateful for her chance at the Ironman World Championships—finally.

"So, you ready?" Gray asked as he set the tripod on the roof deck.

"Not quite. I need a few more things from the car." Liza assessed the space amongst a handful of early wedding guests. Downtown Seattle loomed just beyond the edge of the roof deck, its picture-postcard view better than any backdrop she could supply, the iconic Space Needle presiding on the far western edge of the city. But light was an issue. In an hour, darkness would prevail. The grooms had insisted on photos at dusk—so romantic, they'd said. Experience taught her otherwise. She'd brought the backdrop as an insurance policy.

"I meant for the race, but sure," Gray said.

"Oh! I never think I'm ready for a race," Liza said. "Be right back, I need to run and get a couple of lights from the car. Would you mind just keeping an eye out here? And if you see the guys, tell them it's time— we're losing daylight!"

"Will do. I've never known Gregg to miss a photo op—I'm sure they're close."

Back at the car, Liza grabbed two stand lights and her phone, which she'd left in its holder mounted to the dashboard. Her form-fitted dress didn't have pockets, and she didn't have time to look at her phone while working, but she grabbed it anyway. A quick glance showed a text from groom #1, James, saying they were five minutes away—sent five minutes prior.

"Crap!" Liza blurted and slammed the door. Losing daylight and grooms that were now in place. She scanned the phone for any other important messages:

> Kate—*could wait.*
> Last week's client—*could wait.*
> Nathan—*she'd open that one.*

Good luck tonight, babe. I'm going to hit a karaoke bar and home by midnight. Facetime when you get home? XOXO

With a smile, Liza typed back that she couldn't wait to Facetime, to have fun singing, and she loved him. She'd much rather be snuggling into bed with Nathan when she got home that night, but at least technology gave her something to look forward to. She'd see his face and hear his voice and pretend they were together.

Soon.

For now, she was Liza, the wedding photographer, about to record a couple's most special day in digital history.

# # #

This time, the walk to Brazen was familiar. Invigorating. Twenty minutes to clear his head of the week—the meetings and stylists and publicists. Since he'd been in San Francisco, he'd been immersed in agent Julian DeMarco's "create a rock star" program, which had very defined steps: new hair, new clothes, media training.

"Trust me," Julian said as Nathan sat on a stool in front of a stark white wall, three people hovering around him as if he were an exhibit at a zoo, a photographer prompting him to smile and not smile. To pout and posture. To channel his sexiest head tilt.

"For them to look at later," Julian said about the photos. "So they can build you a complete look."

"I don't know, man," Nathan said at the suggestion that his new look should include a black leather jacket with multiple silver buckles. "It's not really me."

"That's just it." Julian clasped hands in acknowledgement as he too, hovered. "Nate Staples is *not* you. We have to find him. You supply the voice, but *Nate* is an *image*."

Walking to the edge of the Mission en route to the Castro district, Julian's words circled in his head. Nathan reflected on what was being asked of him: to let go of his notions of who he was and lean into becoming who he could be. Someone fans would love. Someone who would sell music. He wanted to be a rock star, right?

"You've been Nathan all your life," Julian said. "It's time to be Nate. It's time to reach your potential."

Could he do it?

Could he let go of Nathan and embrace the potential of Nate?

He'd already let go of his past once in his life when he transitioned. Could he squash the voices that said he was betraying everything he'd worked so hard for—his authenticity—to be, as Julian said, an image?

In a pair of slim-fit black 501s—no more baggy denim, he'd promised—a white V-neck T, and the once-questioned leather jacket, Nate Staples arrived at Brazen. Same sign out front announcing Karaoke. Same rainbow flag in the window next to the door. Head held high, its fresh dark highlights woven into his chestnut hair, he tossed open the door and headed to the bar. He knew the drill.

"Hey," Nate said, giving the bartender a casual smile. "Jason not working tonight?"

"He is," the woman said. "Smoke break. What can I get'cha?"

"Okay, cool. Can I have an Anchor Steam and get my name on the karaoke list? Nate Staples."

"Sure, doll. It's busy tonight—looks like eight in front'a ya. What'cha singin'?"

"'Landslide,' please."

"Don't know it."

"Fleetwood Mac? 'Landslide?'"

What person who worked in a karaoke bar didn't know "Landslide?"

"I'm just joshin' ya, kid. I know your song. You're good to go. Cheers."

Beer in hand, elbow resting on the bar, he surveyed the crowd. Some were there the week before; some he didn't remember. The scene was consistent—a Karaoke singer on stage, doing his best Elton John, his rendition of "Rocket Man" not interrupting the laughter and conversation and general milling taking place. Hands patted backs, drinks were swigged, conversation rumbled.

If anything could rile a bunch of queers, it was Stevie Nicks, Nate told himself as he took a draw of his Anchor Steam. The local's beer, it was more bitter than his preferred Rainier, but he liked it. It was something to hold *and* it took the nerves down a notch.

"Hey sexy," a voice said as a hand landed on his lower back. "You came back for more, huh?"

"I did," Nate smiled, tipping his beer in acknowledgement with a slosh. "Damn. Sorry about that. I'll go get a paper towel."

"Don't worry about it. I got it." Jason bent, bar towel in hand, and made quick work of the spill.

"Thanks. Guess I got a little carried away. Anyway, yeah, back for more."

"I'm glad. You look great—love the jacket."

"Really? I wasn't sure about it."

"It works," Jason said, straightening his bow tie. He was once again dressed in dark denim, no shirt, and a black satin bowtie, his defined abs on proud display. "How are you going to top 'Lights'? You have another Bay Area classic stuffed up that jacket of yours? Maybe a little Joplin?"

"Not Joplin, but kind of Bay Area, as a matter of fact."

"Oh yeah? What'cha singing?"

"You'll see."

"Alright superstar, good luck. Love the James Dean thing you've got happening." Jason traced a Z pattern with his forefinger in the air before walking away.

The heat on the back of Nate's earlobes had to be the overhead lights. Didn't it? Shaking his arms, he attempted to focus on the task at hand. It was his second "live show" since he'd been in San Francisco, but it was one song. Just one song. In less than five minutes, his performance would be over, and he'd go back to his tiny apartment and anonymity to wait for what the next week would bring.

Julian said they'd start auditioning band members on Monday, and Charles was coming to town to participate. Something to look forward to. As he watched the rotation of Karaoke-goers, Nate rehearsed the lyrics in his head. The bar had a teleprompter, but he wouldn't use it. To respect the music, he memorized lyrics.

Three-piece tux woman was there again, this time singing "Hallelujah," and killing it with her incredible range. Nate clapped as she finished and congratulated himself on his timing—there was one more after her before his turn. He didn't want to follow her again.

"And next up—" the female bartender's voice echoed through the bar. "Oh, hang tight."

After a brief pause, she was back. "Looks like we lost one. Next up, Nate Staples."

"Dammit," Nate said under his breath and bounced towards the small stage, just as he had the week prior. "It looks like we're starting a bit of a tradition, huh? Thank you very much, Shellie. That was beautiful."

Shellie straightened her suit, took another bow, and handed off the mic.

"Alright, y'all. I've been going through a lot of changes lately, so I picked 'Landslide' to sing for you. Help me out if you know it."

Nate stood in the center of the stage, in the single spotlight, and took a deep breath. The opening bars set him up with perfection; it was time. He did what he did so well: Sing. With feeling. With heart. Because he got the lyrics. And because he lived them. When he hit the chorus, he hit the deck, both knees on the stage, mic cupped in both hands, he sang about being afraid to change because of a life built around a person—or perhaps an image of a person.

By the end of the song, he had them singing along, just as he'd requested. Who could resist a good sing-along song? No one could. Especially not when there was booze involved.

"Thanks, everybody," Nate smiled as he bowed to applause, song carried through completion. "I'll see you next week. Hit me up if you have any requests—I clearly need to step up my game!"

Walking off the stage, it hit him. He'd always thought the person the narrator had built their life around was a lover. Now, he wondered—was it actually the narrator? Was all the fear of change and of getting older centered around letting go of an image of oneself to become someone different.

TEN

Liza rolled over in bed and clicked the power button on her phone—2:11 a.m. She'd been half attempting to sleep and half waiting for Nathan to call for two hours. Nothing on either front. Sleep was elusive; so was her promised Facetime call.

Hugging a pillow, she flopped back onto the mattress, reminded once again why she didn't favor long distance relationships. It wasn't forever, but she was getting a glimpse into what life would be like when Nathan was on the road. People made it work all the time, she told herself. They could make this work.

Hi, said the text. *You still up?*

Hi, Liza replied.

As fast as she hit send, her phone rang with a Facetime call, a smiling, leather jacket wearing Nathan on the other end to greet her. Aside from the new jacket, his hair looked different, too. Were those highlights?

"Hi beautiful," he said from his futon in San Francisco, looking more comfortable amidst its well-worn fabric, the usual steel in his eyes amplified by bright fluorescent light. "I'm sorry it's so late. Karaoke went long. How was the wedding?"

"Hi," Liza said, the middle-of-the-night frog in her throat adding a few extra syllables as she coerced her vocal chords to work. "It's okay. I wasn't sleeping. The wedding was beautiful. Gregg's brother married them and they had a lovely ceremony. James sang his vows. Almost made me cry."

"You're going soft!"

"I said *almost*," Liza laughed. "I have a soft spot for singers. How was karaoke?"

"It was super fun. I followed the suit woman, Shellie, again. That's why I'm late. We talked a bunch and I asked her to audition for the band. To sing backup."

"Really?"

"Yeah, she has incredible range. And she's quirky."

"We love quirky," Liza said, ruffling her hair with her free hand.

"We do. Anyway, she's into it, so I'm excited to see what Julian thinks."

"That's great. So, what did you sing?"

"'Landslide.'"

"Oh, I love that one!"

"Yeah, it was awesome. Have you ever thought about the line where she talks about building her life around someone and being afraid to change? This part—"

Nathan sang the chorus—a reminder of the lyric, and an appeal to Liza's soft spot for singers.

"So pretty, babe. I wish I'd been there."

"I know. That's the hardest part of all this. I'm doing all this work and making all these changes and you're not here. It got me thinking, that line about being afraid to change because you've built a life around another person—it's not about a lover. I always thought it was about building your life with someone and then realizing it wasn't the right life. What if it's about being afraid to change because you've built your life around *an image of yourself* and you don't know how to change that?"

"Too deep for 2 a.m.," Liza said. "But it totally could be. Are you feeling like you're making too many changes?"

"Yeah, I did feel that way. Last week was a lot. But I think the song opened my eyes to why I was scared to change. Funny, huh? A random song I chose for karaoke taught me something!"

"That sounds exactly like what should happen," Liza said. "Things happen for a reason."

It may have been too early for song lyric analysis, but without effort, the conversation flowed again. Just as it always did. They didn't struggle with dead air. Didn't want for topics. Didn't worry about running out of things to say. Nathan told of the bar and its cast of characters: the older woman bartender who wore a tiara in her hair and called him 'doll.' Shellie's three-piece suits and voice of an angel. The hang outs and hook ups that happened around him. How the San Francisco bar scene was so similar to Seattle's, and yet so different. There was something about the air, he said. Maybe it was the salt from the Bay. Maybe it was the fog. It just *felt* different. People were people. But there was something special about the place.

"I really miss you," he said. "Only three weeks 'till Kona. After your race, I'm not letting you out of my sight!"

"I miss you, too," Liza frowned all the way to her forehead. "I'm so proud of you. But I really hate this."

"Me, too. Could you maybe get away?"

"Come to San Francisco?"

"Yeah!"

"When?"

"I know you have a wedding on the weekend, but what about after? Charles will be here next week, so maybe after he leaves? We could have a little fun in the evenings. I could show you around my 'hood a little. We could hang out like normal."

"Oh, now it's your 'hood?!" Liza leaned against the headboard and smiled into the phone. "You're becoming a San Franciscan?"

"Just for a little while. Whatd'ya say? Come down for a few days? You could run through Golden Gate Park and I'm sure there's a pool. It'll be fun. Please?"

"You don't have to ask me twice. I miss falling asleep with you. This—" Liza hugged her extra pillow, "isn't the same."

"So, you'll come?"

"Hell yeah I'll come!"

"And you'll be okay for training? I don't want to mess up your schedule."

"I'll be okay. But I should try to sleep now. I have a long ride/run brick in the morning, and one more next Saturday, then I'm going to start tapering again. It's actually perfect timing. I'll be in taper mode to see you."

"I can't wait," Nathan stood, shrugging off the leather jacket he initially hated and now felt made him look more butch than his preferred buffalo plaid. "Get some good sleep, love."

"Sweet dreams," Liza said, placing her hand to her lips and blowing an air kiss. "I can't wait to see you. And we'll talk about that jacket then."

# # #

She'd procrastinated enough. The house was spotless—not a speck of dust to be found on a baseboard or a hint of mold in the fridge. No laundry uncleaned. No toilet unscrubbed. Emily Hall had nothing left to do, except what she really needed to be doing all along: write. She owed her editor the first 100 pages of her second novel in a less than a month, and she had zero pages written. She had ideas and plot points. She had character names and alternate character names.

But she'd yet to put fingers to a keyboard.

Starting was the hardest part.

Starting meant she'd have to finish, which was perhaps harder than starting. The fact was, she was scared to start.

So, she did what any respectable writer would do: Pulled on a pair of sweatpants and her coziest hoodie, brewed a full pot of coffee, set her phone to mute, and bribed herself. Two thousand words. Two thousand words before Angus woke up would earn her a new pair of shoes from Nordstrom. Four thousand came with a new handbag. She wouldn't get crazy and expect six thousand. Though Angus could sleep long enough, six thousand was pushing it. Two thousand would be perfectly acceptable—a solid B+.

With a mug of coffee taking its regular place on the desk, Emily fired up her laptop. She shifted in the seat, took a sip of coffee, and then stared at the screen, cursor beckoning her to type something. Anything.

She flipped the hood of her sweatshirt over her head and flipped it back down. Took another sip of coffee, its nutty warmth filling her body with liquid motivation. Fingers poised, she stared. That damn cursor just blinked.

Her idea was to write a memoir-style novel, told from the viewpoint of London Greer, one-half of the couple whose story was soon to unfold. Emily closed her eyes and started typing—she didn't need to look at the screen or keys. She needed to feel the character's story. She knew it would be a story of falling in love, then out of it. Of misery apart. Reuniting and rekindling. Of long distance and too-close-for-comfort. Her goal was to tell a relatable story—one where the characters had human traits and flaws. Where they were selfish at times and giving in others. She purposely sought out to write a made-up memoir, which had to be easier than writing a true memoir, right?

Somehow, someway, the words spilled out. Clunky at first, and then with more grace, she found London's voice—which really meant she found her voice. In their meeting, Jen had told her it was a good idea. But was it a good idea because it really was—or because Jen wanted a baby and a central theme of the book was about trying to conceive as a same-sex couple?

Emily had come by Angus the old-fashioned way. She didn't know the struggles of same-sex couple parenthood firsthand, but she could imagine. She'd heard it time and again from friends and occasionally from lovers who'd been through it: insurance didn't cover expensive fertility treatments. An audience of would-be parents could relate to her character's struggle—if only she could summon the emotion attached to it.

Which gave her an idea.

Jen wanted kids. Maybe she'd share some real-life insights into what it was like to venture into baby-making outside of a heteronormative situation? Would that be crossing a line, Emily wondered? Asking her publisher for such personal information to help write a book she'd promised she could deliver? She imagined the scenario in her head—going to dinner, asking questions with journalistic precision, pretending to be all-business, not letting on that she may have ulterior motives.

Chiding herself for once again for imagining something that couldn't be—she'd been doing that a lot lately—Emily re-focused her runaway thoughts on the book's prologue. The internet would provide all the answers and background info she needed to write the book. Much as she was tempted, she'd leave Jen out of it.

ELEVEN

"I can't believe this was my last day of work," Kate said, taking a pull on the beer that'd just arrived at their table. "Twenty years of my life. Woosh! Gone in an instant."

"How does it feel?" Christine asked.

"Surreal."

"I bet."

"I know I don't have to go to work on Monday, but I have that Friday night feeling. Like, better have some fun for a few days because Monday will be here in a minute, and for two nights, I don't have to worry about work. But—I *really* don't have to worry about work. Which is just—weird." Kate signaled with a raised finger for their server to return to the corner booth at Prospect. It wasn't a Friday night without a visit to the local haunt. "Can we get two glasses of sparkling wine?"

In a feat of speed, two flutes of wine were on the table, bubbles floating to the tops in rapid succession.

"Enjoy it," Christine said. "You've worked hard for this moment. Cheers to the unknown, the magic of new beginnings, and the ranch."

"Cheers to all those things—especially the new beginnings," Kate said.

"Have you thought of a name for the ranch?"

"I have a few in mind. I can't decide which!"

As they talked, Kate inched away from her side of the booth, the want of closeness drawing her like a magnet until their thighs touched. She was going to miss this easy proximity, the instant electricity in her veins when their bodies found each other.

"You two want any food?" The server reappeared with a tablet, stylus poised to take their orders, long sleeves rolled up to her elbows revealing elaborate tattoo sleeves.

"We're good for now, yeah?" Kate said.

"Yeah," Christine said with an easy smile, "we're good."

"Okay, let me know if you change your mind." As fast as she arrived, the server was gone again, tending to the regulars and one-timers, the crowd building as Happy Hour got into full swing. She was winning in the speed department that evening.

"So, you've talked all around it, but you haven't told me one single name idea! What's your baby's name?"

"Well—I was thinking Galloping Gallatin Grange. Nods to the mountains and the horses. And I love an alliteration. But I'm torn between that and naming it after the dogs. Something like Lucky Lab Ranch. Or even D+ H Estates. I really don't know!"

"Mm-hm. I see the problem."

"You do?"

"You're addressing this like an engineer. All logic. No heart." Christine reached for Kate's hand, bedside manner appearing.

"Really?"

"Maybe you need to dig a little deeper. Find a name that *means* something to you. This is going to be your home—do you want to go home to 'Galloping Gallatin Grange?'"

"I thought the alliteration was good. I found a "G" word that means ranch!"

"Okay, so you'd get an 'A' on your English paper for your vocabulary, but it doesn't roll off the tongue. 'Lucky Lab,' maybe. 'D + H Estates' sounds like a winery."

"Ouch," Kate said. "Talk about brutal honesty! This is why people don't share baby names before they're born."

"And it's why they should," Christine chuckled, right on cue.

"Wow, you're on fire tonight! Good thing I have a thick skin built by two decades in tech."

"Do you want to brainstorm some ideas? Maybe you just need some help to spark your emotions."

"Okay, Dr. Downer, let's brainstorm."

"Can't let go of the alliterations, huh?"

"Not even a little," Kate smiled, squeezing Christine's hand. She could take the heat.

"Alright, keep in mind there's not a lot of room for creativity in my day job. Patients don't really like it when you 'brainstorm' with them, so this may not work. But how about a word association game? I say a word—you say the first thing that comes to mind. I bet we'll find your name in there somewhere."

"I'm in," Kate said. "Hit me with your best shot."

"Shot."

"What?"

"That's your first word," Christine said. "Shot."

"Cuervo."

"Landscape."

"Painting," Kate said, sliding back across the table so she could look at the woman pummeling words at her. Christine had pinned back her silver-flecked hair with a barrette in each side. Clear-frame eyeglasses sat on the bridge of her nose with authority. Her nose was strong, not a hint of a crook in it. When she smiled, her eyes twinkled; the fine lines around them making a brief appearance. She wore a black mock turtleneck sweater that emphasized her long neck.

Leaning forward across the table, hands clasped creating a V shape with her arms, Kate urged her mind to focus; not to get lost in the eyes behind the glasses. Not to jump forward in the evening, to when they'd land in bed laughing.

"Horse," Christine said, breaking Kate's trance.

"Black Beauty."

"Cowboy."

"Cowgirl," Kate said, "Keep it coming. I could do this all night."

"Romance."

"Novels."

"Happy," Christine smiled. She too, could do this all night.

"Love."

"Love?"

"Yeah, I'm happy when I'm in love," Kate admitted, sitting a little straighter in her seat.

"Are you happy now?"

This was the moment. The moment that had been building for months. A feeling not assigned words yet, for a hundred reasons—and for no reason. In a split second, was living in an impressionist painting, the scene discernable, but muted. And she had a decision to make.

Spill the beans and risk alienating the one person who she worried about alienating. Stay silent and risk alienating the same person.

It was a lose/lose—or a win/win. A coin flip.

Kate cleared her throat and waited one more beat, searching for answers in those twinkly pine-colored eyes staring at her, unrelenting. She'd just upended her entire life by quitting her job and buying a ranch. What was one more major decision in the mix of mixing it up? "I'm very happy. I'm undeniably giddy, in fact."

"Me, too," Christine said, reaching across the table to unwind the V of Kate's hands and hold them in hers. "I'm beyond happy. And that's something I haven't owned in a very long time."

"Are you saying what I *think* you're saying?"

"I don't know. Are you saying what *I* think *you're* saying?"

"I'm saying I'm in love with you," Kate blurted. "Totally, madly, can't-see-straight, in love with you."

No turning back now. That impressionist painting was hanging on in the background as she waited, teeth biting lower lip. Feet bouncing to an imaginary beat. Breath held.

"I'm saying that I'm in love with you, too. I didn't think I'd ever again feel for someone what I do for you. You've renewed my spirit, Kate. And you've renewed my life."

"Well, that's a relief."

"I know!"

"My mom will be so happy to hear we had this talk," Kate laughed.

"As will my dad! But this doesn't solve the problem. The ranch name."

"How about—Second Chance Ranch?"

"Kate! That's brilliant! See—you just needed to lead with your heart, not your alliterations."

# # #

Friday nights were for drinking wine and charting the week's book sales in her basement. It'd been her routine for nearly a year, and she liked it. Watching sales numbers was a guilty pleasure—seeing her authors' success felt like her own. Because it was.

That Friday evening, however, didn't involve wine. Jen Scott was off alcohol indefinitely, the final stages of pregnancy prep in full swing. When 8:00 rolled around and she'd run sales numbers for all her authors, she had time on her hands, and no crutch. Wine would dull the sadness of singledom, or at least, let her forget about it for a while.

Faced with her own company and no vices as a distraction, Jen caved. She swiped her phone screen and pulled up the dating app she'd reluctantly signed up for at her sister's suggestion. No, that's not the right word. At her sister's *insistence.*

Jen told Maggie it was futile. The dating apps were full of the same people and the same BS. Everyone who was single was on all the apps, a recycled ocean of washed-up fish with the likelihood of making a match almost nil. And she would know—stats were her life.

"You never know," Maggie insisted. "What if someone just came out of a relationship they've been in for a long time?"

"Then I don't want to date them," Jen shot back. She definitely did not want to date someone coming out of a long-term relationship. She'd been that person. She'd dated that person. That person wasn't ready. And she didn't have time to help heal the wounds associated with a divorce or long-term relationship break-up.

"Okay," Maggie said, "what about someone who hasn't dated much so they're easing into apps?"

"Also don't want to date them. I don't have time for insta-love or insta-drama."

"Sister, listen to me. If you keep up all these rules, you're never going to find someone and you're going to end up raising that kid alone. Which is a perfectly fine thing to do, but I believe you want a partner to share your life. Do you not?"

"I do," Jen told her sister, weeks before. Before she ran into Kate. Before she travelled the road to the past. "I miss having someone to share my life with."

And that's why she was sitting cross-legged on her couch, hair pinned into a loose bun on the top of her head, coziest sweatshirt with the neck cut out a la "Fame" fame keeping her warm amidst the chill of fall. She had a death grip on her phone as she swiped—mostly left; rejections—to reveal the next prospect.

"Nope," Jen said aloud in response to a twenty-five-year-old with a purple poodle and a tongue ring.

"Next," she said to a man who'd somehow wrangled his way into the lesbian listings. It happened time and again, and she always wondered, "why?" She didn't want to date a man, even a man who was in tune with his feminine side.

With a fire crackling in the fireplace, she swiped. Favorite Indigo Girls record on the player, she swiped some more. After twenty solid minutes of fruitless effort, she started negotiating with herself. "Just swipe right on *someone,*" she told herself. Find someone *good enough* to get the ball rolling. Certainly, she could swipe right on someone she'd never met, never seen out at a bar, never heard about through the gayvine. There had to be at least one person in the Inferno app with whom she could potentially have a conversation.

The last swipe turned out to be the most important one.

Emily Hall was on Inferno. Of course, her profile was well written. And charming. Her photo showed a feminine woman in a wrap dress, shoulder-length chestnut hair curled, sincere smile the foundation of her thin face. In the photo, she looked like a runway model, her make-up understated but well-done, her figure impressive. Jen knew Emily practiced yoga—and it showed. A femme woman who was into fashion and could express herself well. AKA, Jen's type. If you don't count her ex-wife. Or the firefighter. Okay. Let's call it Jen's *evolved* type.

If they didn't know each other, this was a woman for whom she'd swipe right. But they did know each other. They more than knew each other—Emily was one of her authors. There were professional boundaries she needed to mind.

She couldn't date an author.

Could she?

"Hey," Maggie said when she answered her phone. "What's wrong?"

"Why do you always answer with 'what's wrong?'" Jen asked with a "pfft" instead of a question mark.

"Because it's Friday night. Friday nights are numbers nights. You don't call me on Friday nights unless something's wrong."

"Crap," Jen said as she tossed another log onto the fire.

"So, what's wrong?"

"Nothing's wrong, per se. I just need your advice about something. But first, how are you?"

"It's 9:00 on a Friday night and I answered your call on the first ring. You do the math."

"Ah, sorry. Still in a dry spell?" Jen asked, already knowing the answer. Her sister wasn't shy about sharing her dating adventures. If she answered on a Friday night, she was in a dry spell.

"Yep. And you?"

"In more ways than one. I haven't had a drink in two weeks."

"Good girl. Let those hormones do their jobs! So, what's up, then?"

"I took your advice and set up an Inferno account."

"It's about damn time! You can't meet someone if you don't look!" Maggie said.

"Yeah, well. As I told you, it's the same recycled pool of people that it always is, except—"

"Yeah?"

"Remember that author I told you about, the English teacher with the fifteen-year-old?"

"Rings a bell."

"Well," Jen said, sitting and recrossing her legs on the couch, the fire more interesting than before, its crackles and pops setting the stage for her revelation. "She's on the app."

"And? You like her?"

Silence, save for the now-roaring fire.

"You like her!" Maggie shouted, just as she had when they were kids and she'd figured out one of her sister's secret crushes. "You like Emily!"

"Maybe," Jen said. "But it's wrong, right? I can't swipe for one of my authors."

"Why not?"

"We work together!"

"But do you? You run the publishing company. She has another job. She's written one book that you're publishing. I hardly call that 'working together.' Hang on—"

Jen heard muffled voices in the background. Her sister was clearly not at home.

"Sorry about that, I'm back."

"Where are you?"

"Just a bar," Maggie said, the shrug in her shoulders coming through the airwaves loud and clear. "What? It's not for lack of trying. I'm trying, too."

"No judgment. Do what you need to do," Jen said, and meant it. Her sister's marriage had imploded at about the same time as hers. They'd always been close, but simultaneous divorces brought them closer.

"You need to swipe for Emily," Maggie insisted. "Swipe. What's the worst that can happen? She doesn't swipe back? She says she's not interested? Or, you find something with a future with someone who meets your quality bar? Just saying—I don't see a lot of downside. Swipe."

"Are you sure?"

"Didn't you call me so I'd tell you to swipe?"

"Maybe."

"Then fucking swipe! Just do it. If she doesn't swipe back, no loss. If she freaks out, tell her you were drunk and you're sorry. If she's into you, well, I don't have to tell you what to do there. I gotta go, hon. I'm going to go chat up a very handsome young man hanging out by the bar alone."

"Thanks, Mags. Really. Go do your thing. Love you."

"Love you, too. Let me know how it goes!"

Jen envied her sister. She had the gumption to walk up to a stranger and start a conversation based solely on physical attraction. That had never really been her game. She wouldn't dream of approaching someone she didn't know with no purpose other than trying to arrange a hook up.

Which brought her back to her phone. And Emily.

Maggie supported the swipe.

Her loneliness condoned a swipe.

Her professional alter ego questioned it.

"Oh, what the hell," Jen said as she swiped right—the modern equivalent of "I like you"—on Emily Hall's profile.

TWELVE

"You ready?" Nathan yelled towards the back of his rental apartment in the Mission district, pulling on his new favorite accessory—the leather jacket. As it turns out, people can change.

"Give me a minute! Beauty takes time!" Charles Martinez shouted. His hair needed a touch more fussing; eyebrows needed one more pass with the tweezers.

"I'm sure you look great. We need to leave in five!" Nathan sunk into the futon to which he'd become accustomed and missed his comfy couch back home. Just a few more weeks in the rental and he'd be free to go to Kona to see Liza race, and then—finally—he could go home. Though he missed Seattle and the reliable comfort of his own home, having Charles in town for the week helped. Immensely. A sense of normalcy followed Charles and his prissy banter.

"Okay, how do I look?" his friend asked as he runway-walked through the tiny living space, pivoting on one toe and returning.

"You look like Ricky Martin!"

"Perfect. You be my entourage and I'll pick up a groupie or two tonight."

"Dude."

"What?"

"You are not bringing a guy back here tonight."

"Who said I'd bring him back here?" Charles asked, flipping the collar of his black blazer up. "I'm going home with a local, baby, mark my words. Let's go."

The walk to Brazen went faster with company, the friends re-living a week that resulted in them having a band—again. They'd auditioned bassists, guitarists, keyboard players, back-up singers, and a few all-rounders who could play multiple instruments. When Charles arrived in San Francisco that Monday, they had a lead singer and a drummer. Now, they had a five-piece band and three backup singers, one of whom was Shellie, the karaoke phenom Nathan invited to audition.

"Nice job this week," Charles said as they walked past an Italian restaurant blasting opera music to its patio and beyond. "You really stepped up and owned being Nate Staples. I noticed."

"Thanks, man. I'm getting there."

"It shows. I didn't trust Julian at the start, but he knows what he's doing. I get it now."

"Yeah, it was a rocky start," Nathan said, looking at his feet as they moved over concrete. He'd traded his comfortable Chuck Taylors for a pair of black leather wingtips—all part of the transformation. "He's pushing me hard—in good ways. The last few weeks have been intense. I just hope it all comes together like he says it will. It's a big sacrifice if it doesn't go anywhere."

"You still missing home?"

"Yeah, but not as much. I'm figuring out San Francisco. It's different. But also, the same. I'm meeting people—that helps. Karaoke helps, too. Something to look forward to."

"Your Shellie find was brilliant. I can't believe you found her singing karaoke! She's going to up our game a ton—so many possibilities for duets, and more depth to the sound. You think she'll sing tonight?" Charles walked proud—head held high, thumbs hanging out of his slacks pockets, sex oozing out of his well-groomed pores. He'd donned a slim-fit black suit, white shirt, and black tie that evening, his Nordstrom discount once again proving beneficial in providing the perfect outfit for the occasion. He'd trimmed his beard close, leaving just a hint of stubble; jet black hair blown into a perfect raised part.

"Right? She blows me away. I hope she sings tonight. It's nerve-wracking to follow her, but worth it. You ready?"

"For?"

"To sing?" Nathan asked.

"I was born ready, you know that!"

"Gonna tell me your song?"

"No chance in hell. You'll hear it with the crowd."

"Suit yourself. I'm going with 'Heaven.'"

"Bryan Adams or Kane Brown?" Charles knew his fair share of country music—hat tip to Texas for turning him on to country as a kid.

"Adams. I've been working on putting a little gravel in my voice—figured that was a good one to try it out."

"Good choice. Oh, look," Charles said, when they were about fifty feet from the bar's entrance. "It hasn't changed a bit."

"Feels like coming home?"

"Yep. To my early twenties—when I was so happy to be out of Texas and in the gayest place on earth. Even if it was only for a couple months. Sometimes I wonder what would've happened if my dad hadn't gotten sick—I doubt I would've gone back to Texas. But probably wouldn't have made it to Seattle, either."

"Things happen for a reason," Nathan said, remembering what Liza told him. "And it's my honor to welcome you back to the gayest place on earth. After you." Nathan held the door and noticed the sign out front. In block letters, it said, "Karaoke Tonight," just as it had the past two times he'd been there. The butterflies in his stomach were present, but less pushy. Maybe Brazen was becoming his home, too.

He'd only sung for the Saturday night crowd—didn't know what to expect from a Friday. At first glance, it looked the same. The place was packed. People were talking and laughing and enjoying their social time. There were definite regulars he'd seen before, including Shellie, who was nursing a mixed drink near the stage.

"I'll have an Anchor, and—"

"—get your name on the list for Karaoke," the bartender finished.

"Hey Jason," Nathan said, motioning to his right with his head, "This is my buddy, Charles."

"Hi Charles," Jason said, sliding a draft beer across the bar in Nathan's direction. "What'cha havin'?"

"Dirty martini, Absolut." Charles flashed his Ricky Martin smile. "And your number."

"Tempting," Jason said, a rendition of "Piano Man" happening behind them on the stage. "But I don't date the clientele." He winked at Nathan when he said, "clientele."

"Ouch," Charles said, pushing a twenty towards the shirtless barkeep. "But I understand. Thanks for the drink. Keep the change. Hey—can I get my name on the list, too? Charles Martinez."

"Okay, Chuck. What'cha singin?'"

Charles leaned across the bar, the distinctive aroma of beer taps co-mingling with whiskey mash, muddled with Jason's cologne and sweat, a musky/salty/hoppy combination. "Livin' La Vida Loca," Charles whispered into Jason's ear, lips brushing his earlobe as he delivered the message.

"Got it. And what're you singing this week, sexy?" Jason nodded, looking towards his favorite customer of the two in front of him.

"'Heaven,' Bryan Adams." There was that pesky heat on the back of his neck again.

"Okay, got it. Chuck, secret song. Nate, 'Heaven.' Have fun, boys."

They found a spot in the back corner of the bar, perfect for Nathan to watch the other singers and Charles to scan the crowd. He'd promised he'd go home with someone that night; he needed to scout his options.

"So, the bartender's into you, huh?" Charles asked with a poke to Nathan's waist.

"Hm?"

"The hunk behind the bar. With the abs. And eyes—damn. He's into you."

"He's not."

"Dude. Listen to me. You're missing it. He's into you."

"Okay, so? What if he is?"

"Aren't you a little curious?" Charles asked as he downed the martini, his allocated one glass of hard liquor now consumed. With vodka for dinner and olives for dessert, it'd be soda water for the rest of the evening—his waistline insisted.

"No."

"Okay, but he is."

"Well, that's great. I'm in a relationship."

"Not even a little bit curious?" Charles continued, the way only a brother could. They may not have been biological brothers, but they'd been best friends for over a decade—they were chosen brothers.

"No," Nathan said, the red from the back of his neck moving to his cheeks. He wouldn't mention that Jason had given *him* his number, unprompted.

"You are!"

"I'm not."

"The red on your face says otherwise."

"It's hot in here."

"Yeah, it's smokin' hot in the bartender department!"

"Alright, alright. Can we just drop it? I'm in a relationship. It's already hard enough being apart—I don't want to talk about this."

"Suit yourself. Oh, look, it's Shellie! Shhhh. I want to hear her."

Shellie, as usual, took command of the stage in a three-piece suit—purple that night, to match her tips—and stood in the spotlight. She took a deep breath, closed her eyes, and opened with gusto, channeling a young Cher turning back time, right down to the tongue flick. When she was finished, the crowd was mesmerized—and Nathan made a mental note: Work up a Cher cover.

"Alright my Brazen family," Shellie said. "For the third week in a row, I'm happy to present, Nate Staples! But before I do, I'm even happier to report that Nate has a band—that I've just joined. So be on the lookout for us singing together, soon. Nate, take it away!"

# # #

The walk home went as Charles had predicted: Nathan placed one foot in front of the other and ambled back home from the Castro—alone. Charles's theatrical rendition of "Livin' La Vida Loca," had sold the Ricky Martin image he was going for, and after he sauntered off stage with a huge grin, Nathan didn't see him again. It was just as well—he needed time to clear his head.

The sidewalks were damp—it had rained while they were in the bar. In the 2 a.m. glow of streetlights, Nathan looked beyond parked cars to shiny oil spots in the empty streets. Filled with Rorschach blots, the streets had a story, too. The undulating hills told of cars and motorcycles. Rain slowly eroding pavement. Of dreams formed and dreams lost by those who travelled the well-worn city streets daily.

With "Heaven," playing on repeat in his mind, Nathan walked. He'd chosen the song because he thought it was beautiful, but there was more to the story. It nodded to his life with Liza, too. In some ways, growing up together. Getting to know each other as they evolved and having memories to reflect on from many years in the past. They had so much history together, and while their romantic relationship was new, their memories ran deep.

"Nothing can take you away from me," repeated in an endless loop, the line hitting him on a cellular level.

He wouldn't admit it out loud—to anyone.

Hell, he didn't want to admit it to himself.

Curiosity about the bartender was growing. In the quiet crevices of his mind, when he wasn't thinking about building the band, wasn't pushing his creative boundaries, when he was still and surrounded with quiet, thoughts of Jason broke through. Like a thief in the night, they were unwelcomed and took parts of him he didn't want taken.

Can you hold space in your heart for two people? Can you truly love someone if your mind wanders into unknown territory with another? He'd never considered being with a man. Not before his transition, and not after. Was it power of suggestion? The power of someone wanting him? Or was it more? Was he attracted to the bartender, or the *idea* of the bartender? Was he just lonely?

A hundred questions swirled without answers, serenaded by Bryan Adams with his own voice. Nathan told himself it was curiosity, that's all. Nothing on which he would act. Nothing for which he would risk his relationship with Liza Barrett.

Liza, who had one more big workout and one more wedding to shoot—the next day—before she headed to the Bay to spend time with him. Liza, who'd supported him through his transition, through breaking up the band, chasing his crazy dream. Who'd encouraged him to sign with Julian and see what happened. Who'd listened when he said he didn't want to talk about the pile of letters from his family she'd found in the kitchen—and hadn't brought it up since. Liza, who was a loving and supportive partner.

It was too late to call, so he pulled out his phone and sent a text for her to see when she woke.

I can't wait to see you! Have a great ride today and then get some rest. I love you, Liz. XOXO

# # #

Ah, Saturday. Emily Hall's favorite day. After teaching teenagers about literature for five days straight, she reveled in the downtime that was the weekend. Her time. With Angus at his dad's, she had two full days to do whatever she wanted. As she relaxed into the comfortable final pose of her morning yoga practice, a hint of fall sunshine peeked through the high windows of her family room, that last weekend in September. Emily breathed out. Allowed her mind to think about nothing at all. No Holden Caulfield. No lesson plans. No grilling Angus about whatever he was up to that day. Just peace in her head and quiet in her house.

Rolling onto her side, Emily sat up and bowed her head, saying a moment of grace for the blood running through her veins and the air that filled her lungs. "Namaste," she said to no one, and popped to her feet. "It's going to be a good day."

Drip by drip, the coffee pot announced its hard work, until there was enough in the carafe for a full cup. Waiting for that first taste of Saturday morning, she thought about what she'd write that day. The week had yielded twenty-five pages in her new novel. An encouraging start. Another twenty-five would keep her on pace to meet her first deadline; beat it, even. She liked the world she was building, where two people could find each other in a sea of sameness, their souls unknowingly meant for each other. A world where they could face obstacles and sometimes prevail, sometimes fail, and sometimes separate, only to re-find each other and pick up where they left off. Thoughts of asking Jen for insight into the upcoming plot arc—the couple trying to conceive—floated in the back of her mind, and she dismissed them as soon as they popped up. It wasn't needed.

With the coffee ready and the day's scenes developing in her head, she grabbed a mug from the dish drainer and took a long sip of a full vessel, the distinctive aroma of a dark roast filling her senses every bit as much as that first sip. She'd gone out of her way the night before to grab a pound of her favorite Kaladi Brothers beans.

Her Saturday ritual continued at the dining table, the daily newspaper replaced with news brought to her through the media of the times—social media. A swipe of the phone brought it to life, its excitement displayed in the colorful icons that looked back at her. Instagram. Facebook. Email. Her bank's app. The weather. They all had a place on her home screen. As did Inferno, the dating app she hadn't looked at in months. She hadn't yet deleted it—there was a piece of her that always had hope—but she rarely opened it. That morning, a red dot in the corner of the app's bold "I" icon indicated new activity.

Before she checked her social feeds or email, her index finger instinctively hovered over that red dot.

"Probably nothing," Emily said to herself as she tapped the icon.

That couldn't be right.

Jennifer Scott had swiped right on her profile. Dangerous territory.

For all the reasons she told herself not to ask for help with the more personal aspects of her book, she shouldn't return the swipe. Even if she wanted to.

Jen was her publisher. And Kate's ex-wife. There had to be rules against dating your publisher. There were definitely rules about dating your friend's ex-wife. Especially when you knew so many intimate details about their relationship as it dissolved.

Maybe it was a drunk swipe? Or a late-night mistake?

But.

Maybe it was on purpose. Maybe Jen felt the electricity she did when their hands had touched at their last meeting. Maybe, it wasn't in her head.

She checked her texts to see if Jen had sent an "oopsie, my mistake," text. Nothing. The data suggested Jen was serious.

She shouldn't return the swipe. Should she?

Conversations with Jen came easily. They shared a love of fashion and books. Jen wanted kids, and of course, Emily had one. They hadn't had a shortage of things to talk about, and they'd barely scratched the surface.

And yet.

This was an awkward position. Jen had signed her for two books—the first of which wasn't yet published, and the second still unfinished. Barely started, in fact.

If she returned the swipe, there might be something there. But there might not be, and their working relationship could get awkward.

If she didn't, she might miss out on something potentially great. And, their working relationship could get awkward.

It was an impossible choice.

Weighing the options, she remembered what Mallory told her when they broke up over the summer: *Relationships are all about timing.* And she needed to stop apologizing so much. She could own her actions without guilt or regret.

"To timing," Emily said, raising the mug of coffee in a solitary toast.

With the flick of her finger, she'd returned the swipe.

And with a sharp inhale, she realized what she'd done.

No turning back now.

THIRTEEN

The last time Liza'd been in San Francisco had been for a symphony concert at the Masonic Hall. Her mom's orchestra had toured the west coast that summer, and she'd missed them in Seattle—she was racing Ironman Canada. Failing to qualify for Kona in Canada that year—like all the other years before it—had crushed her. So, she'd flown down to see the concert and spend time with her moms.

Liza called the woman who'd carried her, "Mom," and her other parent, "Mama." She was the spitting image of her mom—same fiery red hair, same all-American smile, same obsession with excellence. They were no-nonsense, Type A types. But they both had a creative streak. Her mom, Ruth, played first violin for the Boise Symphony and threw pottery. Liza'd also been a first violin, but unlike her mom, sports were even more compelling than music. That must've come from the donor—a man she'd never met, nor cared to. When she gave up the violin to pursue triathlon, her mom was disappointed, but understanding. She knew the urge to compete—to win—had to come from within, and if triathlon did it for her daughter, triathlon it was.

Liza beared no physical resemblance to Dorothy, AKA, Mama. Dorothy was tall and curvy, an olive-skinned example of Italy's finest with a faint accent to prove her heritage. Though their physical appearances were opposite, they shared a sense of humor and a fascination with photography. Her parents were totally different and totally in love, even after all the years they'd been together. It was a classic Irish/Italian love story, with a twist: both lovers were women. She told people she had the most *normal* unconventional childhood imaginable.

As she disembarked the plane from Seattle, Liza remembered the relief she felt when she saw her moms after the symphony that cool summer evening. They'd played Tchaikovsky. Her mama had squeezed her hand so hard during every violin spotlight that she wondered if she'd be able to grip the handlebar brakes the next time she rode her bike. She could still see her mom up on the stage in that first seat, leading her section, and felt the fire she kindled for music, even after thirty years of being a professional violinist.

"Liza, amore, there will be another race," Mama Dorothy said while they waited backstage for her mom to appear after the show. "And another after that. The important thing is you keep trying. And have a little fun along the way. When's the last time you *relaxed?*"

"I don't know how to relax," Liza said. "It's not in my DNA."

Dorothy laughed. "Yes, I understand that part all too well. Forty-two years with your mother has taught me all about your DNA. But you must find a way. A life too serious is no life at all."

"I've just been trying so long. I'm always so close. But it hasn't happened yet. I don't know if I want to do it anymore." Never mind that Liza didn't know if she wanted to do it any more every year after she just missed the cut. Then, swore off racing. Then, missed it too much, licked her wounds, and got back in the water. And on the bike. And in her running shoes. Like an addict who vows to quit drinking every New Year's Eve, Liza swore off triathlon every fall. And was back at it full-force every winter.

"Okay," Dorothy said, patting her shoulder for Liza to lean on. "I'll tell you what I tell Mom all the time when things are hard and she gets wound up like a top. It's what my mama, bless her soul, told me when I kept trying to get into university in America and not succeeding. 'Just find an American man and he will make it work out for you.'"

"Mama!"

"I'm kidding! But that *is* what she told me. In my day, European women didn't move continents by themselves. She was trying to help. Little did she know what was in store for me. I did make it to college in America—as you know. I had no idea where this place called 'Boise' was, but I was so happy to go there. I didn't give up. Because you know what?"

"Hm?"

"If I had gotten into my first choices—any of them—I'd have never met your mom. I'd have been in North Bend, Indiana or Los Angeles or New York. You mom wasn't in any of those places. She was in Boise. I was meant to go there. There is a lesson in failure, amore. Things work out the way they're supposed to. You will make it to Kona. When it's time. It's not time. You still have things to learn. All in time. Don't give up." Dorothy hugged her daughter tight into her bosom, as Liza imagined her Sicilian grandmother doing for her own daughter, and all was right with the world. When things were hard, Liza was like any other human—she wanted her mom(s).

Snapping back to the moment, Liza watched the parade of bags circle the baggage claim belt in San Francisco International and realized her mama had been right. It had taken two more tries, but things had worked out for her. She'd qualified for Kona—which was in less than a month— she could afford a little time to relax. It didn't have to be all serious, all the time. She was in town to be with Nathan.

Nathan, who'd come into her life years before. Who'd supported her as a friend and had really stepped up his game as they'd become a couple. She laughed out loud, ignoring the throng of strangers surrounding her. In some ways, she had "found an American man to make it work out." Not that it was his doing that she'd finally qualified. But the comfort and security she found in their relationship certainly hadn't hurt.

I'm about to get on the BART, Liza texted, swim bag tossed casually over her shoulder, roll-a-board suitcase by her side. *And I can't wait to kiss your face. Be there in an hour. Or less!*

# # #

"Hi," he said, working the gravel in his voice on purpose, his front-stoop greeting practiced many times that day. Ever since he'd sung "Heaven," he kept practicing the sultry side of his voice, trying to draw it out on command. Hands folded behind his back, Nathan watched as Liza approached against the backdrop of dusk. "God, I've missed you."

"Look at you, Nate Staples!" Liza blurted, leaving her bags in the street and running straight up the granite steps to him, arms immediately slung around his neck. "I've missed you, too!"

"I'm sorry I couldn't meet you at the airport."

"Don't be sorry. Work is work—I get it. But you've forgotten something."

"I have?" Nate asked, as he pulled a bouquet of red roses from behind his back.

"Oh, that's sweet, thank you," Liza said, taking in the presence of her boyfriend. He'd left Seattle "Nathan Stapleton." It only took a second to see that he was now "Nate Staples." New skinny jeans. Buffalo plaid replaced with a black V-neck T-shirt. The leather jacket he'd worn on a Facetime call. No Chucks? What the hell? Nathan was wearing wing tips. It didn't make sense, and yet it all made sense. He'd gone to San Francisco to become an artist—an image—and the work was clearly happening. Liza stood on her tiptoes and leaned into the man in front of her. She breathed in new cologne—musky—felt the stubble of his freshly-grown beard on her cheek, and whispered in his ear, "this," just before she kissed him.

She'd been waiting three weeks to do that again.

To reach his soul through his lips.

To feel his heart beat so close to hers.

His appearance may have been different, but his kiss was the same: Soft. Tender. A hint of cinnamon from the gum he'd chewed right before she arrived.

When she opened her eyes, Liza sighed. "That's better."

"So much better," Nathan said, hugging her in tight, no longer needing to conceal the flowers. He hadn't seen Liza in street clothes since they'd been to the symphony. She was always in some workout wear or another. That day, she'd worn bootcut jeans and a blue blazer, her white dress shirt unbuttoned past the collarbone, a silver pendant necklace resting just above the top button. "And you look amazing. Come on, let me show you the place. Though—prepare to be underwhelmed. It's not home. Fair warning."

"I'm sure it's not *that* bad."

"It is. But it's just temporary."

Following Nathan into a different home was—different. She'd been living in his house alone. He'd been in a rental, alone. The easy routine they'd barely developed in Seattle had been eradicated, and as they climbed the stairs to the fourth floor in silence, Liza wondered, how was this going to go? Would they have enough to talk about? Could she relate to the life he'd been living?

"So, here we are." Nathan opened the front door to expose his modest apartment, the famous futon greeting them just to the right of the entry. "This is my living and guest room, and that's the kitchen. There's a bathroom and bedroom down the hall. That's it. Tiny!"

"But mighty," Liza said. "It's where you put yourself first and took a big risk. Someday, you'll be like, 'I got my start in a tiny apartment in the Mission district.'"

"Maybe."

"Definitely."

"Can I get you anything?" Nathan motioned Liza to the futon. "Drink? Food?"

"Babe. You're not my host," Liza said. "You don't have to wait on me. But I would like to see your bedroom. With you in it."

"Now?"

"Yes, now." Liza took his hand and pulled him toward the back of the hall, dim light provided by an overhead fixture missing two of its three bulbs. "And for the rest of the night. Is that okay?"

"It's more than okay. In fact, it's what I hoped you'd say."

# # #

When they'd become sufficiently reacquainted, it was near midnight. Nathan had to work the next day; Liza had prints to process from the weekend's wedding and needed a swim, too. They'd decided to have dinner at Liza's favorite restaurant—one she'd been to with her moms two summers prior—and take a long walk afterwards the next day. It's what they'd do if they were home.

"I have a surprise for you. Before bed," Nathan said, pulling on some sweatpants and the triathlon T-shirt Liza had given him over the summer when he didn't have spare clothes at her house.

"You still have the T-shirt?"

"Oh, I sleep in this. To remind me of you."

"You don't!"

"I do," Nathan confirmed, a sheepish grin on his face. "Echo Lake triathlon, 2012. I remember it well . . . But, anyway, the surprise."

"So many surprises today," Liza said, sitting up against the once-beige wall, its discolorations varied as those on the futon. With no headboard to support her back, she piled an extra pillow behind her head.

"Wait here."

While he was gone, Liza donned the bathrobe she'd packed, and observed. The rental was nothing like his house—their house. It was decorated with hand-me-down furniture, clearly from someone's grandmother. There was an oak tallboy dresser opposite the bed, a handle missing from the top drawer. The TV on top of it was from the 90s—rounded screen, huge tube. The wall held prints from the Miami Museum of Modern Art, circa 1978.

"Oh, I get the guitar treatment?" Liza asked when he reappeared with an acoustic guitar around his neck, black leather strap embossed with the word, "Nate."

"You do."

"I love it when I get the guitar treatment! Can I make requests?"

"Maybe," Nathan said, clearing his throat as he strummed, playing and replaying a C major chord. "But first, I have something I want to play for you. When I got here, I was kind of a wreck."

"Really?"

"Yeah, I freaked out a little. I was worried I made the wrong choice. I shouldn't have blown up the band. I shouldn't have signed a solo deal. I shouldn't have come to San Francisco. This place is kind of a dump, so that didn't help. It was a pretty classic meltdown."

"Babe, why didn't you tell me?" Liza asked, leaning across the bed for emphasis, C major still on repeat. "I could've been there for you. I should've been there for you."

"I don't know, I guess I didn't want you to know I was weak."

"That's not weak! That's human."

"Yeah, well. I felt weak. And scared. But I refocused on why I was here. I thought about how hard I've worked to get here—how I'd be an idiot to walk away from a chance at my dream. When the stylists were trying to change me—I resisted. And then I refocused *again*. It's been a hard few weeks, but—" Nathan shifted from strumming to picking; a melody emerged, "—it gave me this song. I hope you like it."

I was lost in a concrete jungle
Every tree unfamiliar
Every stream a raging river

I thought I'd found my way out
But it was just a white out
I was in a dream

And every time I turned a corner
I saw your face
I heard your voice

And I wonder where I am without you
I wonder who I'm turning into
I know there's a higher meaning
I know things aren't what they're seeming

Is this mirage my reality?
Or is it something meant-to-be?
If I find my way out unhindered
Will I be the man you need?

And I wonder where I am without you
I wonder who I'm turning into
I know there's a higher meaning
I know things aren't what they're seeming

Is this mirage my reality?
Or is it something meant-to-be?
If I find my way out unhindered
Will I be the man you need?

"Wow," Liza said as he drew out the word, "need" to finish the song, his alto voice lower than usual on the final note. "That's beautiful. And vulnerable. And really different from your other songs."

"Yeah, I wrote the words in like fifteen minutes, and Charles helped me with the score last week."

"Maybe you needed to be a little scared?"

"Maybe. Charles told me to find the angst."

"I think you found it. Have you played it for anyone else?"

"Nope. Except Charles, because I needed his help," Nathan said. "I wrote it for you. I wanted you to hear it first."

"Well, I think you should play it for people. Like Julian."

"I will. When it's ready. I still need to work out some phrasing."

Sitting in bed, the clock striking midnight, Liza knew. Nate Staples wouldn't be a secret for long. He'd toiled with Maplewood for years, and they were good. But there was something new in his voice. In his lyrics. Like a piece of coal under pressure, unassuming in its appearance but undergoing massive transformation, Nathan was becoming a diamond before her eyes.

"I can't believe you wrote me a new song." Liza kissed his cheek before retreating to the non-headboard wall. "I thought 'When You Love Her' was amazing. But *two* songs; that's really incredible."

Nathan laughed as he released the guitar from its strap and slid into bed. "I've been writing you songs for years, Liz. You just never knew it."

FOURTEEN

"So," Jen said, a tentative smile forming on her lips, arms crossed tightly across her chest. "This is a little awkward, huh?"

"A little." Emily returned the smile. "But I teach 15-year-olds. I'm okay with awkward."

"Me, too. Well, not the teaching part. Just the awkward part. Which I suppose is getting worse!"

Emily laughed. "It's okay. Let it be awkward. I'll be honest and say, I've never had this kind of conversation."

"Me either. I didn't really think past asking you to dinner! Thank you for meeting me on a school night."

"It's my pleasure. I never get to go out on random Tuesdays. In fact, I say we talk about the elephant in the room and then have a nice dinner. I've heard they have great dolmas here."

"What elephant?" Jen looked around the restaurant, half standing to get a better view. "Just kidding. So—were you surprised?" Her giggle was involuntary, hands now smoothing the white linen tablecloth at the Greek restaurant she'd selected. It was near her house, but importantly, they were usually incredibly slow.

"Are you two ready—" the server started from three steps away, only to receive a cut-throat hand signal from Jen as he reached their table. She was a regular and had never seen him before, but he understood. "Okay then, I'll be back soon." This server was an over-achiever. They'd been there five minutes and already had drinks and a request for orders. Unheard of.

Watching him walk away, Emily considered her response. It was a loaded question—the server had provided an intensity break. Should she tell the truth—she'd considered asking Jen out under the guise of book help? Or, save face and just answer the question? Maybe both? "Surprised? A little. I thought you'd made a mistake. An accidental swipe, maybe. Then I thought about how well we connect. And I had to admit that I've had a crush on you since we met at the cat café. But—"

"Really?"

"Yeah. But we work together. And you're Kate's ex-wife. Not that everyone doesn't know someone who's dated their ex-wife, it's just—"

"I know. I'm sorry I put you in a weird position," Jen said, studying the woman sitting across from her. She was well-put together. Stylish and smartly dressed. Make-up tasteful and earth toned. But more than that, she had kind eyes. She was wearing a cold-shoulder sweater with a tight weave, the mocha color picking up flecks of those warm eyes, her wavy toffee brown hair sitting on her shoulders. In the past, Jen would have focused more on the put together part—the outfit; earrings; hair style. But older age had taught her—those things don't matter. It's the heart of the person that matters. Their spirit.

"Don't be sorry. You opened my eyes to—potential."

"Yeah?"

"Yeah! It's been a long time since I've met someone I've found interesting." Emily wouldn't mention that she'd met Kate because they'd been on a few dates. It was never meant to be—they wanted very different things. Hindsight told her to be grateful they'd never slept together. Or *that* would be awkward.

"Me, too. Mid-life dating's hard, isn't it?" Jen knew it all too well—mid-life dating *was* hard.

"So hard!"

"So many rules. And requirements. And—so much baggage."

"So much baggage," Emily parroted and noticed the server was working his way back in their direction. "Should we order so he can relax?"

"Let's. Definitely get the dolmas. And their baba ghanoush is out of this world."

Order placed, waters refilled, and deep breaths taken, the elephant awaited.

"Okay, so what's your baggage?" Emily asked, half joking, half serious. She'd been through enough brief relationships. It all came back to checklists and compatibility of each other's traumas.

"Don't you think that's second date material?" Jen asked, the tablecloth as smooth as it'd ever be. Was the pendant light over their table brighter? It seemed brighter.

"I think, 'what the hell?' It all comes back to this anyway, so we may as well get it all out first. I'll tell you mine."

As Emily talked about coming out later in life, her divorce, and the ways she contorted herself to be someone she thought society wanted her to be, Jen listened. Their stories were different, but similar. An ex with strong opinions. Trying to make it work and suffering in silence until she couldn't suffer any longer. A mid-thirties revelation.

Summoning courage. Saying something. Ducking and covering for the aftermath of breaking up a marriage—both from their exes and all their friends. That divorce doesn't just affect the couple in question—it trickles down to all their relationships and often changes them permanently. Emily spoke of co-parenting and questioning everything she'd done. Blaming herself for imploding her family. The hurt and anger and sadness. Losing friends. Making new ones. Getting to a place of peace with Kevin, through what seemed like impossible circumstances. Of his opinions about her writing. Especially his opinions about her writing.

"Wow," Jen said. "That's very honest, thank you. Are you worried I may be like Kevin?"

"In what way?"

"Opinions. About writing. I mean—we're different people, but in some ways, we're kinda similar. And I'm your publisher!" Jen told herself she should've trusted her gut and *not* swiped. There was no way this would work. Emily was a sensitive writer. A good writer. But a fragile, inexperienced one.

"That could be a concern," Emily shifted in her seat, the spotlight now on her. She told herself she should've trusted her gut and *not* swiped. This was her publisher, after all. She was going to have opinions about her writing. And if she didn't, she wouldn't be a very good publisher. "However, I trust that your opinions will come from a place where you have my best interest in mind."

"Absolutely. And—I wonder—what if you worked through the editor? I've been giving him more and more responsibility. Just an idea, but what if I'm out of the picture on your day-to-day? It's about time I delegated."

"You'd do that?"

"I would." Jen nodded a confirmation.

"I think that's a great idea," Emily said. What a grown-up suggestion. Maybe she did the right thing after all. Funny how first dates were like a ping pong match. Constant assessing. Constant wondering if it's a waste of time or if the potential relationship has legs. Deciding for or against someone only to change that opinion six times before the end of the date. "Okay, so, I've told you my bruises. Let's hear it. What are your battle scars?"

With a sigh, Jen started. "You drive a tough bargain. But, okay. The biggee is usually that I'm trying to have a baby. But you already know that. I'm running out of time, and it's my biggest life priority now. That's usually enough to send 'em running for the hills. How do you feel about that? It's a lot for a relationship. Especially a one-date old one." Before her date could answer, the server appeared with their order, arranging plates on the table with the skill of a master jigsaw puzzler. He had the perfect location for each plate and fit their generous order in the space allowed. The neighborhood haunt had stepped up its game—they should've had to wait at least twenty more minutes.

"Wow, that was fast!" Emily smiled at the efficient young man who could've been one of her students. "Thank you."

"You bet. Enjoy," he said, and was gone as fast as he'd appeared.

"You must be good luck. They're usually much slower," Jen said. "Anyway, what's your position on babies? Angus is almost out of the house—a baby is a backward step for you."

"You definitely shouldn't go into sales," Emily said. "That's a good pitch against seeing where this goes!"

"Ah, yes. The presumptive close." When in doubt, make a joke. But she wanted to know. Was Emily open to more kids? That was jumping the gun—a lot—but she'd had so many promising dates that were dead on arrival once the baby bomb was dropped.

"Is that what it's called? Presumptive close? Well, you're good at it. And you're right. Angus is just about grown. But I don't have a firm position on babies either way. I love kids. I couldn't do what I do if I didn't. I'd always thought I'd have two—a boy and a girl—but that isn't how it worked out. But would I run away if you get pregnant? Is that what you're asking?"

"You writers and words. That's what I'm getting at, yes."

"Words matter!" Emily insisted. "The answer is, no, I wouldn't run away if you get pregnant. I may run away for other reasons, but wanting to have a baby is not one of them. How's that?"

"It's perfect," Jen touched Emily's hand across the table, warmth radiating straight to her heart, just as it had at the cocktail bar. Maybe swiping was the right thing to do. What a weird concept to spill your worries and emotional triggers before deciding to date someone. She could've saved herself a lot of heartbreak if she'd tried this approach in the past.

"Good. I'm glad that's settled."

"I guess there's just one more thing," Jen said. "Before we decide to go on another date."

"What's that?"

Jen leaned forward over their table, its puzzle perfect arrangement reminding her the underlying premise of why they were there, nuzzled her nose close to Emily's, and breathed in the fresh scent of citrus. She waited a beat. Emily didn't flinch. Didn't pull away. She stayed in the moment—a good sign. Under the spotlight at a table for two, surrounded by others enjoying their dinners, Jen pressed her lips to Emily's. Softly. Sweetly. As if they'd done it a hundred times.

"I wasn't expecting that," Emily said, and then whispered, "but I'd like you to do it again."

# # #

The grass along the walking trail that traced the edges of Greenlake showed signs of fall. Squishy underfoot, it nudged Kate back onto the gravel path, though Dallas and Hunter preferred the sniffs buried deep in the sod.

"Let's go, boys," Kate cajoled, tugging at their leashes in a reminder that she was the boss.

The late September air was crisp. Almost cold. It was—remarkably— her last September in Seattle. She was headed to Second Chance Ranch in less than two weeks and determined to squeeze every drop out of her remaining time in the city. That meant walking the dogs twice a day, getting coffee from her favorite espresso stand where the road and trail converged, and breathing in the dampness that mingled with pine and goose poop. Canada geese were everywhere, setting up residence along the lake, just as they did every year.

"Dallas! Leave it!" Seven years old and still lacking impulse control, the black lab lunged for one of the many geese that had taunted him since paws hit path.

"I thought that was you," a voice announced just as Dallas decided he would indeed leave it.

"Well, look at you," Kate said, drawing a flattened hand toward her body—a silent request for her dogs to sit. "Want to walk with us?"

"I'd love that," Emily Hall said, patting both pups on their heads—one with each hand—tails wagging excitedly against the ground in appreciation of new attention.

"Great! Let's go, boys," Kate again commanded. The mid-morning cloud layer burned off as they walked, its haze giving way to a welcomed sun break that lit the lake and caused both women to pull sunglasses into place from the tops of their heads.

"Did you know Seattleites buy more sunglasses every year than anywhere else?" Emily asked.

"I didn't. But I believe it. It's lucky I grabbed these—I lose them so often and then—look out!" Kate pulled Emily off the path with her and the dogs, missing a collision with a guy on a Segway plowing through the usual crowd of walkers and bike riders. "Look where you're going!" He was long gone, and Kate's voice wasn't loud enough for him to hear her, but she yelled anyway.

"Geez!" Emily yelled, too, brushing her thighs as if she'd landed in dirt. In fact, she was standing upright, but brushing off felt obligatory. "Thank you. That was nuts."

"Welcome," Kate said as she surveyed the dogs—they seemed fine. Hunter had his nose glued to the ground, and Dallas had already found another goose to stalk. "Just when I wonder if I'm doing the right thing in leaving, some jerk on a Segway reminds me—I'm doing the right thing. Who even rides Segways anymore? This city is getting out of control. The millennials are taking over!"

"Oh, come on now," Emily said, beginning to walk again. "Every generation says that about the generation after them. Remember, we're lazy Gen X. We're narcissistic and won't amount to anything. And we did just fine. He was a one-off."

"I guess so. But I still think the city is growing too fast."

"You've mentioned it."

"It is. Anyway, what's going on in your world, professor?"

"Oh, nothing," Emily said, head turned toward the lake as they walked counterclockwise around it, a kayaker in the distance catching her attention. "Angus has a girlfriend, so between time with Kevin and her, he's not around much. The house is quiet, but I kinda like it."

"How's the book coming?"

"Really well, as a matter of fact. I have a solid frame—want to hear it?"

"I'd love to," Kate said, tugging her dogs closer to her—a constant activity. She couldn't wait for 20 acres and the ability to let them wear themselves out without being attached to them.

"Okay, so, it's kind of a chance encounter that turns permanent, until it isn't—"

Emily told of an unlikely story of a long-distance relationship that turned into a long-term relationship that led to a breakup. Of years passing. A reunion. A family. She said the characters were driving the plot, and while she knew what needed to happen—she didn't know how she'd get there, and that was the best part. Writing this book was like reading a "Choose Your Own Adventure" novel. She got to make the decisions. It was she who called the shots.

"The characters talk to me. It sounds weird, but I hear their voices. They have a life inside my head. Which is either really deranged or will work out great," Emily said, turning her attention from the kayak and the ripples it created across the top of the lake to Kate, whose eyes were hidden by mirrored sunglasses.

"Sounds interesting. Can I read it? I love a romance novel."

There it was. Again. The question Emily tried to avoid answering. She loved to write. Teaching literature. Talking about books. And hated the thought of people reading her work.

"Of course, when it's farther along. I haven't even shown it to the publisher yet."

"Jen?"

"Yeah."

"I still can't believe—of all the publishers in the world—you found Jen. I mean, I'm so excited for you," Kate backtracked. "But what are the odds? You and Jen?"

"Yeah," Emily said, hands finding the pockets of her track pants, right hand getting tangled in the headphones she'd stuffed in there when she saw Kate. "About Jen."

"Hard to work with?"

"No—"

"No?"

"Not at all. She's wonderful. Insightful. Listens to my ideas."

"Really?" Kate asked, automatic leash tug happening. Five steps forward, one tug to realign the dogs. Five steps forward. Repeat. "So, it's working out, huh?"

"You sound surprised! Yeah, it's working out," Emily confirmed. "But there is something. Actually, I kinda hoped I'd see you this morning."

"Okay?"

"With Jen—I just wanted to let you know—"

"Oh my God! You're sleeping together!"

"Oh—no! Well, not—yet. But we went on a date. Not a publisher/author date. A *date* date."

Gravel crunched under feet as Kate processed and Emily waited. Step, step, step. Crunch, crunch, crunch. Sun warming their backs. Geese cackling. Wings flapping.

"Well, that's—great," Kate said, lifting the sunglasses back onto her head and smiling, not breaking her stride. Her hair's roots were nowhere to be seen. Her romantic roots were another story. "Think you'll go on more?"

"I hope so." Emily smiled, right hand now fully entwined with those earbuds. "Are you okay?"

"Of course. Our relationship is so far in the past."

"Are you sure?"

"I'm sure! That ship sailed a long time ago. See where it goes. It actually kinda makes sense—you two, together. I can see it."

"Yeah, me too. But I don't want you—"

"Em—this isn't about me. It's about what you want. And what Jen wants. If you like each other, see where it goes. I'm happy for you!"

As Kate convinced her friend to date her ex-wife, she convinced herself to be happy for them. It had only been one date. Experience told her the rubber didn't meet the road until three months in. Give it time.

"Thanks. I'm happy for me, too. I wasn't looking—in fact, even Angus lectured me about needing to date. But I wasn't feeling like the parade of random strangers. This just sort of happened."

"I'd say if Angus is on your case, it probably happened at the right time."

"It did," Emily said, nodding. "It really did."

"Hey—I'm glad you told me," Kate said as they approached her turn to head home. A turn she'd made hundreds—probably thousands—of times before. The lake had been her backyard for so long. The site of countless walks to clear her mind. To heal breakups. Decipher mixed signals. Connect with friends. "I'm gonna miss this."

"The lake?"

"Yeah. And—this," Kate said, pointing to Emily and back to herself. "Running into you here. Serendipitous catch ups."

"Me, too."

As they hugged goodbye—"not for the last time," Kate said—the weekend regulars did their thing. Dogs and walkers and bikers communed with nature, Segway guy nowhere to be seen. Birds chirped in trees, local sparrows sang their songs from above. The sun peaked in the sky, its cheery orb a reminder that while the days were getting colder, there was still hope for warmth.

FIFTEEN

"Kate?" Christine asked, again. Her conference call ran late—a rare Saturday activity—and she emerged from her home office to find her girlfriend and dog in a serious snuggle fest on her couch, Sadie curled in a dog-shaped ball in Kate's lap.

"Hm?"

"I said, hi. You okay?"

"Oh, yeah. Sorry. Sucked into status updates. Hi," she said, tossing the phone with which she'd been consumed onto the couch as her lips were captured in the most perfect hello by the most perfect woman.

"I've missed you," Christine said, sitting on the couch in spite of Sadie's side-eye stare that said, "go away, we're cuddling."

"I missed you, too," Kate sighed. "Remind me. How are we going to do this from states away? Some things just don't translate to FaceTime."

"We'll make it count when we're in person. Like now."

Christine nuzzled into the nape of Kate's neck, an attempt to memorize the softness of her skin. The curve where her shoulder and neck met. The freshness of her scent—like a meadow in summer. She tucked a stray tendril of hair behind Kate's ear and noticed the hole high into its fold from an abandoned piercing—a nod to her rebellious years, no doubt. She kissed Kate's jawline, before again landing on her lips, finding a hint of cherry flavor on her cupid's bow lips. Christine had studied these lips. Watched them talk. Smile. Laugh. Felt them brush hers. They sent a surge of electricity through her entire body when they did that last part.

With an involuntary sigh, Christine retreated. She wanted to burn every aspect of Kate's presence into her brain. Round eyes the color of the ferns that had dotted the edges of the hiking trail where they'd first met. Tiny indentations just above her nose that formed an upside down "V" when she was lost in thought. Defined cheekbones. The always perfectly blonde hair, with just enough spunk to make it seem like she didn't bother to style it, when Christine knew she took ample time getting it that way.

She'd done this—the studying, the cramming it all in—before. In fact, it was all she knew. Long distance was her entire frame of reference when it came to relationships. She relied on memories and pictures and "looking forward." To the next visit. The next vacation. Next time to hold and be held. They hadn't even spent time apart yet, and she was doing it.

"What?" Kate asked. "Do I smell weird?"

"Oh, God, no! I was just making a mental picture. Sorry, I didn't mean to freak you out."

"You didn't, I just got self-conscious there for a minute! What's the picture look like?"

"Well," Christine said, nudging Sadie off Kate's lap and laying her head in the spot her dog was determined to keep. "It's a picture of a strong woman. Someone who's not afraid to go after what she wants. Who's driven. Who's been through her fair share of fights, but still comes out swinging. And—someone who had a wild side. Who pierced her cartilage to fit in, but later found it impractical, so abandoned it as she figured out who she was. She lived in Doc Martens and black denim when she was younger, but played plenty of George Strait alongside her Depeche Mode. Because as she reminds me often, you can take the girl out of Tennessee, but not the other way around. A woman who smells like flowers in spring and tastes like sunshine and a—" Christine drew her thumb and forefinger close together "smidge of cherry Chapstick, which I like, for the record. A woman who's captured my attention, imagination, and my heart."

"Wow, you got all of that from a kiss?"

"I did. Was I close? About the Doc Martens?"

"One-hundred percent. But it was The Smiths. Not Depeche Mode."

"Ah. They're very different. Pardon me," Christine said, working her hand behind Kate's head and drawing it towards hers, heart beating through the ends of her fingers, heat rising as their breath intermingled.

As they made out like teenagers on a parent's couch, Christine let go of the meeting. The patient who had filed a malpractice suit. The uncertainty of her future in medicine. A tongue in her ear jolted her. How was that possible?

"Sadie! No, baby. Go to your bed. Go!" Sadie trotted off with head dragging, her apricot fluff catching the afternoon light filtering through the Mission-style stained-glass window in Christine's family room.

"Looks like she wanted in on it," Kate laughed. "I don't blame her though. You, Dr. George, are the best kisser."

"Yeah?"

"Oh, yeah," Kate said, "I'm going to need a lot more where that came from to get me through our first time apart."

"I'm pretty sure I have an endless supply," Christine said, sitting up. "But, about that."

"Kissing? I like endless supplies."

"That's a given, but I have some bad news. I don't know if I can drive to Montana after all." Christine blinked back the mist in her eyes as she finished her thought. "I'm in a tough spot at work—I may not be able to leave until later next month. I'm sorry, Kate. The timing is terrible."

"What's going on?" The concern in Kate's head escaped with a crackle in her voice.

"I'm not sure yet. That's why I was on the call. A patient filed a malpractice suit against me and a surgeon—we just found out, and—"

"Oh my God. Are you okay?" Kate shifted closer and her hand found the top of Christine's thigh, her voice tender.

"I don't know. It's new news—I'm a little numb right now."

"I'm so sorry. What happened?"

"She's claiming a surgeon and I colluded to convince her to have surgery that her health insurance didn't fully cover to meet a quota set by the hospital. We think it's baseless, but it's something we have to deal with, and we have to be available in person to meet with lawyers for the next few weeks."

"Wow. That's a big claim," Kate said.

"Yeah."

Sitting together in silence, Christine breathed. She had to tell Kate about the suit and its impact on her move—who knew when she'd be able to leave Seattle for more than a day or two. Her fall vacation was erased by a patient with a bone to pick.

The thing was, Christine knew that Sheila Hanson needed the surgery. She knew—with every ounce of her being—the only reason Sheila was alive to file the suit was she'd had an angioplasty—a routine procedure to widen blocked arteries. Sheila had first seen her with two 95% blocked coronary arteries and a severe case of angina. The procedure had been both essential and effective. And now, this. A malpractice suit that had nothing to do with her. A suit that was more about insurance than medicine and had the potential to dramatically impact her career.

"Is this common? Are you worried?" Kate spoke slowly.

"It's not uncommon, but I've never experienced it. So, I'm a little worried. But I also stand behind our medical decisions. I worked with Dr. Jha to assess the best course of action for this patient, and we agreed. Every diagnosis holds a certain degree of risk—but this one was pretty cut-and-dried."

"So, it's a disgruntled person who received a bill they weren't expecting, and they're blaming you?"

"That's how I'm interpreting it—now. Maybe there's more. Who knows," Christine sighed, again. "Sometimes I wonder why I do it."

"Why you practice?"

"Yeah, I have my days. I think about how precious life is and how it can be gone in an instant, and I wonder, 'is this how I want to spend my days?'"

"Babe," Kate insisted. "That's exactly why you do it. Because life *is* precious and you have a gift. You help people live. You help them give their families the gift of having them around. I think that's a damn good way to spend your days. Don't let this woman have that power over you. Don't let her discolor your entire career."

"I know. But sometimes I feel a little like, 'why can't you just say, *thank you*, and go enjoy your life?' Today is one of those days. I spun the malpractice roulette wheel—we all do it, every day—I was the unlucky winner."

"I think it's going to be okay. Granted, I don't know anything about the medical system beyond what I've seen on *Gray's Anatomy*, but this sounds like it's going to work out in your favor. And if it doesn't, there's an opening at the ranch for an on-site doctor. I just wrote the job description this morning. The pay's for shit, but the benefits include fresh air, wide open spaces, and a cute blonde and her mischievous, but lovable, Labrador retrievers."

"Do you have any candidates?" Christine forced a smile under the weight of reality.

"Just one."

# # #

"What's new?" Kate asked, shoving the phone between her shoulder and ear as she shuttled a load of laundry into the dryer, her house now mere days away from being someone else's, the navy sweatpants and Pixies T-shirt she was wearing the only remaining clean clothes available.

"Oh, nothing much. Darlin', where are you? It sounds like you're in a clothes dryer."

Noting her mom's ability to pinpoint her exact location, no matter where she was, Kate laughed and closed the door to the laundry room. "Close. I was putting clothes in the dryer."

"On a Saturday night, you're doing laundry? Honey, is something wrong with you and Christine? Did you have a fight?"

"Everything's fine, Mom."

"Are you sure? You don't sound fine. You had the talk? Oh no! It didn't go well?"

There was nowhere to hide. Glenda Conrad knew her daughter and knew when she was being lied to—even over the phone.

"We did. It went really well. That's not it."

"The way you're huffing and puffing, it sure sounds like it. Sweetie, just tell me what's going on. Maybe I can help?"

"I don't know, Mom. I don't think you can help with this one," Kate said as she eased onto the last bit of remaining furniture in her living room—if you could call it furniture. She'd shipped a container of belongings ahead, leaving only what would fit in her Jeep for the drive to Montana. As it turns out, not much fits in a Jeep. Add two, 100-pound dogs, and well. She was living in an empty house with an air mattress and a refrigerator containing partially eaten Thai take-out and three beers. No, make that two-and-a-half beers.

As she settled into the air mattress, Dallas and Hunter found their spots—one on each side. They must've thought they were in trouble— they'd become more attached to her hip than ever.

"Try me. I bet I can help," Glenda insisted. "A mama knows."

"Alright, Chris can't drive with me to Montana after all. And I just found out the people buying the house want to close early—on Friday—like in six days. It's been a lot of news in a short period."

"Why can't she drive with you? I thought y'all were planning this all along? You shouldn't drive all that way alone. A single woman? It's not safe."

"It's perfectly safe!"

"I beg to differ. But what happened?" Glenda pressed.

"Something came up at work. She feels horrible, but it isn't going to work out, timing-wise." Though it wasn't her battle to fight, something inside said to protect Christine. Malpractice was no laughing matter, and she didn't want to color her mother's view of her girlfriend before they'd even met.

"Well, that's too bad, dear. How about I fly in and drive with you? I wanted to come to the ranch, anyway. We could play mix tapes and sing road trip songs. It'll be fun. I'll just ask Sissy to cover my Sunday School classes a bit early. Oh, and I can have your brother watch the house, and—" Glenda's voice trailed.

There it was: the rule of threes in full force. The third big thing of the day. Her move had done a 180 since she'd walked around Greenlake earlier that morning. Her companion changed. The date changed. The outcome changed. Thoughts of romantic horseback rides through hayfields that led to picnics by the pond evaporated as her mom ran through her travel to-do list.

"Mix tapes?" Kate asked, recalling a phrase she hadn't used—or heard—in ages.

"Yes! You load a bunch of songs onto your iPod and then play them while you drive. It's fun!"

Never mind she didn't have an iPod, or a cassette tape player, it was cute that her mom was trying.

"How about we just listen to satellite radio? And I'd like it. If you want to drive with me. Maybe come a day or two early? You can meet Chris."

"Oh, yes!" Kate heard Glenda's clap through the phone. "I'd love that! I can't wait to meet this woman who's stolen your heart. She'd better be all you say, darlin'. My daughter deserves the best."

"She is. She totally is. Did I tell you we named the ranch?"

As Kate recounted the evening that had resulted in the "I love you" conversation and the name of her ranch, she realized how far she and Glenda had come.

When she and Jen had gotten together, Glenda was against it. She wondered who would take care of her daughter ("I will!" Kate insisted). Wondered how a woman's companionship could rival a man's ("Trust me!" Kate said.) How Kate could ever be open about her personal life in a world with so much intrinsic bias and judgment. ("Times are changing," Kate predicted.) Glenda was a travelled, educated woman. She insisted her concerns were about wanting her daughter to have an easier life, and kept this up, through Kate's marriage and subsequent divorce. When she and Jen split, Glenda was concurrently against it and pushing for it—hoping her daughter would come to her senses, find a nice man, and settle down. All while adoring Jen and suggesting it was Kate who needed to make all the compromises so they could stay together.

As if either were an option.

Since then, she'd mellowed. She may not have understood, but she accepted. Perhaps they'd grown closer after her dad died. Maybe, as Glenda got to know adult Kate—every Saturday for eight years—she leaned into wanting her to be happy over anything else.

"Second Chance Ranch," Glenda echoed as Kate told her the new name of her Montana homestead. "I like it. Do you think you'll get married there?"

"Mom, we've been down this road, you know I'm not going to change."

So much for progress.

"Kathryn Ann! I'm asking if you and Christine will get married. Your second chance at happiness. Don't be so defensive!"

"Oh," Kate said, her hand finding Dallas's belly. "I don't know. It's only been a few months. I don't want to be a U-haul away from another divorce."

The truth hurts, doesn't it? Kate thought more about divorce than marriage. Jumped to the back of the book before reading the plot—just to see what happened so she didn't get too attached to characters that may not make it work. Was she doing that in real life? Wanting the best, but assuming the worst—because experience led her to believe the outcome she wanted was out of reach?

"Let me give you some advice, darlin'."

"Mom, it's okay, I don't—"

"You listen to me. If you only think about how things will end, you're going to miss out on all of life's joys. Do you love her?"

"You already asked me this. I do."

"Okay. Can you see your life without her?"

"No," Kate said, Dallas now fully rolled on his back to maximize his evening belly rubs, head resting in her lap, little black hairs aloft around them. "My life has gotten so much better since we met. It's just—"

"No, 'it's just.' Your daddy did this same thing to me when we were dating. He wasn't sure; he couldn't commit. We were too young. And the excuses went on."

"I didn't know that!"

"Yes," Glenda said, "he put me off for a good long while." Glenda drew out the words "good," "long," and "while," her drawl especially effective at emphasizing her point. He'd been dead eight years and she was still upset about the length of their courtship.

"Huh," Kate said, looking around her living room. It felt less like home and more like an empty canvas, waiting for the artist to finish their painting. The partly sunny day had given way to rain after sunset, which was lightly rapping the windows as she talked to her mom.

"I'm not saying get married tomorrow. I'm just asking—have you thought about it? Is this person your person?"

Good question. Was she?

"I think so. I hope so. But I don't know if she feels the same. About the future. We're still in the honeymoon phase. We haven't been together long enough to know if we annoy each other. If we want the same things. If we can fight and find our way back to each other. If—"

"Too many ifs! All relationships take work, Katie, you know that. There isn't such a thing as happily ever after. Happily ever after is code for 'work.' So, I think you need to ask yourself—do you want to do the work with her? That's the real question."

Aside from the fact that Glenda had a half-dozen pet names for her, she had a point.

"I do."

"Okay, then. Now you know. What you do with that information is up to you."

"It is," Kate said. "Thanks, Mom. So, when will I see you? Tuesday? Wednesday? I'll take you for sushi in Tangletown and to the market for dim sum and, there's this new Japanese place in Capitol Hill—"

"I'll see you Tuesday," Glenda said.

"Okay. And Mom?"

"Yes, dear?"

"You'd better book a hotel—I don't have any furniture."

When she hung up the phone, Kate had only one thought: food. Okay, two thoughts. A quick text ought to solve both.

Hey, stranger. All done with your errands? I know it's only been a couple hours, but, want to meet me for sushi and . . . more? Can the boys and I sleep over?

SIXTEEN

"**Okay,**" Nathan said as he held open the door, "are you ready for this?"

"I'm more than ready!" Liza said, "I can't wait to see how you've been spending your Saturday nights without me."

"I can't wait to show you!"

For a month, Brazen had been his Saturday night home, its regulars now claiming him as one of theirs, its dimly lit confines providing courage, keeping secrets, and giving him a creative outlet while he transitioned once again. This time, it was a transition from Nathan, the electrician with a garage band to Nate, the singer. The artist, even.

"Hey sexy," Jason greeted as he slid an Anchor Steam across the bar. He'd stopped bothering to ask Nathan's order. "Who's your friend?"

"Thanks," Nathan said, right hand on Liza's back, an off-key rendition of "I'm Too Sexy" beginning on the stage behind them. "Jason, this is my girlfriend, Liza."

"Well, well, well!" Jason's tight abs bounced ever-so-slightly as he engaged, his uniform of tight pants and bowtie san shirt as predictable as early morning fog in the Bay. "She exists! Nice to meet you, Liza. What'll it be?"

"You as well," Liza smiled. "Can I get a soda water and lime?"

"You bet. Are you singing tonight?"

"Oh, no! I leave that to the talent. I'm here to support my man." Liza's smile did what Liza's smile did best: sold her point. And in a bar full of gay men, her point was simple: Nathan was *hers*.

"Fair enough. Gotta keep an eye on this one," Jason said, eyes meeting Nathan's with a wink. "So, what's it going to be tonight? I can't predict with you, Nate Staples."

"What's that mean?!" Nathan asked, right hand still resting against Liza's back, the warmth of her skin radiating through her sleeveless dress. He had the hottest date in the bar, no question.

"Oh nothing," Jason smiled. "What'cha singin'?"

"'Annie's Song.'"

"Don't know it."

"John Denver? You fill up my senses?" Nathan shook his head—his song choice wasn't *that* far out there.

"Hang tight, let me look—" Jason typed on a small computer behind the bar. Must've been the brains behind the karaoke machine. "Ah, okay, here it is. I don't think anyone has ever sung that one. Like I said, unpredictable!"

He may have been unpredictable, but he'd chosen the song for many reasons. It was romantic. It suited his voice. It told a story of undying love. And if ever there was a story he wanted to tell while Liza was present, it was a story of love and commitment and beauty beyond human characteristics. As he shifted in his wingtips, Nathan reminded himself to breathe. To stay calm. He prayed his hand wasn't sweaty on her back, that his cheeks weren't betraying him. Amidst the familiarity of hops and whiskey mash and the lingering tobacco wafting off the guy standing next to him, he searched for stillness.

"Okay, you're all set. 'Annie's Song' it is. You sure you don't want to sing, sweetie? A duet, maybe? I'm sure they're getting tired of *this one* by now." Jason motioned in Nathan's direction with his head as he placed a paper coaster and drink in front of his new customer.

"Oh, no. I don't sing. Trust me, you don't want that." Liza leaned into the bar on tiptoes to grab the drink that awaited, the smooth concrete cool under palms. Her soda and lime looked like a mixed drink but didn't impede her ability to train. It also helped her meet her hydration goals. Always training, one way or another.

"Alright, well, let me know if you change your mind. You two have fun."

As he had the prior three weekends, Nathan surveyed the bar for a place to stand. It looked the same, but different. Same groups of people laughing and drinking and coupling. Same tiny stage. Same neon beer signs providing most of the light. A new interpretation of the term "beer googles." Perhaps everyone looked better in "beer light."

For weeks, he stood back and observed. Talked to people. Made acquaintances. But that was through the lens of Nate, the singer. Nate, the mystery man with the tousled chestnut hair. With the skinny jeans and leather jacket.

Now, he took his regular place at the back of the room with a woman on his arm. Not just any woman, mind you. The love of his life. A striking redhead with a killer figure in a tight dress and high heels that emphasized her defined calves, earned by thousands of miles on a bike. A woman with piercing green eyes and the most perfect smile. In other words, a woman any woman in that bar would die to go home with. And some of the men, too.

The truth emerged, sip-by-sip, the Anchor Steam in his hand providing comfort while he realized the image he'd been creating for weeks was just that: an image. Would he be less accepted with a date by his side? He was, after all, in a gay bar with a beautiful woman on his arm. They were obviously more than friends.

What did that say about him?

It either sold his image—the rocker with swagger who could get any woman, just as his co-worker had suggested before he left Seattle—or undermined it. He hadn't considered it, but by walking into Brazen, week after week, and making a name for himself, he'd—well, made a name for himself. He was presumed gay. In his daily life, he worried so much about passing—fitting in. Looking the part. Now, the coin had flipped. He was still worried about fitting in—but in a different way.

They didn't know him, beyond his stage name and his penchant for old music. They didn't know his backstory. His history. And he didn't know theirs. He'd created an alternate universe where he played a role in the cast of characters. That universe was comfortable. Comforting. Until now. Liza's presence outed him as straight—the very thing he'd wanted his entire life. Until now. How ironic.

"So, the bartender's into you," Liza said, 'I'm Too Sexy,' still happening on stage, in a grating, this-has-gone-on-too-long, way.

"What?!" She'd jolted him out of his trance and back into the moment.

"Babe. That guy has it bad for you."

"No, he doesn't. He's friendly. He's working the tips."

"If that's what you think," Liza turned toward the bar, looking for the Chippendale's-worthy bartender, then back again. "But he was definitely flirting with you. So you know."

"I don't think so, but whatever. Oh, there's Shellie! I want to introduce you."

Perfect timing, Shellie. Changing the subject would sell his indifference, right?

As he introduced the two women in his life, Nathan wondered—had he made a mistake? Had he opened Pandora's box by bringing Liza into his underground San Francisco world?

"Next up, Shellie Carpenter. Shellie—" the husky voice boomed, "it's your turn."

"I need to run, but it was so nice meeting you!" Shellie hugged Liza, then Nathan, and headed for the stage, her three-piece suit understated that week. She went with a traditional black tuxedo, punctuated with a rainbow bowtie, her obsidian hair swept in an updo, but tips purple as usual. No confusing Shellie's preference.

"She's sweet," Liza whispered in Nathan's ear as his new band member took the stage. "Reminds me of Janelle Monae."

"She hates that," he said. "I made the mistake of saying something once and it didn't go well, so don't mention it, okay? And just wait. You won't believe her voice."

# # #

"Thank you! Thank you very much," Shellie bowed, as she did each week, at the end of her carefully-selected song. And as she did every week, she'd brought the house down.

"Shellie! Shellie! Shellie!" someone chanted from the crowd, starting a full-on group request—they wanted her to sing another.

"You're too kind, really."

"Brick house!" A man shouted from the front row. "Come on! Sing 'Brick House!'"

"I'm sorry, guys, I don't know that one. And I gotta say, the feminist in me isn't a fan. So, how about this? Nate Staples, where are you? Get your ass up here!" Shellie held her hand, mic still in it, above her eyes and searched the crowd. "Oh, wait. Jason—can we jump the line? This once? And can you queue the one we talked about?"

Under the spotlight she stood, waiting.

In the back of the room, he stood, hiding.

"Babe, go! You came to sing. Just go," Liza insisted.

"I don't know—we didn't plan this," Nathan whispered.

"So? You can't leave her hanging like that. She's in your band now. Go!"

As the crowd chanted "Shellie!" and she stalled, looking for her new front man, Nathan worked his way to the stage. With "excuse me" and "sorry" punctuating each sentence, he made forward progress. It was a small room, but the walk to its front felt like a run across a football field with linebackers trying to tackle him. Only these linebackers held cocktails and reeked of too much musky cologne and hair product. Not that he'd ever played football, but still.

"There he is!" Shellie encouraged. "C'mon, Nate. You're a fan of the oldies. What do you say we bring out an oldie, but goodie? Think you've got a little Kenny in you?"

"Loggins? Or Rogers?" Nathan half-yelled as he ascended the steps to the stage. Two could play at this game.

"The Gambler, of course," Shellie said as she signaled to the bartender for another mic. Before Nate, she'd been the ringer at Brazen. Now, she had to share the stage, but welcomed the company. Especially since his agent had signed her to a six-month contract as a back-up singer. Maybe Nate Staples was her ticket out of karaoke in the Castro and onto bigger stages.

"I think I can swing it," Nathan said, flipping the collar of his leather jacket up, running both hands through his hair to create a part down the middle. "How's that?"

"Yeah, sexy!" A man yelled, complete with cat-call whistle.

"Thanks—whoever you are," Nathan said, "See, they think I have it. I think the question really is—do you have a little Dolly in you?"

"Oh, that's sweet of you to ask," Shellie joked as she pushed up an imaginary bra under her suit jacket. "I think you meant, does Dolly have a little Shellie in her?"

"Oh, that's how it is? Alright, let's go! But before we do, I have something serious to say. I'd like to dedicate this one to my girlfriend. Liza's in the audience tonight, and I can't tell you how much it means to me to have her here. Here's to my island in the stream!"

"Aw, that's sweet," Shellie said, resuming her lead in the impromptu skit. "Sorry boys, he's taken. But we love him anyway, right?"

# # #

"Why do I feel like we're looking at the future of San Francisco music?" A voice asked from her side, as the duo onstage broke into the chorus of their song, which was definitely not from the future. Kenny and Dolly would've been proud.

"Because, we are," Liza said, matter of fact, eyes trained on Nathan and Shellie across the room. "They have some serious chemistry."

"Oh, definitely," the voice said, its owner now standing close enough to identify. Jason. Spray-tanned, perfectly plucked, discreetly Botoxed—Jason. "Shellie's been coming here for years. Voice of an angel. But she hasn't taken it anywhere. And then, in walks this lanky guy out of nowhere, starts singing these old songs with so much soul, and she stepped up her game like ten notches. He's pretty special. I didn't realize he had a girlfriend. You're a lucky lady."

Didn't realize he had a girlfriend? Hadn't he acknowledged her as if he knew about her a half hour before?

"Thanks," Liza forced a smile to disguise the gears churning in her mind. Had Nathan not mentioned her to the bartender he was clearly friendly with? "He's super special. But not just for his talent. He's a genuinely good guy."

"How long have you two known each other?" Jason asked, bar towel flung over his shoulder, crossed arms hiding his abs. For the moment.

"Oh, geez. Like twelve years."

"Wow, that's a long time to be together. Congratulations."

Under the cover of semi-dark, amidst a crowd looking for a release from their daily grind, Liza half listened to the lyrics coming from the stage and half listened to the man standing next to her. The discomfort in her head expressed itself in her body and she shifted against the wall, the drywall smooth against her exposed arms. Jason wasn't the only one with muscles.

"Hm? Yeah. Oh, no. We've only been together since the summer. Our relationship has been a marathon, not a sprint, I guess." She couldn't help it. Liza thought like an endurance athlete. Distances determined effort. And theirs *was* a marathon in the making.

"Ah, I see. Endurance is a good thing," Jason chuckled, his right arm outstretched to take her empty glass. "Anyway, can I get you another?"

"I'm good, thanks. But, hey—"

"Yeah?"

"Don't take this the wrong way. I see how you're looking at him. And that's cool. But the thing is, I love him."

"Understood," Jason said with a smile and a half bow. "Good to meet you, Liza. Let me know if you need anything else."

As he walked away, Liza turned her attention back to the stage. This experience was a mind trip. She was in a gay bar—a place she should be comfortable and relaxed—watching her partner sing, something that she loved doing, and the knot in her shoulders was as tight as it was on race day. But this wasn't a race. It wasn't a competition at all. Was it?

When she broke up with Jackie, they'd lost their connection; they had different priorities. Jackie was so far in the closet she could find all the missing socks lost in the dark corners and match them up. Liza'd never been in a closet, except to search for sporting equipment. She'd told her moms she was gay when she was seven, they'd believe her, and that was that.

Now, she felt the suffocation of being stuffed into a closet from a different perspective. She had a boyfriend. A serious boyfriend. Who'd done nothing wrong. Whom she loved, as she'd just boldly informed the bartender.

So why did she feel the need to march up on stage, grab the mic, and tell everyone in the room, "You don't understand! I'm gay!"?

SEVENTEEN

She fought back a scream as she injected herself with yet another cocktail of hormones, the magic in a vial that would help her body become a receptive host to an embryo. An embryo who happened to be hanging out in a freezer across town. It'd been more than six months of this routine—doctor visits, hormones. Pills, injections, tests. Picking a donor, harvesting eggs. Hoping they would be viable. Frustration with the process. Excitement about the process. Fear. Worry. Optimism. As she pulled up her PJ bottoms, Jen Scott winced, the fleshy side of her butt sensitive to even the light brush of fabric over it. She noticed a new bruise had formed overnight, her skin appearing more like she'd been in a fight with a tiny-fisted opponent instead of performing a medical task.

How she'd love to have someone with whom to share this experience. The plotting and planning and learning. So much learning. Unintentionally, Jen had become a reproductivity expert, especially for those in their "geriatric" years—a term to which she took offense but accepted. She was forty-four. Not exactly a young mother. But if Janet Jackson could do it—at 50—dammit, she could, too. Years of searching for a parenting partner had turned up empty, so there she was. Alone in her bedroom, raindrops pounding on the window with determination, the grey cloud cover with silvery light behind it setting the mood of the day: gloom, with a chance of sunbreaks. Her personal sunbreak was a planned walk with Emily later that afternoon, rain or shine. They were true Seattleites with the mindset held by long-time locals—don't let the rain interrupt your life.

Nothing would ever happen otherwise.

Thinking back on their date made her smile. It was easy and comfortable, even when it was uncomfortable. They'd talked for hours about their pasts and what they wanted for their futures. As she pushed herself up from edge of the already-made bed, Jen grabbed her phone, an early morning habit of looking at overnight sales taking over. Those sales numbers had a way of directing her days. But instead of her author dashboard, she opened her texts and started to type before realizing was 6:14 *a.m.* Way too early to text Emily without seeming desperate. And, as she told her sister—and herself— repeatedly, she wasn't desperate.

How much texting was appropriate, anyway? They'd sent a few the day before. Nothing important. Nothing deep. Jen had carefully timed her replies. She didn't answer immediately—that would seem needy. She didn't let too much time go by, either—that would seem indifferent. Dating was so much easier before timestamps and the ability for constant contact.

With hours before her sister would be up, hours before it was appropriate to reach out to Emily, and a fresh stream of hormones coursing through her veins, Jen decided there was only one thing to do: paint the nursery. She'd had the paint for months, its cheery pale green waiting to be needed, to be wanted. There it sat, stacked in the corner of the room with brushes and rollers, blue painter's tape and tarps, just waiting for her to take action. She wouldn't be able to paint once she was pregnant. And yet. She hadn't mustered the energy to do the work.

Or had she perhaps not wanted to jinx herself?

Painting a nursery was a big commitment. Painting meant there would be a baby. What if there wasn't? What if the embryo didn't attach? What if she couldn't carry it? What if she miscarried?

"Oh, to hell with it," Jen said to herself, the empty cavern of a room clad with uncluttered hardwoods and empty walls echoing back to her. "No time like the present."

In bare feet and paisley PJs, Jen set her mind to the job at hand. Inch-by-inch, she unfurled the painters' tape and tried to stick it in a straight line over the baseboards, stopping every so often to ball up a mess of stickiness into a blue softball and start over. Two hours into the project, she'd covered everything she didn't want painted green in tape and tarps. Progress.

With a new commitment to finishing what she'd started, Jen stood back and took it in. She stared at a blank canvas and imagined bringing her child home, swaddled tight in a baby blanket printed with teddy bears. Imagined rocking the baby on the rocker she'd picked but not purchased. Envisioned placing a sweet angel, unspoiled and unjaded, into the white wooden crib she planned to put in the center of the room. For a moment, she could see her family.

When the phone buzzed, she returned from the daydream. Where was that coming from? There were no pockets in her PJs. She'd had the phone when she started. The room was empty save for the tarp—ah, wait— under the tarp was a possibility. There it was, in the corner of the room, lighting up through the canvas, giving away its location.

Hey! I wondered if you wanted to get brunch instead of a walk? It's pretty gross outside!

Emily had broken the text barrier first, a relief. That little buzz from her phone offered an out from the project at hand, an opportunity to get out into the world without getting drenched. But she needed to paint. She'd sit on it a minute. Change her clothes. Think of a witty reply. A witty reply seemed important when declining an invitation to brunch.

Painter's overalls found (with no paint on them—yet), second cup of coffee consumed, and a clear mind, Jen replied.

I thought you were tough! I'd love to, but I started a project I need to finish. Want to come help me paint? Or can we push it to late lunch?

It was a long shot, but there was a hidden offer in that message. The words said, "want to help me paint?" But what she *meant* was, "want to come to my house?"

# # #

"I didn't think you'd actually come," Jen said, from her entryway, its slate tile a dead giveaway of her home's era. It was built in the late '40s, when odd-sized green slate was all the rage in Seattle. No two tiles were the same, but they fit together with precision.

"Of course I'd come! You don't know this—yet—but I'm excellent with a paintbrush and roller. And you can't beat my price."

"There's a price?!"

"Just this one," Emily said, as she stepped into the foyer and drew Jen closer. First, their bodies. Then, lips. Then, a tight hug to seal the moment, never mind the damp raincoat.

"Consider yourself hired! I'll open a PO right now. Come in and give me that jacket—you got me all wet. Oh! I mean—"

Emily laughed and handed over her raincoat. "So formal. Hiring and POs! And I want a tour. Where's this nursery going?"

It'd been so long since Jen had shown someone new her home. Since she'd focused on getting pregnant and growing the business, she'd barely dated, never mind met someone worthy of bringing home. But this was different, she reasoned, as she toured Emily Hall around her modest living space. Even if it went nowhere, Emily was still one of her authors—someone she trusted, someone she hoped would be in her life for a long time. Her house was a far cry from the old Craftsman she and Kate had owned on Capitol Hill, even from their cabin in Sun Valley. But it was hers, and it was home. She'd grown to love her Phinney Ridge neighborhood, its narrow streets lined with charming Tudors and Craftsmans, the odd mid-century shoeboxes, as she referred to them, sprinkled here and there. Those post-war homes were made of red Roman brick, thinner than standard brick, and a dead giveaway of the era.

It had been two days since they'd seen each other, but the conversation flowed. Saturday happenings. Angus's attempts to get his parents to buy him a car for his 16th birthday, which was the next week.

Jen's fertility updates. A conversation about the local music scene, sparked by a deep-dive into Jen's record collection, which included local up-and-comers like Thunderpussy and old-school favorites from Modest Mouse to Death Cab for Cutie.

"You're more into music than I knew," Emily said, holding a signed Brandi Carlile record. "You've even met Brandi?"

"Oh, that'd be because of Kate," Jen admitted. "She used to drag me to random shows all the time, and it turned out, I liked it. I got that Brandi album at a special concert we had for work. The perks of working for a mega-corporation."

"How hip of you," Emily said. "My students would be impressed. They're always shocked when I know about a current band."

"Why's that? They don't think you're hip?"

"They do not. I'm old in their eyes, remember. There's no way I could be anything close to dialed into what they like. But part of having a teenager is exactly that—I'm dialed into what Angus likes so I can relate to him, and there's the whole parenting thing. I need to make sure he's not getting into undue trouble. Some trouble I expect, but I keep a close eye on him."

"Ah, yes, parenting. About that—it's just—I haven't had anyone to talk to about the fertility stuff, aside from my sister, who's supportive, but not that interested. So, you need to tell me if I bore you with it, or it's too real, or—"

"Hey," Emily said. "I'll tell you if it's too much. Promise. But this is something I know about. I'm happy to talk about it, anytime. There's so much they don't tell you—it takes experience and friends with experience. It's okay."

They lingered in the kitchen, Jen's favorite spot in the house, she'd said, because it was where all the action happened. There was a reason people hung out in kitchens—aside from access to wine. Meals brought people together. Creating food for others was one of life's great joys, she said. Not that she'd done that much lately, but she thought of the first meal she'd cook for Emily as they stood amongst the white cabinetry and colorful pendant lights that hung from the ceiling, their soft light highlighting an eat-in bar. The window over the sink looked out on her backyard, two huge rhododendrons in sight beyond the patio. They wouldn't bloom again until spring, but their presence held an ongoing reminder—life has seasons. There's a time to prepare and time to bloom.

"Thanks," Jen said, "that means a lot."

"I get it. Trying to get pregnant is a big deal. Being pregnant is a bigger deal. I can only imagine what you're thinking as you do this. It's temporary, by the way. The crazy emotions and the highs and lows. Having your body overtaken by an alien. You forget all that once the baby comes."

"Yeah?"

"Yeah. And then your life gets overtaken by an alien!"

"Encouraging," Jen said, the corners of her mouth turning up. Emily was funnier than expected. Easier going, too. She wasn't the uptight image her on-trend clothes and put-together appearance projected. She was softer. More human.

"I'm kidding. What do you say we go paint your future kiddo's room? Green is the perfect color for a little alien!"

EIGHTEEN

Her last night in San Francisco came faster than she expected. Faster than she wanted. Thoughts of her training schedule and to-do list and adult responsibilities that she'd shoved away for a week bubbled to the surface as Liza walked to one last dinner with Nathan before heading home. Coit Tower stood in the distance, its slender concrete shaft presiding over Telegraph Hill, the haze of sunset giving way to the bright white lights illuminating it.

"I'm not ready to leave." Liza swung Nathan's hand in hers, the tiniest whine escaping with her sentiment.

"I'm not ready for you to leave," Nathan said. "This week went too fast! Finally, I'm feeling at home in San Francisco, and a lot of that's thanks to you."

"I have that effect on places!"

"Is that right?"

"Definitely. I make your house feel more like home, too. You just don't know it yet."

"Touché. I can't wait to see that for myself." The "Nate Staples" look stayed in the closet that evening. He was wearing his finest flannel, comfiest 501s, and signature Chuck Taylors.

"And—I like seeing you this way."

"What way?"

"Like Nathan. In your Seattle grunge wear. With the Chucks and the flannel. I've missed *you.*"

"Aw," Nathan said, the steel in his eyes shimmering in the light of dusk. "I haven't changed, babe. I'm still me. The clothes and image are just that—an image."

As they hopped off a post-card ready streetcar and walked, Liza took in the distinctness of the neighborhood. Nob Hill looked different than the Mission, and the activity around them changed, too. People dined outside at small tables near corner restaurants. A guy on a longboard flew down the hill they'd started walking up. A lesbian couple held hands as they walked and talked enthusiastically. She could imagine her moms vacationing there in the '70s and feeling comfortable—feeling accepted—by the diversity of the city's people. Envision them feeling at home amongst the evening chill, reveling in the canyons between the pale-colored Victorians. She knew where she was, and yet, she felt she could be in any city in Europe. And wasn't all that—the fancy building facades and the Bohemian culture—also *just* an image? Didn't people make assumptions about San Francisco based on what they'd heard, what the city wanted them to see?

"I know, but—" Liza started, her free hand landing in her hair, head turned to follow the lesbian couple up the hill.

"But?"

"I like it when Nathan shows up. No matter how big you get, I'll always see you as Nathan first."

"Liz—are you okay?" Nathan squeezed her hand.

"I'm fine, just a little sad. I didn't realize how much I missed you until I got a whole week with you."

"You sure? You've been quiet today. I was going to ask at dinner, but now's as good a time as any."

"I don't know. I guess last night threw me a bit."

"How so?"

"All of it. I mean, you've been telling me about the bar and the people and karaoke, but seeing it all in person made it real. And there I was, with my boyfriend who knew everyone, and was parading around on stage, and I felt like—an impostor. You have this whole separate life and I felt like I was watching it from the outside."

San Francisco is a lot of things. Quiet is not always one of those things. Streetcars screeched. Bike messengers yelled. Cars and motorcycles zoomed. The guy with the Bluetooth speaker strapped to his backpack was sharing his music with everyone within 500 feet. And still, Nathan heard her perfectly. Any other sentence, he may have missed part. Any other sentiment, he may have overlooked. Not this one.

"An impostor? Because?"

"Because—I was in a gay bar, and for the first time ever, I didn't really feel at home. It was weird. I felt like I was in some sort of reverse closet."

"Here let's go sit on that bench," Nathan motioned. They were close to the tower now, and its park-like setting provided them with a private place to talk at the right time. "I think I understand."

"Yeah?"

"Yeah, I had a similar feeling. I've been going there for weeks. They think I'm gay. I mean, I'm a guy alone in a gay bar—not a stretch. But then—"

"You show up with your girlfriend and that's a real headscratcher."

"Exactly."

"Because queer isn't as black and white like 'gay' or 'straight.'"

"Right—not at all."

"So, it was weird for you, too?" Liza asked, looking for the truth in the eyes that had never lied to her. Hoping her suspicions were just insecurities.

"It was weird."

"But not like, 'this *feels* wrong.' Right?"

"What do you mean?" Nathan asked, pointing to a low branch on a dogwood tree nearby. "Hold on—look over there!"

"What? I don't—"

"In the dogwood. Look—a parrot!"

"What the hell?! That *is* a parrot."

Their serious conversation just took a left turn to—parrots? On the branch, the bird was barely visible in the waning light, its plumage near camouflaged by the green of the tree's leaves. But it was a parrot. In the city. No rainforest to be found.

"Oh, yeah, we have hundreds of 'em," a voice interjected. "Sorry, I wasn't eavesdropping, I just saw you pointing. Happens all the time. Some house parrots got free a couple decades ago, and now, we have the Telegraph Hill parrots. It's charming. I think?"

"Thanks," Liza said, looking for the source of the voice. They were alone on the bench; there wasn't anyone else around.

"You're welcome."

"Do you see her?" Liza whispered, her hand finding Nathan's thigh, the softness of his old Levi's instant comfort. Maybe it was in her head? Maybe she was more shaken up than she realized by the Brazen bar experience.

"No," Nathan said, craning his head.

"But you heard that, right?"

"I did."

"I'm real," the voice said, as dusty work boots hit the ground with a thud, followed by a twenty-something in overalls with a paperback book opened, thumb holding her place. The pine tree to their left recoiled from its inhabitant leaping southward. "I just like to read up there. It's where I go to get away from it all. This city can get to you. People everywhere. No personal space."

"Totally get it," Liza said with a smile, sanity in check, and imagination off and running. How very *Tom Sawyer* to read a book in a tree. How did she get up there, though? It was a big tree.

"I'm Lemon," she said, "And yes, that's my legal name. My parents had a unique sense of humor. I was a surprise. At least they didn't call me Lemonade."

"Nice to meet you, Lemon," Nathan said, hand outstretched. "I'm Nathan."

"Liza," Liza offered, "Thanks again for the info on the parrots. Fascinating."

As the three chatted, Lemon pulled a camp chair from under the tree and told of her travels—which consisted of stints in almost every neighborhood in San Francisco. She hadn't quite made it to the Inner

Sunset yet—not a lot of trees, she said—but she'd done time in Golden Gate Park, the Presidio, and of course, the Castro. She'd been in North Beach about a month; it was time to start thinking about moving along. She told of the best places to watch the sunset, where to score a cheap shower, and that if you wanted free donuts, you needed to wait behind the donut shop in the financial district—not the chain, the one that also serves Banh Mi sandwiches—at around 4:30 p.m.—closing time meant they gave away what was left. She wondered where Liza and Nathan were visiting from—she assumed they were visiting.

"Oh, I'm putting together a band," Nathan said. "My agent is here, so I came down to work with him."

"A band, huh? Cool! I loveee music. Huge Janis Joplin fan. She was so misunderstood. What a tragedy! She died so young! I'm originally from Texas, just like her. But I can't sing!" Lemon laughed.

Liza wasn't known for indulging random "life story tellers," as she called them. Lemon's cost was starting to exceed her benefit. "Well, Lemon," she said, clearing her throat for emphasis. "It was nice chatting with you, but we have dinner plans—"

"Oh, of course, sorry. Gets a little lonely in the trees. Don't get a chance to socialize much. My apologies. Y'all have a nice dinner. Welcome to San Francisco," Lemon grabbed her camp chair and headed into the darkness of a stand of pines, her long braided hair bouncing against her back as she walked.

"I thought she said she needs to get away from it all, and goes into the trees? Then, it's lonely in the trees? That doesn't even make sense," Liza said, grabbing Nathan's hand to resume their walk.

"I don't think you can take much of that seriously. But the parrot was fun, huh?"

"It was."

"Is it okay if we finish our conversation at dinner?" Nathan asked. "I need to come down a little from that."

"Totally. And I have this strange craving for a Lemondrop. Want to get a drink first?"

"Lemondrop? I don't remember the last time I saw you with a drink—wait, I do. The symphony! You sure?"

"Yep," Liza said. "I'm sure."

# # #

Going to a bar hadn't been on that evening's agenda, but then again, neither were parrot sightings or strangers falling from trees.

"What'll it be?" the bartender asked as she placed paper coasters in front of them, their rounded-edge squares filled with travel-poster style images of the Golden Gate Bridge. Cushy stools with red vinyl upholstery lined the long bar—the kind with the brass grommets and the footrest all the way around so you always have a place for your feet. There were no tables—unless you count the pool table in the front window, where a heated match was underway. A hint of oregano wafted in from the Italian restaurant next door, its distinctive aroma making a pizza sound incredibly appetizing right about then.

Liza laughed as she read the coaster:

Visit San Francisco.

And then go home.

Clever twist, and she could relate. She felt that way about the influx of people moving to Seattle. "I'll have a Lemondrop. Go easy on the sugar, thanks."

"And I'll have an Anchor Steam, please," Nathan said. The bar was smooth under his hands, but in a different way than Brazen's. "Is this—"

"Old bowling alley flooring—from the lanes," the bartender answered before he asked. Her name tag said, *Karla, San Ramon.* "Came outta the old alley at Broadway and Van Ness."

"Thanks," Nathan nodded as she handed him the drink he'd come to associate with his time in the city by the bay. His leg tapped to the beat of the Beatles song on the sound system. At least, he told himself he was time keeping. He may have been deflecting, too. Pretending to be into a song he didn't even like until Liza's martini came.

"Here you go, hon," Karla said, delivering a not-too-sweet Lemondrop to Liza's coaster. "Cheers."

"Cheers," Liza turned to Nathan and smiled. "To you."

"Cheers to you, too."

"Woo," Liza's all-American smile turned to a pucker after just one taste. "That's—lemony."

"Do you want her to add some sugar? That looked pretty intense!"

"Nah, it's okay. I'll get used to it."

"So—" Nathan shifted in his stool, the Beatles beat dropping away and easing into a mellower song he couldn't place. That was going to drive him crazy. It sounded like Carole King, but was it? Had to be.

"So?" Liza leaned into the bar and turned to face her boyfriend, head propped in one hand, eyes picking up the green in her sweater—which for once, had sleeves.

"Where were we? Before the parrot debacle?"

"Ah, yes. Serious talk."

"Yeah, 50 Shades of Gay sound about right?" Nathan asked, making himself laugh and smoothing the fronts of his jeans. If you couldn't have levity in serious moments, well then—you couldn't have levity.

"All good here?" Karla interrupted. That was starting to feel like the theme of the evening: interruptions.

"All good," they echoed.

"50 Shades of Gay," Liza repeated, when Karla'd retreated. "That's funny!"

"I'm not all songs. I can do books, too."

"Clearly. But seriously, you felt weird, with me, in the bar? That was weird, right?"

"It was, but not a *bad* weird. Just an 'oh, I hadn't considered this,' weird. If that makes sense?"

"It does," Liza said, taking a tiny sip of the sourest Lemondrop ever.

"Seriously, babe, let her add some sugar," Nathan said, raising his hand to summon Karla. They were never going to complete this conversation, but watching her pucker after each sip wasn't conducive to a productive discussion anyway.

Drink re-mixed, nerves soothed, James Taylor on the sound system, Nathan started again. "Okay, the third time's the charm," he said. "It was different being in the bar with you, but there is no one I'd rather have been there with. I was so excited to show you one of 'my places,' and have you there to watch me sing. It's not like when Maplewood played, I know, but it's all I have right now, so it made me so proud knowing you were there watching."

"I was proud to be there," Liza said. "I was just really aware of being different, and it wasn't something I was expecting. It's maybe something I need to get used to—"

"Or not," Nathan stopped her. "I'm not going on a Gay Bars of the West tour. I'm going on a tour. It just so happened I made my weekend home Brazen—it felt natural. I'm most comfortable in a queer-friendly environment. But I'm only here two more weeks and then with you in Kona, home for a while, and we're going to cut a demo and start touring early next year. Julian has a few dates lined up already."

"True, but—that's not what I'm really getting at."

"No?"

"I'm just wondering—and you know you can be honest with me. We have to be honest with each other for this to work."

"I agree," Nathan said, hand finding hers on the bar. It was trembling. That didn't seem like Liza. At. All.

"I'm wondering, are you attracted to men? Now? We never really talked about that back when you transitioned—or when we got together. I mean, I know I'm not. Attracted to men. Well, not counting you and Ryan Gosling, but come on, he's pretty. Anyway, it could happen. I'm just curious if you've considered it."

"Wow," Nathan said. The most efficient conversationalist he knew couldn't get to the point. She rambled her way through it.

And.

She knew.

"I'm sorry, that was a lot, I just wondered—"

"It's a fair question; don't apologize. You want another?" Nathan signaled to Karla for one more. For both of them. It was a "one more" conversation.

Parrots and interlopers seemed like so long ago, but that crazy story only happened a half-hour prior. This crazy story might drag on a while.

"Okay," Nathan sighed, a long draw of a fresh beer filling his senses and delaying his response time. "Yes, I have thought about this."

"I figured."

"And. It's complicated."

"Also figured. There's no right or wrong answer, but it's important we talk about it. Otherwise, I'll just keep wondering, and that'll create doubt and worry. When Jackie and I broke up, it was about doubt and worry, and I don't want that for us," Liza said, a sip of the second drink not making her pucker. Turns out sugar is important, in certain situations. That would cost an extra mile on her run when she got home. Or maybe two—one for each drink.

"That makes sense. I'm sorry if I've made you worry. I didn't think it was that big of a deal—it's nothing I plan to act on."

"So, you are?"

"I mean—sometimes. For instance, yes, Ryan Gosling is very pretty. Lately, I've realized I'm attracted to *people*. Sometimes men, sometimes women. But Liza, listen to me. I love you. With all my heart, since we met, I have loved you. You didn't always know it. I didn't have the courage to tell you when I first knew—I had a big journey to go on before I could tell you. If you hadn't come to me first, hell—I probably still wouldn't have said something. But trust me when I say, I'm with *you*.

Only you. People are going to flirt with me—it's bizarre, but it comes with the singer thing. But bottom line—as long as you want me, I'm yours."

"And you're not into Jason?"

Thank you, vodka.

"What?!"

"I told you, he's into you. I'm just curious—"

"I'm not into Jason, or anyone, but Liza Barrett. She's the love of my life and the one I want."

"Good answer," Liza threw her arms around his neck and tugged. He smelled of barley and a new bodywash.

"And you weren't tempted by any of the women in the bar? You're not missing your Gold Star status?"

"Sometimes, yes. I've always been a lesbian. Since I was seven years old, I've had an identity. And that identity is different now. But I wouldn't take back my Gold Star for anything because that would mean I wouldn't have you. And Nathan Stapleton—Nate Staples—whoever the hell you want to be—I'm yours, too. I love you. And I'm so proud of you. Prouder than you know."

"All good here?" Karla asked, one last time.

"We're good." Nathan signed a pretend bill in the air—check, please.

"So, to recap," Liza said, her finger collecting all the sugar from the rim of the martini glass. "There are parrots in San Francisco, we love each other, and I shouldn't drink vodka."

"Sounds exactly right," Nathan said. "We're skipping dinner, huh?"

"Right. Take me home or lose me forever." Was that a slur in her speech?

"Doesn't it go, 'Take me to bed, or lose me forever?' The 'Top Gun' reference?" Nathan signed the check and stood, wrapping her arm around his shoulder to slide her off the stool.

"Whatever. Take me home," she laughed. "In a Lyft. I don't want to walk."

"Wow, you *really* shouldn't drink vodka. I've never known you to voluntarily take a car home. But okay, let's go. And Liza?"

"Mm?"

"I'm glad we had this talk."

"Me, too."

NINETEEN

"Mom!" Kate Conrad yelled, a sea of people obstructing her path. She'd seen her mom come down the escalator from the terminal. "Mom! Glenda!" It was pointless, so she kept walking, squeezing through openings here and there, pushing past strollers and roll-a-boards and the people tethered to them. "Mom!"

"Katie!" Glenda saw her this time. "Look at you! You look wonderful! Not working is working for you."

"Hi Mom," Kate said, hugging her mother tight around her narrow middle. How she stayed so thin year-in and year-out was a mystery. "Did you have a good flight?"

"As a matter of fact, I did. I sat next to this nice young man from Memphis. He flew out to visit his grandmother. Isn't that so sweet? He told me that he's going to take her to visit her friend somewhere, where was it—?"

This is the point at which Kate tuned out. Her mother loved uncovering stories about strangers on planes. She invested hours into someone she'd never see again, and genuinely enjoyed it. Meantime, Kate just wanted to get the luggage, out of baggage claim, and away from the growing crowd. Everywhere she'd been that day, there was a crowd. She didn't expect solitude. It was still the city. But in the middle of the day, she'd hoped for less—less traffic, less hassle. Fewer people with fewer bags. "What's your bag look like?"

"Oh, it's a roller bag with a gold band around the middle. Black," Glenda said, stepping toward the carousel that teased her with each new suitcase that spun past. Like a proper Southern woman, she'd dressed for her flight: Navy blue slim-fit slacks, burgundy cashmere sweater, and a simple string of pearls to accentuate her still-taut neck. No one needed to know she'd had a little help in the neck department, nor that her real pearls were in the safe-deposit box back home. Those pearls were impostors. Good impostors, but impostors, nonetheless. Not a strand of her silver hair was out of place, its perfect pixie cut on trend.

"That one?" Kate asked.

"No," Glenda peered to confirm—it wasn't her bag.

"Okay, let me know when you see it. Are you hungry? It may be a few hours until dinner—Chris doesn't get off work until six."

"Oh, I'm fine, dear. I had a nice snack on the plane. Oh! There it is!"

"This one?" Kate asked as she lugged a *huge* bag off the carousel. A nod told her it was indeed the one—unsurprisingly. She probably should have provided clearer instructions on what would and wouldn't fit in the Jeep for their big drive later in the week. Glenda insisted on having the right outfit for every occasion. For a moment, Kate was twelve again, standing in the curbside bag check in station at the Knoxville airport, waiting. Waiting for her mom to remove enough weight from her luggage so they could go to France for spring break. It was just the two of them—a girls' trip to Paris—and Glenda had packed four bags. Four very heavy bags. Her dad laughed from the Suburban as Glenda ran items—one at a time—back to the truck. He'd thought it was hilarious.

Probably because he'd been in Kate's shoes before. He understood. Young Kate just wanted to get going. As did adult Kate, then. "Mom, I don't know if this is going to fit in the Jeep with my things and the dogs. We may have to ship some of it ahead."

"Darlin', you're not still driving that old Jeep are you? I thought you were going to buy a truck?"

Not the point, Glenda.

"I'm going to," Kate said, dragging the bag behind her as they did the baggage claim game of Frogger in reverse. "I just haven't. Yet."

"Well, we could go shopping tomorrow if you want? I love test driving!"

"I don't know," Kate said, noticing the smile on her mom's face. She seemed genuinely interested in driving trucks. "Too much change in a small period. Maybe when we get there."

"But sweetie, that drive will be so much more comfortable in a nice new truck. With automatic. And power windows! The dogs would be happier, too. Do you need money?"

"No!" Kate insisted as she pushed the button to the elevator that would take them out of there. Out of the hustle and bustle of an international airport, and into the hustle and bustle of stop and go traffic. She'd taken care to put herself together that day as well—she knew her mother. Appearances mattered. So, she'd pressed a pair of chinos and a white button-down oxford, the Polo logo stitched in bright red. She'd visited her stylist the day before for a fresh cut and root touch up. She'd even worn tinted lip balm. Picking up her mother at the airport to go meet her girlfriend was serious business. Skipping over any outfit or appearance feedback would only set the stage for a smoother meet-and-greet later.

"I could chip in? A housewarming gift, maybe?"

"I don't need money, Mom. I can afford to buy a truck—I've just had a lot going on. And—"

"And?"

"I'm not ready to let go of the Jeep yet." Kate and Jen had bought the Jeep together to leave in Sun Valley at the cabin, and that yellow 4x4 was the only material item she had left from their marriage. It reminded her of a different time—and an old country song wherein the guy got the Jeep while his ex got the "palace" in their divorce. In their case, Kate got the Jeep, Jen got the Range Rover, and neither came out with a house.

"So, keep it. But let's go find you a truck tomorrow. A nice F-250 or Silverado. Something big and sturdy. The new GMCs come with a tailgate that folds a bunch of different ways. Or you could go with a Ram, for more power if you're going to be hauling a horse trailer. It'll be fun!"

Since when was Glenda an expert on new truck models? And why was she so intent on this, of all things?

"I'm curious," Kate said as the parking garage elevator arrived with a ding, their airport journey nearly complete. One more elevator, one more short walk, and they'd be on their way. "How come you know so much about trucks?"

"Oh, no reason," Glenda said, looking directly at the closing elevator doors.

"No reason? Those are a lot of details about features for someone who's never driven a truck. Did you—?" Kate had led her mom directly to the Jeep, its sunshine yellow paint easy to spot amongst the row of silver mid-sized SUVs.

"Oh, darlin'! No! James reads all the car magazines—he told me all about them. When I told him about your ranch and you needing to get a better vehicle."

"James?"

"Yes," Glenda said, that big smile plastered across her face again. "The gentleman I've been seeing lately."

Gentleman?

"Mom, do you have a *boyfriend?*"

"Oh, I wouldn't say—"

"You do!" Kate said, heaving the suitcase into the Jeep. Seriously, what did she have in there?

"Maybe."

How the tides turn. There she was, nervous about introducing her mom to Christine, and Glenda was as nervous about mentioning James.

"Well, get in and tell me about him!"

Kate navigated out of the parking garage maze while Glenda talked, telling of meeting James Darling (yes, that was his real last name, she said—ironic since she used 'darlin' more than anyone) at a charity tennis event. They'd bid on the same item in the silent auction—two tickets to the Grand Ole Opry and a backstage pass—they both loved country music. James had won and asked Glenda to join him. The rest was history. They'd been thick as thieves since that trip to Nashville, three months before.

"Mom, this is wonderful!" Kate said, shifting down as I-5 northbound traffic came to a crawl. She wasn't going to miss this traffic. "Why did you wait to tell me about him?"

"Well, darlin'—I know you miss your daddy. And I didn't want you to think I was trying to replace him. I miss him, too. But I get lonely. I didn't want to say anything until I knew if it was something that could last. I haven't told your brothers, either."

"I don't think you're trying to replace him. No one could replace him. Everyone wants a companion, Mom. There's no shame in that. If you're happy, I'm happy for you."

"Thanks," Glenda said. "And speaking of happy, I can't wait to meet this Christine whose stolen your heart. You sure you can't convince her to move to Montana with you?"

"I'm not sure—yet." Kate said, downshifting again. At this rate, they'd get to Christine's just in time to leave for dinner. "It's not out of the question. We're not there yet."

"It might just take time, dear. Time will tell."

"I know, Mom. Let's not think about that right now. Tell me more about James."

# # #

"Your mom is so sweet," Christine said as she pulled the duvet over her shoulders and sunk into a double stack of soft pillows. One wasn't enough. Two were perfect. She'd clicked off the lamp and her eyelids were heavy and begging to close, if just for a moment. After a day of being 'on' at work and 'on-ner' with Kate's mom at dinner, there wasn't much energy left to give, but she wanted a few moments alone with her girlfriend before doing it all over again. The clock read 12:11 a.m. She pushed away thoughts of patient appointments and the impending board meeting waiting the next day.

"She has her moments," Kate laughed. "She was so excited to meet you. She couldn't stop talking about you on the ride to her hotel. *'Christine is so smart!' 'Christine is so successful!'* You're every mother's dream son-in-law. I'm sure she's told all her church friends how I'm dating a doctor."

"Son-in-law?!"

"I'm only kidding." Kate folded the covers neatly just below her armpits—sheet over duvet, tight tuck. Christine would learn. "I'm sure your dad must've had similar thoughts—wanting a son-in-law? And then you brought home an Air Force Pilot. Best closest thing, I figure. How's he going to feel about an unemployed software developer who lives on a ranch?"

"He's going to *love* you, just like I do." With Sadie snuggled between them and snoring, and Dallas and Hunter on the floor—also snoring—Christine sighed.

"Everything okay?"

"It will be. I have a board meeting tomorrow about the suit. I'm trying not to think about it. It's been sitting on my shoulders all evening, waiting. I didn't want to bring it up around Glenda, but it's getting to me."

"Come here." Kate tapped her shoulder. "Why don't you snuggle in and tell me about it?"

Outside the bedroom window, a Harvest Moon shone, its ethereal glow providing soft light amidst a backdrop of darkness. One more night together and Kate would be on her way to Montana. Christine sighed again, knowing. She'd planned on being on that journey. Wanted to be on that journey. And now, the clock was ticking, and she was consumed with a senseless lawsuit without a timetable.

"I've been over it in my head. Over and over and over it. She needed the procedure. Yes, we have surgery quotas. But, I ignore them. I'm not a surgeon. I don't recommend procedures a person doesn't need, or I don't think will help their problems. Dr. Jha is one of the best—she doesn't have to work to meet quotas. She has a waiting list. It doesn't add up."

"So then, it'll probably blow over?"

"I hope so. In the meantime, it's making me a little nuts."

"I doubt you're nuts," Kate said, "This sounds really—human. You pride yourself in your work. Someone's accusing you of something you didn't do, and it's only natural to want to clear your name. Not crazy."

"I feel crazy," Christine reiterated, little chuckle escaping as it did when she was insecure. "I've been down both paths with this. In one scenario, the case disappears before it turns into anything. It's just an obstacle. In another, she gets to court with it, and manages to convince a judge that Dr. Jha and I colluded. I don't know what that scenario looks like for my career."

"Have you talked with Dr. Jha? What does she think?"

"She's as befuddled as I am."

"I have an idea. When I get blocked with a work problem, I diagram."

"I don't know, Kate—"

"Just hear me out. Your mind is spinning out of control with paths this could take. You're stuck on 'what if.' But there are only a few ways it may go. You already outlined a couple. Let's just draw it out. Get it out of your head and onto paper. Then, it's less scary. It's words on paper. Potential outcomes. But those outcomes don't define you. Okay?"

"Okay, tomorrow. I'm so tired." Christine rolled to her side, the allure of sleep pulling her out of the conversation.

"Okay, tomorrow. But one more thing—" Kate said before placing a kiss on Christine's cheek.

Too late.

As fast as she'd rolled, she'd fallen asleep.

# # #

Kate was up with the sun, which hadn't actually "come up," per se. The last day of September was shrouded in a protective layer of greyness, its cool morning air no longer a fluke. It wouldn't be long and the days would be impossibly short, the nights excruciatingly long. At least in Montana, she'd see the sun.

"I made coffee," she said as Christine ambled down the stairs into the kitchen, her fitted black pantsuit a departure from normal workwear. "Wow, you look nice. Is this for the board?"

"Thanks," Christine said, one hand already on a travel mug and the other on the coffee pot. "Can't hurt."

"We agree," Kate looked to the three dogs lying at her feet by the kitchen island. Dallas and Hunter had become accustomed to staying at

Christine's and had made themselves at home—both with the house, and with Sadie. "Not that they know, but they pretty much agree with whatever I say. I gave them bacon."

"Lucky dogs! So, what are you up to today? It's your last day in Seattle—wow. I can't believe that."

"I know, me neither. I want to do this, but I'm going to miss you so much. I pretty much change my mind every day."

"I'm going to miss you, too, but you have to go. It's your dream," Christine said. "Who knows, I may not be that far behind."

"I love this idea! Just say the word." Kate smiled her best "move in with me" smile. "But I do have a favor to ask. Would it be okay if I leave the Jeep here for a while?"

"Don't you need it?" Christine had already grabbed her overcoat and was headed for the garage, which, typical for the era, had room for exactly one vehicle: *her* Jeep.

"Well—that's what I'm doing today. Mom wants to go truck shopping. Thinks I need a 'better vehicle.' She's not wrong. It's time. I'm picking her up shortly and we're going to go find a suitable truck, load it up with what's left at the house, and get ready to head out. She asked me to take her to Ichigo for dinner. She can't get good Japanese food in Tennessee. And I doubt I'll find it in Bozeman. Join us? We'll celebrate a positive board meeting and the unknown that is Big Sky country."

She'd planned this for a month. She'd signed papers to sell her house, to buy the ranch. Between logistics and moving companies and trying to spend as much time with Christine as possible, the month had expired. Just as they always had when she was in a good place. When things were going well, the days were like minutes. When things were tough, they stretched on for eternity.

"Of course, I wouldn't miss it. And go Glenda. She's been in town less than a day and she's already convinced you to get a new truck. Impressive." Christine said. "Of course, leave it here. If you don't mind, Jess can drive it from time to time. Sometimes she doesn't feel like riding the bus."

"Thanks, love," Kate said, standing to hold her girlfriend for a fleeting moment before they both headed into the world. "Mm, you smell as good as you look."

"Sandalwood."

"It's nice." Kate drank in the sweet smell of sandalwood as they kissed. It wasn't a kiss of extreme passion. No, this kiss was more—a statement of building love and respect. A hint of the future masked in the realness of the present. "Good luck today."

"Thanks, I need it," Christine said as she turned on her heel. "I love you, Kate Conrad. See you tonight."

"I love you too," Kate yelled after the shadow who'd already disappeared.

What was it Shakespeare said? Parting is such sweet sorrow? Yes, that was it.

And yes, it was.

TWENTY

The day he'd been waiting for had arrived. Conversely, the day she'd been dreading had arrived.

It was Angus Hall's sixteenth birthday.

While he slept, Emily wondered over coffee and old photo albums: How did she have a sixteen-year-old? While liberating for him—he was taking his first major step toward freedom, toward adventure unknown—the day hung heavy on her heart. Her baby—that sweet, innocent, funny little boy with the wild locks and dimple in his left cheek—was one step closer to being a grown man. The boy who'd once told her he wanted to marry her someday, who'd held her hand in grocery stores, who'd called to her in the night when he had bad dreams or feared the monster under his bed, had given way to an independent thinker with taste for the finer things and one goal: a car of his own.

She and Kevin had talked it over. Plenty. They wouldn't have to shuttle him back and forth to work and athletics. He could drive himself. But with a car came great responsibility. Was he ready? And if they gave it to him—if he didn't have to buy it himself—would he appreciate it?

"Only one way to know," Kevin had argued.

"But, that one way could have horrible consequences," Emily said.

"Em—at some point, we have to trust him. Trust the job we did raising him."

"I know. But I'm not ready."

"So, this isn't about him. It's about you."

Damn Kevin and his astute observational skills.

Though they'd told him no, he was absolutely not getting a car, on the curb in front of her house sat a faded red 2005 Honda Civic. For Angus. Not a dream car, but not a slouch, either. It was a practical first car. It would get him where he needed to go, safely. And it was only fitting it was built the year he was born. The writer in both appreciated the metaphor.

"It beats my first car," Kevin laughed.

"What, you mean that primer-colored '76 Dart wasn't your dream vehicle?" Emily asked, when he told her he'd found Angus the perfect starter vehicle.

"It was not. But I loved it."

"I know," Emily said. "I remember you picked me up in that rust bucket for our first date, and I was like, 'does this thing even run?'"

"It did, didn't it? Most of the time. Man, those were simpler times. When I could change the spark plugs and dump in a quart of oil and be good to go."

Kevin had a point. Those *were* simpler times. But it didn't have to do with oil and spark plugs. Those times—before marriage and a baby and careers; before divorce and co-parenting and book deals—were fleeting. They'd slipped through fingertips like sand, leaving only memories.

And now, those simpler times were Angus's to have. The excitement of a freshly printed driver's license. The newness of exploring the city without a bus pass—or your parent—taking you there. That was something special. Being able to pick his girlfriend up for a date—Emily didn't want to go there. It was inevitable. Whether it was Raven, his current girlfriend, or the next one, or a boyfriend, Angus would find *his* someone and they'd create memories they'd later talk about as the good old days.

But she was getting ahead of herself. As she looked at an old photo of him in his Pop Warner football outfit, helmet in hand and missing front teeth not stopping him from displaying a huge smile, she laughed. That kid. She was the professional teacher, but he'd done so much of the teaching. A true Libra, he'd taught her patience to wait while he weighed the pros and cons of a situation. When he was seven, he'd spent a week deciding if he'd trade his Matt Hasselback Seahawks card for a Tom Brady card. He'd weighed the choice, the potential upsides and downsides, and walked her through each step of his rationale, only to land on keeping the Hasselback because he couldn't sell out his hometown team, even if Brady was a superior quarterback. So very Angus.

She'd seen parts of herself in him—parts she'd hoped not to pass on, but had. People pleasing, for one. But she'd also seen parts of herself she was proud he inherited. His ability to talk with anyone about anything. His interest in keeping things fair. Angus loved to win—but not at the cost of fairness. She and Kevin had done a good job, she reasoned. They'd raised him to be conscientious and respectful. She had to let go and trust him.

Angus, for all his pleading, didn't yet know of his new wheels.

As she sipped the last drops of coffee from the mug in the silence of a still house, Emily thought of her time with Jen. She was on the verge of an empty nest, and Jen was just gathering sticks to build the nest. The duality was noteworthy. Initially, Jen's admission that she was working towards a pregnancy was just that—a fact.

Now, Emily wondered. Did she want to do it again? The lost sleep and teething and learning to read? The delirium that came with working and raising a child? Could she find the love in her heart to raise another? She'd be 43 when Angus went to college. (Assuming he went to college. That was another topic.) Jen was waiting for the "go" on her embryo transfer. If the invitro took, she'd be—gasp—60 when that baby left the house.

They'd been on two dates and she was thinking about the next 18 years.

"Too soon," Emily said aloud and shut the photo album, which concluded around the time Angus was nine. She'd stopped printing photos when she and Kevin started having trouble. The rest of his growing up existed in her head and in her phone, and she made a mental note to remedy that.

"Too soon for what?" Angus asked from behind.

"Gus! Don't do that!" Emily shrieked.

"Sorry, Mom. Too soon for what?" Angus kissed his mom on the cheek and went straight to the coffee pot.

He'd caught her. Daydreaming about her life—her future. Wondering "what if," with the same curiosity of a kid wondering where their path may take them.

"To give you your birthday gift," Emily said. Save of the day. "Happy birthday, buddy. You feel any different?"

"Nah. The same," Angus said as he poured himself a cup of coffee.

"Since when do you drink coffee?"

"For a long time," he shrugged, dumping sugar by the spoonful into his mug. "Got a big chemistry test today. Need to be awake."

She had to hand it to him—caffeine and sugar were one way to ensure alertness.

"Maybe you should have some food with your sugar?"

"Nah, no time. Gotta shower. I'll be ready in 15."

She watched him from behind as he bounded up the stairs two at a time, his left hand protecting the top of his mug—wouldn't want to spill the energy source. "Angus?"

"Yeah, Mom?" he shouted.

"Never mind. It can wait."

She wanted to tell him she loved him, and she was proud of him. She wanted to give him a huge hug, to wrap her arms around his nearly 6-foot-tall body and not let go—not let him get any bigger or older. To freeze time—there, then.

Instead, she packed two sack lunches and thought of her lesson plan for the day. For her students, it was just another Wednesday, just another discussion about a book some had read, some had skimmed, and some had begged friends to summarize for them. For her, it was a day of new beginnings, in more than one way. Was that *excitement* about the promise of Jen getting pregnant bubbling inside her?

# # #

"I can't believe this is your last day in Seattle," Liza said as she hugged her best friend. She'd skipped the athletic wear and donned jeans and a sweater for their going-away coffee date in Pike Place Market. "I'm glad you found time for me."

"I wouldn't skip town without seeing you," Kate said, squeezing just that little bit tighter. "You remember my mom."

"I do. Hi Glenda," Liza smiled and hugged the other Conrad in front of her.

Standing in a south-end parking garage with a view of the Puget Sound, they chatted. Small-talked. Shifted in stances and put hands in and pulled hands out of pockets. Yes, Glenda'd had a pleasant flight. And the weather was so nice that day—beautiful blue sky, not a drop of rain to be found. Weren't the ferries majestic against the backdrop of the Olympics in the distance? What? Kate bought a truck?

"You did?" Liza didn't think she'd see the day Kate gave up the Jeep. "Today?"

"Yep," Kate said, "Thanks to Mom's pushing. It was time. It's that dark blue one—over there. The Ford. She needs a name, but that'll come."

"Wow. Beautiful!"

"She needed something more ranch ready," Glenda put her arm around her daughter's shoulder. "You can't tow a horse with a Jeep."

"No, I suppose you can't," Liza said. Never mind Liza knew nothing about horses, unless you count metaphorical carbon fiber horses powered by pedals. "Can we go find some coffee? I've been up since five and I'm overdue."

As the trio walked towards the caffeine—the original Starbucks—
Liza said it again. "I can't believe this is your last day in Seattle."

She'd known this was coming. Her life had been upended over the
past month because—this was coming. They'd spent time apart before.
For Kate's work trips and Liza's races. For the occasional vacation, when
they weren't vacationing together. But, for the first time since they'd
met—back when Kate was still married and Liza was still rebounding
from Jackie, they were going to be *apart*. Not a walk down the hallway
away. Not a drive across town away. *Away* from each other.

With Nathan's impending tour, and Kate fleeing the city, where did
that leave Liza? Kona was 10 days out. When she got back from Hawaii,
what then? There was a lull in wedding season after October—she didn't
have another one booked until early December. There wasn't much new
blog content to create this time of year—save for the illusive Kona race
report she couldn't wait to write. *That,* she was excited about. *That,* she'd
already begun forming in her mind. How she'd set up the sections, how
she'd describe the racecourse. But that was in Hawaii. Back in
Washington, her boyfriend and best friend were leaving her.

At least, it felt that way.

"Why don't you come visit me after Kona? Bring Nathan. I have tons
of room and you can hike to your heart's content," Kate said.

"I don't know—"

"You should," Glenda chimed in as they stepped into line outside
Starbucks, its single-file tidy against the building. This branch served the
same coffee as any other, but this one, the famed "where it all started
location," meant they'd wait. To say they'd been to the original. Which
didn't matter to Kate or Liza, but it was on Glenda's bucket list so she

could tell all the ladies at church. They wouldn't break her heart by spilling the beans—the *original* wasn't the "first" original. "It would be good for you to decompress for a while, darlin.' All that racing can't be healthy in the long run. Everyone needs to rest."

Leave it to Glenda to mama bear someone else's daughter.

"You sound like my mama," Liza smiled, taking a step forward with the line.

"Well, then. Your mama sounds smart," Glenda said.

"Seriously," Kate stepped forward. "Think about it. Chris can't come for a while—she doesn't know when she can leave Seattle, and Mom will have to go back to Tennessee, eventually. Come keep me company."

While the line inched forward, the sun shone over the quintessential Seattle scene. Cobblestone roads constructed in the early 1900s showed years of wear from buggies and feet and later automobiles rolling over them, tops worn smooth and the spaces between them filled with a hundred years' worth of dirt. Green paint peeled around a standpipe at the front of the coffee shop, its flat-roofed, equally green awning protecting them from rain that failed to arrive that day. A man in a knit beanie sat on the edge of the sidewalk picking a familiar tune, his mandolin case hiding part of the yellow line that indicated where the sidewalk ended and the cobbles began. Liza tossed a five in his case—there was that soft spot for musicians.

"I'll think about it," she said. "Right now, I can't make plans past this race. And I want to spend some quality time with Nathan at home before he goes on tour. I've felt so disconnected from him while he's been in San Francisco. We need together time."

"Understandable," Kate said. "Are you ready for the race?"

"I'm never ready for a race!" Liza took another step forward, her eyes saying what her lips wouldn't—*thank you for not asking about Nathan*. They'd talk about that later. When they were alone. "But I'm ready for the experience. I've been training with this guy, Gray. One of my clients' brothers, and he's helped me bump up my watts on the bike. This one's all about surviving the heat, so I need to cut energy where I can. Biking takes less energy than running, so I've been focused on finding time there. And I've been sitting in the sauna. A lot."

"Where's there a sauna?" Glenda asked, pretending to shiver in the 60-degree air, her stylish Chico's outfit a little too linen for Seattle in the fall. "It's so cold here. I wouldn't mind a sauna. I don't know how you girls live so far north."

"Nathan put one in his bathroom. Perks of living with an electrician," Liza said. "You're welcome to come use it, if you'd like."

"We don't have time. Dinner with Chris tonight and then we're hitting the road in the morning." Kate scooted forward one more step. Almost there.

"But thank you, darlin'. That's awfully sweet of you to offer. This Nathan sounds like a catch! Why haven't y'all lived together if you're in his house? And I thought—?"

The answer to her questions—the one she asked and the one she didn't finish—could wait, because it was her turn to order, and she needed to focus on her non-fat, half-decaf, three pumps of caramel latte, with a sprinkle of cinnamon and nutmeg. Not too much nutmeg, please.

The barista didn't bat an eye when she'd finished her request.

"I'll have an Americano," Kate added, "Black."

"Same," Liza said, hopeful that the coffee ordering process would prevent Kate's mother from finishing her thought. Prevent her from saying what so many had almost asked her, only to catch themselves at the last minute—"I thought you were—*gay?*"

"Shall we walk through the Market?" Liza diverted when they had coffees in hand. Certainly, the fish-throwing guys would continue the distraction. As would the stalls full of dahlias and other colorful floral creations. Surely, the shoulder-to-shoulder mob that moved through the inside of the market as one cohesive unit would erase the start of that conversation and shift it to the more reactive, the more inconsequential.

"Yes, we should!" Glenda enthused with her elaborate drink wrapped in a brown paper napkin, straw inserted into the sippy cup lid. "I want to bring Christine some flowers."

"Well, then, let's go!" Liza said and grabbed Kate's hand. Her friend had been quiet since they'd met. Maybe it was moving jitters? Maybe, having her mom around?

# # #

"Nice deflection," Kate said, her mom three steps in front of them with her face in one of the many bouquets on display along the market's outer edge. The inside of the market was for craft vendors, tchotchke peddlers. The outer edges held farm stands: produce, flowers, meats, and cheeses.

"Right?" Liza said, still holding her friend's hand.

"So, really. How are things with Nathan? How was San Francisco?"

"Oh, Kate. It was—a lot. Good. Informative. Busy."

"That's not exactly what I expected you to say." Kate stepped up beside a family to check on her mom. She was fine—discussing the details of growing in the Northwest in fall with a farmer wrapping colorful bouquets. Glenda Conrad was a friend to everyone and a stranger to none. She could go back to Liza without worry. "Informative?"

"Yeah. He's—assimilating. The agent is creating an image for him and he's taking to it. Nathan's still in there, but Nate Staples is becoming real. It's like I'm watching the preview of the future film."

"The future film?"

"Yeah, I got a glimpse of what it's going to be like when he's on the road. What it's going to be like to be with Nathan *and* Nate."

"Hey, darlin'!" Glenda called.

"Hold that thought," Kate said, a finger in the air showing she'd be right back and stepped closer to her mother for a consultation on Christine's favorite color. Answer: blue. That was easy. Glenda would bring her a blue bouquet. She sure was putting on the charm—she must've really liked the doctor. She hadn't taken this level of interest in any of Kate's girlfriends since Jen. But then again, neither had Kate. "Okay," she fell back again. "So, it's a little weird, then? Seeing him as Nate?"

"Not that," Liza said, head shaking. It wasn't that. "Nate's fine. He's just a more polished Nathan, with a leather jacket and wingtips. And highlights! It was more, going to the bar with him and seeing how everyone looked at him. He's got fans, even just singing karaoke. The ab-tastic bartender has a crush on him. That was eye opening. And kind of alarming."

"He already has groupies?!"

"You could say that. We talked about it; it's fine. But you know—it's change."

"I know," Kate said. If there was one thing she understood, it was change. "Change is *change*. Not much you can do about it, except accept it. And hope for the best."

"It's true. Speaking of change, what's up with Christine? I thought she was driving with you to Montana?"

They'd made their way around the end of the market and settled exactly where Kate expected they would: in front of the fish throwing guys. All day, every day, they tossed salmon back and forth like they were 10 and the Coho was a football. She watched her mom watch the guys throw salmon for sport and deemed there was time. Glenda was into it. As were the dozens of other people who were gathered around, cheering.

"She was. And then, she wasn't. She's dealing with a malpractice suit. It just came up, so she can't leave while they figure out what's going on."

"Shit, really?" Liza said, downing the tail end of her coffee and tossing the famous white-and-green mermaid cup in the trash bin nearby.

"Yeah."

"I'm sorry. Is she okay? Are *you* okay?"

"Hang on," Kate said, once again stepping forward to answer a question for her mom. Which fish would she prefer to bring on their trip? Salmon or halibut? Or crab? Answer: Salmon. Always salmon. "Okay, sorry. Yeah, she's upset. She doesn't think there's any merit to the claim. But it's an administrative nightmare. And it totally blows up our plan. I was really looking forward to a couple weeks alone at the ranch—

just us. Sometimes I wonder if I'm doing the right thing. First good thing to come my way in forever and I'm out the door."

"Wow, that sucks. Tell her I'm sorry to hear it and I hope things work out okay."

"I will."

"And—you're forgetting how you got here. You bought that ranch before you knew she was into you. You've wanted to leave Seattle forever. I can't even count how many times you've told me the city is changing in ways you don't like. And, you know as well as I do, you can't change your dreams for another person. You just end up resenting them. I like Christine way too much for you to end up resenting her."

"I know," Kate sighed. "Triad of Impossibility."

"Yep."

"Things just can't be simple, huh?"

"Never," Kate said as she caught a bag of iced down salmon that was shoved into her body. It wasn't what Liza meant, but her question was apropos of the moment. They didn't need to *add* to the things they were taking to Montana. Especially perishable things. But then again, there was no stopping her mother. Years of experience taught her it was better to embrace it than fight about it. It was why she now owned a brand-new truck. And why she'd find time to procure a cooler to carry salmon 12 hours by car. Before their dinner reservation. In two hours.

"Okay, girls! I think I've done all the damage I can do here," Glenda proclaimed, the bouquet of sky-blue hydrangeas she was holding almost completely obscuring her body.

"I can hear her, but I don't see her," Kate laughed. "Let's get out of here."

Just as they agreed to leave, someone stepped on Kate's foot. Of course they did. She couldn't escape the reminders of city life.

People.

Everywhere.

TWENTY-ONE

The school day was a blur of pop quizzes and cafeteria duty, but at 4:00 that Wednesday, Emily was home, pre-heating the oven. Angus had asked for a paleo birthday cake. First, coffee. Now, low carb? She didn't even know this kid anymore, but by God, she would make an almond flour cake that tasted good.

How do you feel about sweet sixteens? She texted Jen at the last minute. She'd debated all the way home in her head. Angus didn't need to hear that dialogue, which made her sound more like one of her students pondering their crushes than she'd prefer. After a commute's worth consultation with herself, she'd decided, *what the hell?* If she was already thinking about the next 18 years, may as well share some cake on her son's birthday.

Depends, came the reply. *Am I invited? Because if I'm invited, I'm all about them.*

Well then, get on your party hat and come on over. 6:30? There's cake. (That I hope will be edible.)

That was light, right? Right. It oozed of lightness.

"Angus!" Emily yelled as she stirred the batter, the wooden spoon becoming heavier in her hand with each turn. "Do you want vanilla or chocolate?" This would have been good to know five minutes earlier, when she was texting while baking. But she could still make it work.

"Carrot!" He yelled from upstairs.

"Not an option. Chocolate or vanilla?"

"Chocolate!"

Good answer. A little cocoa powder and her yet unflavored cake became chocolate. Kevin would be there in an hour so they could give Angus his present together. Their son didn't seem at all suspicious, even though the Civic had been parked in front of their house for days and hadn't moved. Her stomach churned in anticipation. Anticipation of his reaction, she told herself. Anticipation of her first foray into paleo baking, she suggested aloud. Not the fact that her new girlfriend and ex-husband were about to meet. Not to mention, Angus. She hadn't introduced anyone to Angus since Julie—and that didn't end well.

But wait.

It had been two dates. They weren't exclusive. Except. She wasn't seeing anyone else, and she didn't think Jen was. And. She was already thinking about their lives together ten months in the future. When Jen would be a mom and she—a bonus mom? That was ridiculous. It had been *two dates.*

The recipe explicitly said not to over-stir the batter. How long had she been turning the spoon in the bowl? Hopefully not an amount that constituted too long.

# # #

"I want you to record it," Julian said when Nathan finished playing his latest song, the one he'd sung for Liza. They'd just had their weekly one-on-one, daylight turning to darkness outside the high-rise office window. Nathan had "just one more thing" he wanted to talk about. One more thing to share.

As it was for her, this performance had been all-acoustic—him and his guitar. He'd kept the 501s and Chuck Taylors for this day—remembering Liza said she liked it when *Nathan* showed up.

"Yeah?" he sat taller in the stool, the praise from his agent giving him instant height.

"Oh, yeah. This could be a hit for you. Really, really good work, Nate. Let's get it scored for the band, and—" Julian paused, hand stroking his greying goatee, eyes closed. "How do you feel about strings?"

"Like, a violin?"

"Like, a symphony."

"Well, I love that, but—I don't know how to score for a symphony. Charles already has a drum piece for this, and I can do a bass line and keys, but strings?"

"You don't have to do it, I just wanted to gauge your *interest* in it," Julian said. "I've got a buddy who can do it. I feel like this song can go from good to great with the right accompaniment. I'd like to pass it through my top songwriter, too. A few word choice/phrasing things could be better—Tanya can help with that. We want to nail it for your demo, right?"

"We do," Nathan agreed, the C major chord appearing beneath his fingers on repeat. C major was his comfort chord. The soundtrack to uncertainty. Scoring for a symphony was exciting. Changing the song, not-so-much.

"Okay, it's settled. I want to record three songs next week before you leave. This one—what's it called?"

"'In a Dream.'"

"'In a Dream,' 'Canyon,' and a rockin' cover. I want people to hear the range of your voice. Any ideas?"

This was all part of the formula Nathan signed up for—a new look, a new band, and a three-song demo.

The question lingered in a still office, frosted glass door closed to keep the commotion on the other side *on* the other side. Did he have any ideas for a cover?

Since he'd landed in San Francisco, he'd become more of a karaoke machine than artist—covers were becoming an important part of his identity. Others may have seen it as a step backward, from gigging garage band to singing karaoke in a small bar, but Nathan didn't. He enjoyed the weekends at Brazen—and it wasn't permanent. As he leaned on a simple oak barstool in Julian's office, surrounded by tall metal file cabinets and otherwise bland walls lined with framed gold, silver, and even a few platinum albums, Nathan remembered the first cover he'd performed. Outside his shower, that is.

It was, perhaps ironically, "Goin' to California," by Led Zeppelin. He loved that song growing up, mostly because he dreamed of running away. Of going to California and starting a new life. A life where no one knew him and he could be *him*, without Natalie's baggage chained to his feet. Where he'd fall for a girl with a flower in her hair who could sing, just as the song promised. His mother had played that record on repeat—she had no idea the lasting impression it made on him.

The night he'd first sung the Led Zeppelin cover, he'd been young and green. He didn't know how hard it would be to capture an audience; didn't know how exhausting and exhilarating it was to sing for a crowd. He and Charles had just formed Maplewood and had booked an open mic night at a small club in Seattle's University District. They were allowed three songs—a challenge not unlike the one Julian issued. Three songs to reel 'em in. A good night would mean an invitation back. They'd chosen "Goin' to California," "Drops of Jupiter," and "Canyon," the first song Nathan and Charles wrote together. Talk about an eclectic mix.

On a tiny stage they played, hoping to get the attention of the college student crowd. They didn't succeed—beers and conversation were more important than their burgeoning band—but they did leave with the performing bug lodged in their souls. It had been more than ten years since that evening. They'd been through two pianists, four bass players, and one giant band rift that he'd now patched. Time had passed, but he hadn't forgotten the sheer euphoria that came with singing on a stage. Whether it was a karaoke bar or a dive bar or a backyard barbecue, Nathan felt the same—he loved to sing.

"How about 'Goin' to California?'" he asked, already strumming the opening bars.

"I don't know, man. Classic rock isn't quite where we want to take you, you know? You're more edgy than that, don't you think?"

"Who's edgier than Led Zeppelin?"

"They may've been—in the '70s. But let's look into more recent times."

Nathan—and his alter ego, Nate—disagreed. Along with those opening bars, now came the opening lines, in a gravelly, rough-around-the edges, mind-bending falsetto.

"Should I keep going?" Nathan asked after the first chorus. He'd stood for this serenade and was walking around the edges of Julian's office as if he were on stage, guitar held tight to his body, shaggy hair covering his eyebrows—he hadn't bothered to adjust it to sing. That's how much he loved this song.

"Wow," Julian said, his desk chair now reclined as he listened, arms splayed out and supporting his head with interlaced fingers. "Okay, Rockstar. Let's see where this goes. Keep going."

It wasn't cockiness. It wasn't an "I'm right and you're wrong," statement. No, this was about passion. Nathan could sing new life into that old song—if only given the chance. So, he made the chance for himself. Nate Staples was about confidence and composure. The song meant something to him, and he could make it mean something to Julian. To anyone, for that matter.

"Alright. You've convinced me," Julian said. "But I want a back-up in case this doesn't land when we record it. Can you work up something newer, too? Figure out who you most want to be like—take their best song—and let's cover it. Let me know by tomorrow so I can work on negotiating the rights, okay?"

"Okay," Nathan said. He was almost done with San Francisco. For now. Ten days and he'd be in Hawaii with Liza. Ten more days of intense focus on the band before he could give it a rest for a while. "Let me talk to Charles and Shellie and get back to you."

# # #

"We need one more cover for the session next week," Nathan said when Charles answered his phone.

"Good to hear from you, too."

"Oh, sorry. Hi." Nathan shook the swirling thoughts out of his head. He'd had only one focus as he walked home from Julian's office: find a cover. That was the thing about *needing* to do something. Especially something that should be easy. When it should be easy, Nathan overthought. He'd created a list of two dozen songs he could cover. None were right. None made the statement he wanted to make. For this task, the jukebox that lived in his head was out of songs.

"Hang on one sec," Charles blurted, muffled chatter leaking through the airwaves. It wasn't unusual to hear background chatter when talking with Charles. This chatter—however—seemed different. Rushed. And hushed.

"Okay, I'm back. So, what about a cover?"

"Are you okay? It's hard to hear you over whatever's happening there."

"Oh, I'm fine. That's Moses. He's moving in and needed help with the aquarium," Charles said.

Aquarium?

"Dude. Who's Moses?" Had Charles mentioned something about someone named Moses? Nathan wouldn't forget that name.

"You know, *Moses*. The guy I've been seeing since last week. The dancer. He lost his lease and needs a place to crash for a while."

"Woah!"

"Don't 'woah' me. Liza moved in with you after like 30 seconds of dating."

"Ouch. Sensitive much?" Nathan knew Charles to be a lot of things: a loyal friend, an enormous flirt, and—resistant to moving boy toys into his house. He'd always said co-habitation was bad for breakups.

"Sorry, brother. I didn't mean that. It's a little crazy here right now. There's the Pilates machine thing and the inversion table and—the iguana. It's a lot."

So *that's* what the aquarium was for.

"So why is this guy moving in? You sound completely annoyed."

"Because—I'm doing him a favor."

"And?"

"That's the only reason. We're not serious," Charles insisted. "I told him he can stay for a month. Until he finds a place."

"Okay," Nathan said, his mind already back where it started—on the cover he'd called about. It wasn't worth getting invested in Charles's man of the month. "I hope you don't have to evict the iguana. I've heard they can be mean SOBs!"

"Come on, man! He knows the rules going in. The cover?"

"So, for the recording session Friday, we're gonna do that new song, 'In a Dream,' 'Canyon,' and Julian wants one cover. I said, 'Goin' to California,' and he wasn't totally sold. We need another. A back-up."

"It's easy," Charles said, before yelling, "No! Not there. Put it in the garage."

"Put what in the garage?"

"The treadmill. This guy has more workout equipment than anyone I've ever met."

"He sounds like a great match for you. You can skip dinner and burn calories together."

"Dude. I said, drop it."

"I'm only kidding," Nathan said, hearing the annoyance in his friend's voice. It was now directed at him instead of Moses. Push any further and he'd get responses in Spanish, and the last time that happened—he didn't want to go there. "So, what's your idea? Julian said it needs to be rockin'. Something we aspire to be."

"'I Love Rock 'n Roll.'"

"You want to cover Joan Jett?!"

"Why not?"

"I don't know if I can pull off that attitude," Nathan slumped into his futon. '70s folk, he could pull off. '90s grunge, the same. But punk? And not just *any* punk. Joan Jett? That was a high bar.

"*You* may not be able to, but Nate can. I saw it myself."

"I don't know—"

"I watched you prance around that stage at Brazen with attitude even I didn't know you had. You put on that leather jacket and some new person showed up. And I saw how the crowd was into it—especially the bartender. What are you going to do about that sitch, anyway? Clock's ticking."

"I'll think about it. Let me see if I can hit the notes. And nothing. About Jason. There's nothing to do."

"I disagree. But suit yourself. I'd do something about it in a hot minute, but I respect your high moral ground. Hang on—" There were the muffled voices again. "Okay, listen, I gotta go. But I'll see you next week, okay? I'm gonna to learn 'I Love Rock 'n Roll.' You do it, too. Trust me. Julian said to make a statement. This will."

# # #

"I didn't know what to bring a 16-year-old; I hope he'll like it," Jen said as she placed a small, wrapped box on Emily's kitchen counter. "It's a pair of Airpods. He doesn't have them, does he?"

"You didn't have to bring him anything!" Emily said as she took Jen's jacket. "Especially not something that nice on late notice. He'll love them."

"I wanted to. I feel honored to be invited. It's lame to come to a birthday party empty handed. And, I couldn't bring him my standard birthday bottle of wine, so—"

"Good call! See, you're a natural parent. I'm just going to put your coat in the back bedroom—want to come with me for a second?"

For a moment, Emily was 16 again herself, tiptoeing around her parents' house with a crush. Angus and Kevin were out test driving the Civic—a huge hit! They had a few minutes of solitude before the house was overrun with raucous teenagers.

"So," Emily said as she closed the door to her guest bedroom, its space dark, save for the corner streetlight's glow streaming through half-opened plantation shutters.

"So," Jen smiled. "Do you bring all your lady friends back here?"

"Only the cute ones."

Stealing a kiss against a closed door in her back bedroom felt so risky, and thrilling. Heart racing, eyes fluttering closed, Emily breathed in a familiar smell—baby powder—and stayed in the moment. They'd kissed, but *this*. This wasn't just a kiss. This was—nerves in her stomach. This was anticipation of more.

Not tonight.

But soon.

"I'm really glad you invited me," Jen said as they parted. "I want to get to know your full life—not just the 'single' you. If it's okay with you, I want to know Angus, too."

"It's okay with me," came the reply, before she processed its meaning. "I'm glad you want that. I want it, too."

What the hell? Who was speaking? She'd made a huge deal with Mallory about not introducing her to Angus. They'd broken up over it, in fact.

"Great," Jen said, "Shall we go join the party?"

"Are you ready for ten teenagers talking over each other?"

"Is there a way to be prepared for that?"

"No," Emily laughed. "But you passed the test. Come on, I made some Paleo chocolate cake. Angus is on a health kick."

TWENTY-TWO

She'd lied awake most of the night, Christine sleeping at her side, Sadie tucked into the bend of her knees. Both snored, in the cutest way. When Christine rolled, Sadie adapted. Stood up, turned in a circle, and tucked back in. Dallas and Hunter were sprawled across the floor near her feet—they had no issues getting some shuteye.

Kate had been down this road a hundred times—imagining what their last night together in Seattle would feel like. In her imagination, time stalled, and they'd spent the evening tangled up in bed. Reality was different. In reality, they'd gone to dinner with her mother at her favorite Japanese restaurant on Capitol Hill, and then to her townhouse to grab the last few items and say a proper goodbye.

In the barren living room, she'd popped open a bottle of Dom her boss had given her on her last day at work—if not then, when?—and said one last red Solo cup toast to days gone by, memories made, and the promise of new beginnings.

"Cheers, to the house that built me," Kate said.

"You're quoting songs again, huh darlin'?" Glenda asked, rhetorically. Of all people, Glenda got the country music references. "Cheers to this beautiful, strong woman who knows what she wants and is making it happen. I'm so proud of you, baby girl."

"Thanks, Mom," Kate blinked back the tears she didn't want to form. Not now.

"I'd like to say something, too." Christine raised her glass above eye level. "Glenda, it's been wonderful getting to know you these last few days. I'm sorry we don't have more time together. I can see where Kate gets her charm—and good looks!"

"See, I told you I liked this one," Glenda beamed.

"Anyway, Kate, you're saying goodbye to one chapter of your life. One book, even. But the unknown can be a beautiful adventure, and I can't wait to write the next chapter with you. I'm proud of you, too, for following your dream. Selfishly, I wish that dream were in Seattle, but that's what airplanes are for. I'll see you in Montana just as soon as I can."

"With Sadie?" Kate had grown attached to that little pile of peach fuzz.

"With Sadie," Christine promised.

They hadn't lingered—what would be the point? The house was empty, soulless. In less than 24 hours, it would be someone else's. Kate Conrad's Greenlake days were over. When they'd downed their champagne, Kate tossed her keys and garage door clicker on the kitchen counter, took the trash bins to the curb, and closed the garage door from the keypad outside. She lingered in the drive, imprinting a memory of the home where she'd found herself after her divorce, made a life that was hers, and where someone else would do the same. She nodded to her companions, a silent request to hop in the new truck, and backed away. For the last time.

With Glenda returned to her hotel, Kate and Christine found themselves in bed, the fury of passion turning to comfort of closeness, turning to an attempt to stay as close as possible, as long as possible. When Christine dozed off, Kate thought about her route for the next day. Where they'd stop for gas, food. Where the dogs could get out and sniff and stretch. But her thoughts kept returning to summer. To the camping trip on the coast, when the woman whose bed she was now in spent the night in her tent. Waking up alone, confused. To the moment she was certain she didn't have a future with Christine, much as she wanted one.

She'd made major life changes based on that certainty. That given.

There was a lesson in that memory.

Just when you think you know something—when the odds are nil and hopelessness creeps in—that's when the tide turns. When you want to quit and say to hell with it all, that's the pivotal moment. And in the pivotal moment, people do things you don't expect. Like kiss you with such intensity you can't mistake their intensions. Like tell you they want to give it a try, together.

Goddamn timing, Kate said in her head. She knew good and well that if she hadn't bought the ranch, Christine may not have admitted her feelings. That the pivotal moment came when she announced she was leaving Seattle. The forcing function had forced its function.

An hour before the sun would be up and the time she told her mom to be ready to hit the road, she yearned to stop the clock. To wiggle her nose like Samantha did on the *Bewitched* re-runs she watched growing up, and freeze time. If only for a moment.

"Babe, I've gotta get up," Kate whispered, contorting her body around the woman beside her, hand finding Sadie's head, warmth radiating into her chest. "Stay in bed, sleep. I'll call you from the road."

"Mm," came the reply, more of a groan than a word.

"I love you," Kate said, and placed a kiss on Christine's cheek. "And I love you, too," she followed with a kiss to Sadie's head. "You two have stolen my previously cold heart, and I can't imagine my life without you in it."

As she slithered out of bed, trying to make as little noise as possible, she stepped on Dallas's foot. He yelped and plopped his head back on the ground. "Sorry, buddy," she whispered.

"Kate?"

"Yeah?"

"Please drive safely. I need you in my life for a long time."

"I will. Promise."

"And Kate?" Christine sat up now, hands finding the edges of her eyes, rubbing. "I love you, no matter where you are. I know you're worried. Don't be. I'm not going anywhere."

Kate resisted the urge to get back in bed. To snuggle just a little longer. If she got back in bed, she wouldn't get out. Eventually, she had to leave.

# # #

Each day when Liza Barrett awoke, she looked at the desk calendar she'd mounted to the wall next to the bed. And each day, she took a black Sharpie and put an "X" over that day's spot in the calendar. One less day before Kona. One more day to train. And worry. There were more "Xs" than blank spots at that point. Nine days until race day. Six until she hopped on a plane to Hawaii. Seven until she was reunited with Nathan. Her life was a numbers game—for a while longer. Days, distances, paces, calories.

That day, she had a scheduled 15-mile run, a one-hour swim in the lake, and an afternoon meeting with a potential wedding client. A quick scan of overnight messages revealed a text from Kate saying she and Glenda were on the road; she'd let her know when they arrived. One from Nathan asking her to have dinner with him on FaceTime. And a message from Gray confirming he'd see her at Seward Park for their run at 8 a.m., sharp. He wanted to swim with her too, but may have to bail, he'd said—too much to explain over text.

Liza stayed in bed an extra 10 minutes—a luxury—and through closed eyes, thought about how lucky she was to meet Gray when she did. They'd hit it off right away, and he'd become a helpful training partner. And friend. Someone to help her stay focused on her goal, someone she could count on. And someone who, as far as she could tell, wanted nothing from her in return. Just company. He'd shared with her so many of Nancy Callahan's training methods—minus the doping—and helped her work towards calm and confidence about the big race, which was circled and starred in the big calendar. She'd helped him work through his latest girlfriend issues and plan his summer race schedule. They had common ground that made for an easy friendship. Remove the distraction of physical attraction, and it was an ideal relationship. Sex just complicates things, Liza noted as she stumbled out of bed toward the coffee.

Fueled with caffeine and carbs, she rolled into an empty parking lot. Unless you count the Canada geese who were huddled in a squawky blob in one poorly marked spot—they didn't stick to Greenlake alone. The white line markers had faded to nothing, making parking a free-for-all, for humans and geese. In the distance, the quiet swim beach was calling her, the packed shore of summer only a memory.

Gray yelled to her as he jogged closer, his navy running shorts matched to a navy-and-white running singlet, not-quite-shaved head covered in a lightweight white cap. He looked like a Nike ad.

"Last big run!" Gray shouted. "Let's make it a good one."

"Let's!" Liza agreed as she fist-bumped her training partner under wispy cloud cover, the morning marine layer threating to burn off as they spoke. She'd worn capri running tights with a short-sleeved top—and willed the cool, misty air to hang on a little longer. "I hope you wore your fast shoes. 'Cause we need to put down steady sevens."

"I'm all about it," Gray said, shaking out his arms in a way that indicated he was—indeed—all about it. Aside from Nancy, he hadn't encountered a woman with whom he could run until Liza showed up at his brother's wedding. "I'm already five miles into this journey. What's fifteen more?"

"I thought you didn't do distance?"

"That was the *old* Gray. New Gray puts in some miles. Especially with good company. Ready to roll?" Gray jogged in place and nodded toward the footpath that traced the park. That would get them three miles. From there, they'd run north, hugging the road near the lake until winding into the neighborhoods above the park and then heading back to where they started to get in that swim. Though the race order would be swim, bike, run, logic said to run first so they would be warm enough to make the lake's cooling temperature tolerable.

As they ran in silence, Liza noticed the differences in the neighborhoods. They bled into each other, overlapping like puzzle pieces jammed into place—even if they didn't quite fit—the changes minor at first. Seward Park smelled of old money—many of the turn of the century homes had views of Lake Washington and the old growth forest of the park itself. Madrona was similar: Tudors, Dutch Colonials, neighborhood corner stores and eateries, but the trees shifted from firs and hemlocks to more and more of its namesake madronas. When they arrived in Columbia City, the changes were more noticeable—bigger lots, a prevalence of post-war homes, fewer views. And by the time they hit Beacon Hill, it was like they were in a brand-new city. Modern home after modern home lined the streets of the neighborhood she called home.

"Turn back?" Gray asked from a corner in front of a coffee shop.

"Yeah," Liza nodded, "but let's pop in here. I want a shot."

Quick boost consumed, they were back on the street, and Liza picked up the pace a notch, sidewalk underfoot giving way to the shoulder of the road—they were headed back into residential areas lacking reliable sidewalks. The pace increase was part of her plan, and reason for the espresso. They'd hit seven-minute miles for the first half. Her goal was to finish the run on a 6:30 pace. She wanted to train the way she planned to race, and she planned to pick up the pace in the back half of the marathon.

"So how are things with Christy?" Liza asked, turning her wrist to look at her watch. One mile into the turnaround, she was on pace: 6:50 on the dot. Not talking pace, but they were going downhill, which gave a little extra room in the lungs for conversation. It wasn't time to speed up again, yet.

"Not worth talking about," Gray puffed.

"That good?"

"We broke up."

"Oh, I'm sorry. Want to talk about it?"

"Maybe, but not when you're speeding up the pace on me. We didn't discuss sub-sevens."

"Sorry again," Liza shrugged and offered one of the water bottles from her waistbelt. "I got you coffee! Need some water?"

"I'm good. Let's just talk after, okay? I want to hear about Nathan, too."

A mere fifty minutes after they'd turned around, they were back in the parking lot, dotted with sweat, four water bottles, two sports gels, two double espressos, and fifteen miles—all done and dusted.

"You gonna make the swim?" Liza asked, leaning against her SUV as she caught her breath. She'd clocked a 6:26 final mile—better than expected.

"Unfortunately, no," Gray said, his tall body folded in half at the waist, hands resting on his thighs, breath still ragged from the effort. "I'm meeting Christy for coffee. I need to run home and shower—actually run. And since you put the pedal to the metal on me, that's looking a lot more like a walk. I didn't think this through—I'm a little—tired."

"I can drive you."

"No. Get your swim done. I'll be okay."

"Then let me call you a Lyft. It's the least I can do. Really."

"Alright," Gray conceded. "I'll allow it."

"So formal. Okay, so what's going on with Christy?" Liza dug through the swim bag on her passenger seat to find her phone.

"She gave me an ultimatum," Gray said, unfolding to again stand upright. "I don't do ultimatums. So I ended it."

"Wow, that's ballsy! What'd she say?"

"She wants to get married. Said if I'm not planning on proposing before the end of the year, to not bother."

"Okay, that's just crazy! You were already on the rocks. She wants to get married?"

"Right. So, I'm taking her a box of the things she left at my place and closing that chapter."

"I get it, but I'm sorry, Gray."

"Ah, it's okay. There's other fish, ya'know? I just wish I could hook one more like you—low maintenance."

"Ha!" Liza lowered the phone—Lyft could wait.

"What?"

"I have never been accused of being low maintenance."

"You are, trust me."

"Um—I spend my time obsessing about exercising. I worry night and day that my partner is off falling in love with a groupie—or bartender—or both. And I'm pretty sure he is, so occasionally I accuse him of that, and he has to talk me down. And I've mostly avoided romantic relationships because I can't deal with the worry and stress that comes along with them. I'm more complicated than you know. You see Liza, the triathlete with the pace schedule and brick workouts. Not, Liza, the obsessive worrier and occasionally too-jealous lover."

"I disagree," Gray said, leaning against the car next to her. "You sound like a typical Type-A, but not in a bad way. Nathan's off doing his thing—it's normal to worry some. From what you've told me, you respect him and his dreams. You're confident in your own dreams. You're making it work, together. That, my friend, is what every guy wants."

"Maybe."

"For sure. No one wants to be told what to do or how to do it, or be given mandates and deadlines. Trust me."

"Gray, you're such a good guy," Liza said. "Your person is out there. And you'll probably find her when you're not looking. Always happens that way! It seems like everyone I know met their match when they stopped trying."

"Sage advice, Ms. Barrett. Now, get that swim in. I've got to go down a bottle of Advil and put on a fake smile."

# # #

When he told her, she thought she'd mis-heard. Upon asking for a repeat—a clarification—the same sentence was delivered with the same directness.

Now, the conversation played on repeat in her head.

"Dr. George, we're putting you on a one-month administrative leave. Just standard operating procedure."

"That would've been nice to know yesterday," Christine said to the chairperson of the hospital's board, the breath escaping her nose forceful, the stack of charts beside her looming. "But I understand. I need to tie up a few things here, so I don't leave my patients hanging."

"Of course," Dr. Andino said, again with no emotion. "Take all day. And then go have a nice, long vacation somewhere. Hawaii is nice this time of year."

Alone in her kitchen, Christine browsed the wine cabinet for something appropriate. What paired best with anger?

The 36-bottle custom cabinet flanked her kitchen on the dining room side, and was occupied by creations from Red Mountain, Walla Walla, Horse Heaven Hills—all Washington State AVAs. There were a few Oregon Pinot Noirs, a couple of Italian chiantis. California was noticeably absent. She needed to remedy that.

After a full assessment of the options, a Columbia Valley Merlot made the cut. Not too heavy, not too demanding of the palette. "Go have a nice, long vacation," she growled to Sadie, ever loyal at her side as she cut the foil from the neck of the bottle. "Hawaii's nice this time of year. Thanks, doctor. Maybe I should get caught up in malpractice suits more often."

When the wine key met the cork and Sadie realized there were no dinner scraps coming—no dog biscuits, either—she abandoned her mom. "Now, you?" Christine yelled as she pulled the cork from the bottle, the distinctive pop echoing through her empty kitchen. "I can't catch a break today. Kate left, then this ridiculous forced leave. Now, even my dog has abandoned me?" She swished a micro pour in the glass to open it up, breathed in the plum notes, and downed it as if it were a shot.

The thing about dogs is—though they may understand, they can't talk back. Can't tell you it's all going to be okay or offer advice at the right moment. They can, however, lean in and be with you—in a way only they can. In a way humans struggle to replicate. Sadie had been there for Christine through insurmountable grief, and she'd be there for this. After a brief disappearance, she re-appeared with a plush toy in her mouth, snuggled close to her mom's leg, and sat. Apparently, she needed her own support animal.

"That's better. Thank you, Sadie-pie. Mom needs you today." With the comfort of her pup at her side, Christine leaned on her kitchen counter, the Merlot she'd chosen fruity and fragrant, no hint of tannins, smooth in its finish. Perhaps a little too smooth, because before she knew it, she was three-quarters of the way into the bottle, had moved to the dark living room, and was summoning Meg for their Friday night talk. A turn of a lamp knob or flip of a wall switch could've provided light on the situation—but when talking to Meg, she sat in the dark. It was their routine.

"Why is this bothering me so much?" Christine asked. "It's standard, they said. No big deal. Go take a vacation."

No response.

"They could've told me this last week when we went over it with the full board. They could've told me yesterday, even. Then, I could've joined Kate on the drive. I could've been there for her, like she's been there for me."

Nothing.

"Meg, are you with me? I could use a sign that you're here. Anything."

Christine's phone buzzed from the pocket of the white lab coat she was still wearing, Christine George, M.D., F.A.C.C., stitched above the right breast pocket in black cursive lettering. She'd come straight home from the office, a month's worth of appointments re-scheduled or re-assigned to a different cardiologist and hadn't changed her clothes. Hadn't taken a moment to find her comfiest pair of sweatpants or her favorite hoodie. She'd gone straight for the wine.

The phone buzzed, again.

We made it! I can't wait for you to see this place—it's magical. I'll call you before bed. XOXO

Kate had attached a photo of the ranch house, with her new truck parked in front, and a yellow blur, assumed to be Hunter, running in the back of the frame.

The universe had a way of helping Meg's messages get through.

"I guess this day was coming, wasn't it?" Christine kicked off her cushy work sneakers and placed the empty wine glass on the coffee table. She stretched out on her couch lengthwise, as if she were embarking on a session with her therapist. And she was. She was in a session with her deceased former partner. The person who knew all her secrets, all her insecurities. The one who'd always listened without judgment.

Christine continued to talk to the empty room, working out the details. These plans weren't for a trip to Hawaii, though. She'd head to California first—she hadn't seen her dad in almost a year. Too long. A few days in Santa Barbara would do her good, and Sadie loved to run on the beach.

From there, she'd go to San Diego. To their secret spot below the Torrey Pines Nature Preserve. They'd met at Black's Beach dozens of times in the past. Christine would sneak into town for a long weekend, grab a bottle of wine and a cheese plate. Meg would bring the blanket and a backpack full of extra clothes for when the air became too cool to be comfortable. They'd hike down the trail, catching up on each other's lives, and then spend hours on the beach, watching surfers, waves, and chance encounters turn into romantic evenings for total strangers. When the sun sunk below the horizon, when the oranges and reds petered out to a dark blue sky, they'd don headlamps and hike back up the trail, back to the rest of the world that wasn't coated in a protective layer of salt and sand.

For this meeting, she and Sadie would have their own picnic—wine and cheese for Christine, water and chicken for Sadie. She'd hire a boat to take her five miles out into the Pacific Ocean, well beyond what was required. She'd recite the poem by Mary Oliver that she'd read daily for the weeks and months after Meg died—"Love Sorrow"—and give Meg's ashes to the sea.

It was time. And if she was going to move on with her life, it was necessary.

With a plan in place—a counterclockwise road trip that would take her from Seattle—almost at the Canadian border—southward to near the Mexican border, and back north to Montana—Christine replied to Kate.

Exciting! I'm free all night—FaceTime me when you can so I can see it. Your truck looks right at home there. I miss you already! XO

TWENTY-THREE

When the words came, they came with ease. But when they didn't, they really didn't. She had a week left before her first 100 pages were due to Jen—a week to read and re-read, self-edit—and if she were being honest, self-doubt.

Staring at the flashing cursor on the first page of a new chapter, she checked her progress. Seventy-six double-spaced pages. Only 24 to go. Two dozen pages of thoughts strung together in artful prose. Twenty-four opportunities to further expose the personalities of her two main characters: London Greer and Anne Holmes.

This must be how her students felt when a term paper was due and they hadn't read the book or had procrastinated in doing their research. When they were up at midnight, the night before the paper was due, Googling for Cliff's Notes of the book so they could fake their way through an essay or finding the font that took up the most space on the page to meet their page count requirement. She'd had the deadline since she started writing the book. That wasn't new. She had the plot mostly plotted—also not the challenge.

The challenge was, much as she wanted to think about London and Anne and their relationship imploding when London moved from North Carolina to Oakland—a pivotal point in the story—all she could think about was kissing Jen in her guest bedroom before Angus's birthday party. Of moving things forward, a little more, to her actual bedroom. Of heated breath and roaming hands, and—she really needed to stop thinking about that.

"Just focus for an hour," Emily said to herself as she tucked her chair under the desk, a piping cup of decaf where it belonged, on the coaster to her left. "Then you can call her."

It was Friday night, and it sounded like direction for Angus. How many times had she told him, if he'd just focus on his schoolwork for an hour, he'd have freedom to call his girlfriend? To scroll his screens and play his Xbox and do whatever else it was he wanted to do besides the very thing he needed to do.

"Okay, London, let's see what you've got," Emily said as she silenced her cell phone and flipped its screen face down on the desk. She set Modest Mouse to play through her computer speakers—a nod to Jen's record collection—and zeroed in on the manuscript. London had just made the decision to uproot herself from her home in North Carolina and move to Oakland to be with Anne. They'd spent two years in a long-distance relationship, and they were at a stalemate. One of them had to move, otherwise, they'd never know if it was going to work.

As she typed, Emily found her rhythm. She found London's perspective. More than writing it, Emily felt it. The angst of walking away from your home—with your friends and family—to take a leap. To follow your heart knowing sometimes hearts are wrong. Much like a poker player throwing all their chips in the pot, London was going all in for Anne.

Which brought her back to Jen. And the impending pregnancy. "No," she told herself. "Back to the book." There would be time soon enough. Get the pages done. Then, call Jen.

# # #

The route through Dolores Park was well lit, and by then, the walk was on autopilot. His weekly journey out of the Mission to the Castro went past palm trees clumped together along the curved walking path, the grass vibrant green in the daylight hours, but more of an inky black in the evening.

He'd told Shellie he'd meet her at Brazen that night for a duet. Oh and, he had a surprise.

He'd worked up "I Love Rock 'n Roll." Initially resistant, he set his worries aside, and did as Charles said. He binged-watched Joan Jett videos on YouTube. Practiced stomping his feet in time with the drums. He'd already been working on the gravelly aspects of his voice, and this song favored it.

Walking through the park, leather jacket back in action, he hummed the melody and smiled. It was his last weekend in San Francisco. Five weeks prior, he wasn't so sure he'd made the right decision. He worried he'd thrown away a solid band and years of history for a chance at solo success, and that he'd put distance in his budding relationship with Liza for no good reason.

Maybe he had.

But maybe, San Francisco was just what he needed at just the right time. Maybe Julian DeMarco, with his stylists and symphonies and ideas about what would sell—was exactly the agent he needed. He'd undeniably grown. Changed. Evolved. And so much of that was due to Julian's boundary pushing.

As he walked, his confidence was high, as were his spirits. In a week, he'd have a demo in the can and would be sunning himself in Kona, watching Liza race the Ironman World Championships, and then—finally—home. To say it was something to look forward to was an understatement. Though he'd grown comfortable in San Francisco, he couldn't wait for the relief of home.

"Hey, Shel," Nathan said when he saw her.

"Hey, it's Nate Staples!" Shellie greeted. "Just who I wanted to see. I already added us to the list for the duet—but you'd better get your song in now."

"What's the rush?"

"I want to hear you sing, but I have a date tonight—I need to be out of here by ten."

"Oh! That's exciting, what's her name?" Nathan asked, and added, "Come with me to the bar and tell me more."

That bar had become a familiar setting for his weekend nights, its smooth concrete cool to the touch, the spilled beer and liquor intermingling to create a distinctively sour aroma. The people lingering were now familiar, too. They didn't share names or backstories, just knowing nods and friendly smiles.

As they waited to get Jason's attention—there were other bartenders, but only one existed for Nathan—Shellie told him about Naomi, her date. She was younger, Shellie whispered—a senior at Berkeley studying French literature. They'd met at a coffee shop on campus when Shellie played an open mic night. That was a month before, and they were seeing each other more often.

"She's a senior, huh?" Nathan smiled, knowingly. "Totally okay. You're only 25, anyway."

"Right," Shellie laughed. "Ten years ago!"

"And?"

"And?"

"Your eyes light up when you talk about her. But—what's the deal with starting a date at 10? Why didn't she just come to the bar?"

"Hey, you," Jason interjected before Shellie could answer. "Usual?"

"You know it," Nathan said, while silently willing his ears to remain white, along with the back of his neck. "And can you put me down for 'I Love Rock 'N Roll'?"

"Yes!" Shellie enthused, as she signaled Jason for one more gin and tonic with a single raised finger.

"Charles convinced me," Nathan said as a beer arrived in front of him. "But I still think we should record 'Goin' to California.'"

"I love it! We could always do both. So, about next week—" Shellie shifted the conversation to band matters. When they were recording, how long it might take, if she should take full days off work.

"Don't think I've forgotten," Nathan said as he answered her last question, the beer working its way through his veins, the looseness that comes along with a few sips now pulsing through his body. "Naomi. What's the deal?"

"Oh, nothing," Shellie shrugged.

"It seems like it's not nothing."

"Alright, it isn't. But it's just what it is. She lives with her boyfriend and can't get away until he goes to work on the night shift."

"Shellie!"

"I know." Shellie frowned the kind of frown that said she knew she was in over her head but was going to stay there anyway.

"Is she poly?"

"No."

"Non-monogamous?"

"Technically, no."

"Then, why the—Shel, is she not out?"

"Bingo!" Shellie said, touching her index finger to her nose, eyes closing for emphasis. Her eyeshadow was subtle against caramel skin, a light purple to match her tips.

With that admission, Shellie's shoulders relaxed in her suit. This week, it was navy blue with the faintest pinstripes. The pain in her coffee-colored eyes let loose, tears revealing that she wanted more from Naomi than Naomi could give. She batted her eyes and willed the tears to stay put, lest she smudge the mascara that lengthened her eyelashes.

"I'm so sorry. I didn't mean to hit a nerve," Nathan said as he hugged his friend tight. He understood wanting something from someone who couldn't give you whatever it was.

"It's okay. I just didn't want to admit the fucked up-ness of this to myself. There's something about you that makes me feel comfortable saying things I wouldn't say to anyone else."

"Aw, Shellie. I'm honored. Do you want to talk about it?"

"Probably," Shellie said. "After our song. Look—" Shellie pointed to the screen above the tiny stage and then dabbing the corners of her eyes. "We're next."

# # #

They hadn't rehearsed—together, at least. The plan for the evening was to sing "Shallow" from "A Star is Born," but they planned to flip the lyrics. Nathan would sing the female part; Shellie, the male. This swap was their statement that things aren't always what they seem, and gender roles—and rules—are meant to be broken.

Besides, the song was an accurate reflection of where they both were in their lives. Nate, about to embark on the next step of his journey— cutting a demo and later, a modest tour. Shellie, the same, with the added complication of an unavailable love interest with whom she was more than just a little interested.

As she sang the chorus, those pesky tears reappeared in the corner of her eyes. An annoying reminder of the fact that she was indeed, far from the shallow with Naomi. She willed them to wait and continued, her big voice bellowing through the tiny space.

"I'm sad to report," Shellie said as they finished the song to whistles and applause, "that this is Nate's last weekend in San Francisco. Just as fast as he showed up, he's off again. Whatd'ya say? Want to hear him rock one last time?"

"'Brick house!'" A man shouted. That guy again. "Play 'Brick House!'"

"Come on, Mark, we've been down this road," Shellie said, looking through the crowd to meet the regular's eyes. Every week, he stood near the stage and asked for the same song. She wondered why he didn't just sing it himself. "I'm not gonna sing 'Brick House,' nor is Nate. He has something special in store for you all, though. Nate, take it away!"

"Thanks Shel—but I think I'm cutting the line."

"Nope, I worked it out. You're next," Shellie insisted, took a bow, and jogged off the stage as the opening bars to "I Love Rock 'N Roll" played.

"Okay then," Nathan smiled to the crowd. "Here we go!"

On the stage, he was alone. But in his head, Charles was backing on drums. Shellie was supporting on vocals. And the stage wasn't in a modest bar in the Castro. It was in the middle of an auditorium. His mind's eye made it Madison Square Garden. He'd never been to New York, but in his head, he was headlining, and the seats were packed. People hopped in place and banged their heads and swayed to his punk rock side, which was in there. It just didn't make an appearance very often.

That was in his head.

Back in reality in San Francisco, he was met with—nothing. The regulars continued their conversations, sipping beers, clinking glasses. A few polite souls looked on, unsure if they should dance or sway or—? What should they do? He'd lost them. But how? Especially with that lead in from Shellie—they'd loved "Shallow." How had he had them and lost them in only a couple minutes? On autopilot, he finished, unsure if he'd even sung all the words.

"Alright, well, thank you all for providing me a home for the past month or so. I've really enjoyed singing here and meeting you. I'll see you next time I'm in town!" he said, trying to sound upbeat, while the imaginary balloon that represented his ego deflated with gusto.

What a way to end things.

"Hey." Jason placed a hand on his shoulder—a strong, soft hand.

"Hey," Nathan said, a Tito's Vodka sign buzzing with fluorescence behind him. It'd been a while since he'd flopped, and the feeling never got easier. The wall he was leaning on seemed to weigh 500 pounds—it was hard even to lean.

"So, you're leaving us, huh?" Jason took his place on the wall next to his customer.

"I am. Headed to Hawaii to watch Liza race and then home to Seattle. Where I belong."

"What are you talking about? You belong here!"

"I don't know—not after that send off," Nathan sulked. His head had been held so high earlier that evening, and now, there was a permanent bend in his neck. He considered the floor—polished concrete similar to the bar top, scuff marks from barstools being dragged across it. Random pairs of feet—belonging to random strangers—everywhere. A discarded gum wrapper was just next to his left foot.

"Oh, come on man. You've killed it since you got here! One off song? So what? They can't all be winners. Truth be told, I thought you were going to flop that first night. But you didn't. Don't be so hard on yourself."

"I guess."

"Come back tomorrow night—sing a different song—get a do-over. Go out on a high note. Okay?"

"Maybe," Nathan said. Maybe he should try to go out on a high note. But maybe, he should spend his time practicing for the demo session and finding a new cover. Joan Jett, he was not.

"If you won't do it for you, do it for me," Jason smiled, his eyes sincere, his hands holding a bar rag—a tool of the trade. "I'm going to miss you around here," he added, popping the rag against Nathan's arm playfully.

"Yeah?"

There was that heat again, but was it showing? His ears were on fire, and it took every ounce of restraint he had not to touch them to confirm that they were bright red.

"Yeah. I, for one, think Nate Staples is an incredible singer. And super sexy," Jason said, then turned, the bar rag swinging across his body as he walked away.

"What got into you?" Shellie asked when she re-appeared, fresh drink in hand. That had to be her third—maybe fourth of the night. She'd rolled the suit's sleeves up to her elbows, exposing a left arm loaded with thin silver bangle bracelets.

"Hm?"

"What the hell happened to you? You look like you just saw a ghost, white boy."

"Oh, nothing. Just thinking about what went wrong on stage. I wasn't expecting that."

"It happens. I wouldn't worry too much," Shellie shrugged.

"Yeah, but, that's not an encouraging reception to use the song as one of our covers, you know?"

"Maybe. Maybe you're not a punk? What about 'Shallow?' They loved that. It works for your voice—it's from this decade! And it co-stars—moi!"

"Moi?"

"It means, 'me.'"

"I know what it means! I just thought it was funny that you're slipping in French words—your French lit girlfriend is wearing off on you. Speaking of, what are you going to do about that?"

"Nothing. Go on our date, hopefully get her back to my place. Fool around a bit, and then—cut a demo album with you next week."

"Aw now, come on. Don't deflect!" Nathan stood straighter and turned to look directly at his friend, who he was quite certain was pushing the boundary beyond simply tipsy. Her speech was slowing, her words slurring ever-so. "Do you want a closeted girlfriend who also has a boyfriend? Is that okay with you?"

"Of course I don't, but you don't get it."

"What don't I get?" Nathan asked, tension rising in his shoulders. *You don't get it* was *his* phrase.

"My world is different than yours. You don't get it. You just don't—" Shellie trailed off. There were those tears again.

"You're right, I don't. I'll never understand your lived experiences, but I definitely get what it's like to be different in your community."

"How could you possibly?" Shellie pressed. "You're a white boy living in a white world with your hot girlfriend and your music agent and your new band. Maybe you're a little bi-curious, which got you here and maybe isn't so acceptable, but come on, man. You don't know what it's like. I haven't seen my family in ten years. Naomi doesn't want to lose access to hers."

As her words slurred together, he knew—this was dangerous territory. He didn't hide his story. He told people if they expressed interest in his life beyond singing, but it wasn't something he led with. He and Shellie were at the beginning of their relationship. They didn't know each other's history, but they had more in common than she knew—more than he knew until that moment.

"Shel, come here." Nathan hugged her tight for the second time that night and felt her tremble. If Nate Staples was his image, the suit and the voice and the tips were hers. Beneath the personality and the swagger was a hurting human being. He'd been in her shoes. No, that's not quite true. He was still in her shoes. Those letters from his family were looming. He thought about them daily but pushed those thoughts away. Because dealing with whatever those letters said meant dealing with the past. Dealing with a time period he'd long since abandoned.

"Hey," he whispered in her ear. "I'm so sorry about your family. I do get that one—I haven't seen mine since I was 16. I was too much for them, so they wrote me off. But I didn't let it stop me. You haven't either. So I'll ask you again. Is this what you want? Sneaking around and hiding and waiting for boyfriends to go to work?"

"No," Shellie whispered back. "I don't. But I really like her—so—"

"So, tell her if she's ready to be with you—only you—then you two can work it out. But if she's not ready, you understand, but can't participate. You know it's not fair to either of you. She's going to have to face reality eventually. She's young, Shel. Maybe she's just not ready. You deserve someone who can show up for you. You deserve someone who's ready."

"Damn, Nate Staples. Why couldn't you just ride off in the sunset on the bike that goes with this leather jacket and let me be?"

"Because," Nathan released her, arms holding her in front of him. "I think you're amazing and I want you to think that, too. There are other fish, Shel. You know it."

"I know. But what I don't get is why you haven't seen your family for 20-something years?"

"That's a story for when we're on the road, I think. And I think— you got one more in you?"

"I do, if you'll tell me the story tonight," Shellie laughed, draining the last of her drink, the ice clinking in the bottom of the glass as she tried to drain every drop.

"How about a compromise? Sing with me, and I'll think about it."

"Oh, what the hell? I don't have anywhere else to be." Shellie turned toward the bar to re-up on the karaoke list, and then back when it came to her. "We're singing what *I* want. 'All the Single Ladies.'"

If she wanted to sing Beyoncé, he'd sing Beyoncé. He'd back her up, instead of the other way around. And he'd come back the next night, as Jason suggested, to redeem himself. One last chance to go out swinging. It had nothing to do with seeing the bartender one last time. Really.

TWENTY-FOUR

Meanwhile, back at the ranch, Kate Conrad was actually on a ranch. But not just any ranch—her ranch. Now that all the planning was done, the prioritizing and packing, the goodbye tour of greater Seattle in the books, she was the proud owner of Second Chance Ranch.

Which reminded her, she needed to find a metalsmith to make a new sign for the entry gate.

As the sun rose in the Montana sky, yellow giving way to orange and pink, and then light blue, Kate sat on a rocking chair on her back porch, coffee in hand, dogs at her feet. She rocked and sipped. Sipped and rocked. And listened. It was eerily quiet, save for the tsh-tsh the rocker made as it glided over the knotty pine planks of the back deck. No car engines, as she'd become accustomed to in Greenlake. No whir of activity. Nothing in her field of vision except a field, and the Gallatin mountains in the distance, punching their way into the sky with authority. Instead of her and a city full of people, it was just her and her thoughts, and attentive dogs who would like their breakfast, thankyouverymuch.

"Not yet, boys," Kate said, closing her eyes to take it all in as she rocked. The air smelled of Ponderosa Pine mixed with a hint of horse manure, the woodsy aroma of the evergreens comforting as it balanced out the more *ahem* pungent smell coming from the barn. It reminded her of her days on the Pacific Crest Trail, when her only job was to wake up, eat, walk, eat, sleep, and repeat—while avoiding remnants horses had left behind on some of the more travelled sections. For six months, she zoned out of life outside the trail, and learned more from peat, trees, and wildlife than she expected. She learned how to disassemble her tent without missing a beat, pack a 45-lb bag in less than two minutes, and which foodstuffs were most palatable when you had to eat them on repeat. Learned how to maximize occasional access to running water and the generosity of other humans, as more than one trail angel had saved her days with coolers of cold drinks placed in just the right location, or homemade snacks at just the moment she couldn't eat another PowerBar.

She also learned perhaps the most important lesson of her life: She could do hard things.

Was tossing her life in Seattle in the bin and starting fresh in Montana going to be a hard thing? It was too soon to tell. That Saturday morning in early October, the air was crisp, and the sky woke up around her with a fiery display of her smallness in the scheme of the world. With 60 acres to call her own, she felt she'd made a move in the right direction. There was a calmness about her. A sense of peace rising through her being, starting at her feet and flowing all the way through her usually overactive mind.

This time, the only activity in her brain was enjoying the first morning in her new place, and reliving memories from the day before.

Her mom had been pleasant company for the 12-hour journey, even driving significant chunks of the way, proving what Kate said time and again: You can take the girl out of Tennessee, but not the Tennessee out of the girl. Southern hospitality was Glenda's way, and that meant doing one's share of the work—whatever the work may be. Kate wouldn't be surprised if her mom were up before her mucking horse stalls, even though she'd gone to bed exhausted. That's just the kind of person Glenda was: You do what needs to be done. Period.

"Mornin', darlin','" Glenda interrupted her trance. "Sleep okay?"

"I did. And you?"

"Oh, yes. Like a baby."

"Funny timing. I was just thinking how I was surprised you weren't up before dawn, mucking stalls."

"I thought about it," Glenda laughed, her head finding its way to the back of the rocker she'd chosen, terrycloth bathrobe tied in a tight knot around her waist. "But I'm getting too old for manual labor like that. Reminds me of when you took ridin' lessons and we made you learn how to clean stalls."

"I was pretty sure you did that on purpose," Kate said, draining the last of the contents of her mug. She hadn't found her box of mugs yet, and this one was less interesting than her collection, a plain white leave-behind from the previous owner.

"We did. We figured if you were dedicated enough to clean the stalls and groom the horse, you were dedicated enough to deserve lessons."

"Well, we know how that one turned out!"

"It wasn't a statement about you, Katie. All kids go through a pony phase. But there's more to horses than just the fun part. It's kinda like life. If you want to go far, you've gotta shovel some shit."

"Mom!"

"What? Can't I tell it like it is sometimes?"

"Of course, I just don't—" In that moment, Kate realized something. Her mom was *human*. She had a life and an identity beyond being "Kate's Mom," or "Bud's Wife." She had a perspective. "It was just funny, that's all. Maybe that could be the ranch tagline! Second Chance Ranch: Come Shovel Some Shit."

"Or maybe not." Glenda laughed at herself.

"What put you in such a good mood this morning?"

"Oh, nothin'. I'm just happy to be here with you, on this gorgeous property. I'm happy you're taking the time to have a little fun in your life, darlin'. You've always been such a hard worker. So driven. You deserve to slow down for a while and enjoy your life. And I'm just tickled you finally got your horses. What do you think, can we ride them today?"

"I'd love that," Kate said, "But I need more coffee first. Want some?"

With Glenda's coffee order taken—3 creams, 2 sugars, and can you microwave it for 30 seconds? And stir it vigorously?—Kate headed inside. This wasn't the start to ranch life she'd imagined. She'd envisioned waking up with Christine in her bed, three dogs at the foot, tails wagging in anticipation of what they'd do that day. Of packing a picnic and taking the horses on a jaunt to the pond, throwing down a wool blanket and sipping rosé while they watched the wind blow by. But even though reality didn't match her dream, it was a pretty damn good start. The boxes that movers had placed in every free section of floor could wait, the horse stalls, too. She knew Parker would come take care of the chores soon enough—he'd stayed on as the ranch hand when the property transferred ownership.

"What do you think, boys? Do you like it here?" Kate leaned against the tasteful granite counters of her new kitchen and looked down at her dogs, faithful by her side. Tails thumped the tile floor, and doggie grins emerged. The microwave beeped with Glenda's coffee, interrupting the spell they were trying to put on their mom to give them treats. Treats or no treats, they had no idea just how much they were going to like it there.

# # #

She'd let her dad know she'd be in Santa Barbara Sunday evening, packed a bag for herself and one for Sadie, buckled Meg's urn into the seatbelt of the passenger seat, and started driving. When Christine George left Seattle, the air was cool and the sun was just coming up. When she approached the outskirts of Roseburg, Oregon, it was pushing noon and bright sun beat down on the Jeep's hood, its cheery blue hue reflecting at her with a reminder: this was the start of a bittersweet trip.

Faced with miles of unchanging pavement, Christine glanced over her shoulder to check Sadie—she was snuggled in tight in her plush lambswool car seat, sleeping peacefully as they drove to parts unknown, little body rising and falling with each new breath. Did she have any idea how long they'd been in the car? Probably not. Sadie was always happy to be along for the ride, regardless of how long or where it took her. She'd be thrilled the next day, when they'd made it to Grandpa's house and she was chowing down on some of his homemade dog stew. Her dad swore by making his dogs their own food; said it was the only way to ensure they got the nutrients they needed. Since he'd retired from practicing medicine, he'd become obsessed with the health of his dogs. Would she be like that someday? When medicine was a past life and time was her oyster?

As she refocused on the road, Christine glimpsed the passenger seat, her former partner with her—in a different embodiment. They'd taken dozens of road trips over the years, to National Parks and beaches and deep into the woods where they couldn't be found. They'd collected souvenirs from tiny roadside stands and played music to pass the time. Sometimes, Meg would read to Christine as they drove—articles from magazines, excerpts from whatever novel she was reading, tourist brochures. How many books had she partially read via Meg's narration? How many stories where she didn't know the ending? Too many to count.

This was one story where she knew the ending.

"I never thought about what this would be like," she said, telling herself everyone talked aloud when they were alone, at least sometimes. "But you deserve a resting place in the sun."

The radio playing in the background was tuned to an '80s station that was still coming in from Eugene—staticky, but discernible—and an old favorite came on. "Forever Young." Not the Rod Stewart one. The Alphaville one, wherein golden faces turned to the sun, where some were like water, some like heat—some the melody, some the beat.

"I've always loved this song," Christine said, as she sang along to the part that got her every time, "So many adventures couldn't happen today; So many songs we forgot to play."

A check of the gas gauge said it was time to stop soon and refill— and decide where she'd stay for the night.

"Okay, Sade. How about we make it to Sacramento today? Huh? And go for a nice, long walk when we get there?"

Sadie didn't budge. But it was settled—she'd aim for Sacramento and push on to Santa Barbara the next morning.

# # #

She expected the test results any day now. She'd done all they'd asked of her—injected a never-ending cocktail of hormones into her body, taken a litany of tests, some more invasive than others, filled out forms (and filled out forms, and some more, for good measure). Jen Scott was on the precipice of receiving the news she'd worked toward for going on two years—was it safe to transfer the embryo that was waiting? Was her life about to change forever?

As she sat on her couch, Saturday leisure wear draping her body, hair pulled into a ponytail, Jen tried to focus. She gripped her e-reader in her right hand, but her phone sat at the ready, tucked under her thigh, set to vibrate any time a new email arrived. This vibration proved to be more than distracting when it came to reading the first 100 pages of Emily's new novel, but it was her compromise to herself. Focus on work, but don't zone out so much you miss something important. Enjoy as if she were reading a new novel on a Saturday morning—because she *was* reading a new novel on a Saturday morning.

Jen related to the narrator—London Greer—more than she imagined. The book was a fictional memoir, written from London's perspective, but it touched on so many aspects of looking for a mate in the context of being queer. So many books covered this topic—finding the one, falling in love, telling people—but so few books told it from the context of a queer woman who knows she wants a family. Who knows that to have a family, she has to both find "the one," *and* the one who's willing to do the work to create a family and live life out loud and proud—because two women having a child together meant not hiding in the shadows.

As she read, her phone would buzz, she'd check the mail—spam—and she'd go back to it. Emily's writing style had evolved since her debut novel. She was getting comfortable in her storytelling abilities—the evidence was spilled all over the page in the relatable way that the narrator understood London's perspective. There was depth to the story, to the protagonist character overall.

When the phone buzzed and pulled her back into its grip, Jen didn't look at email. She had something to tend to first.

Your book is INCREDIBLE! I sent it to Darian already for his review, so I'm sticking to my promise not to send notes, but I wanted you to know I love it. I can't wait to find out what happens next . . .

With the whoosh of a sent text, she popped into her email app. It was probably nothing, but she had to check. And as it did every time she saw an email from her doctor's office, her heart rate went through the roof—there sat the email she'd been waiting for. The subject line didn't offer any clues. "Your latest test results" wasn't encouraging or discouraging. Doctors and their neutrality.

She couldn't look alone. The contents of that email would direct the next nine months of her life—and potentially the rest of it. Though

Emily had been supportive and encouraging, it was too soon to drag her into that drama. Wasn't it? It was. There was only one person who really understood—who'd been with her throughout the entire journey.

With a vanilla-scented candle burning on the sideboard behind the couch, her mind racing and heart not far behind, Jen speed-dialed her sister. She tossed her glasses off to the side, sat a little taller on the couch, took a deep breath, and waited.

"Come on, Mags, answer it," she insisted. "Answer."

"Hey," came the breathless answer. "You okay?"

They'd been over it time and again, and yet, Maggie still did the thing she did every time Jen called—asked what was wrong.

"I'm good. Do you have a minute?" Jen wouldn't acknowledge her sister's habit—it wasn't going to change. And who cared? She had much more important things to discuss.

"Yeah," Maggie wheezed.

"Mags, are *you* okay? You sound totally out of breath."

"Oh, yeah. I've been on my spin bike. Gotta keep my date with Terrence. I call him Terry. We're like, virtual lovers, except by lovers, I mean he works my ass regularly and doesn't call me the next day."

"Don't say that to other people," Jen said. "Sounds like an abusive relationship! Listen, I need to share this moment with someone, and I need you to be supportive, no matter what, okay? No matter what I find out when I open this email, you're my supportive sister. Right?"

"Of course, you know I am. What's the email? Oh my God! The test results?"

"Yeah," Jen nodded, though Maggie couldn't see her.

"Well then, what the hell are you waiting for? Open that thing!"

"Okay, I'm doing it." Jen expelled every ounce of air from her lungs as she clicked the message open.

"That was a big sigh!"

"Well, this is a big deal! Okay, here goes. Dear Ms. Scott, blah, blah, blah, after reviewing the results of your most recent testing protocol, I am confident you are ready to move on to the next step of the process. You can safely schedule your embryo transfer. Please call our office to set up a time that coordinates with the appropriate day of your cycle."

"Holy shit!" Maggie screamed.

"Holy shit!!" Jen echoed. "I can't—"

"You're going to be a mom!"

"Let's not get ahead of ourselves. It still has to work, but yeah! I'm one step closer!"

"I'm going to be an aunt," Maggie continued, ignoring the disclaimer. Ever the optimist, Maggie jumped straight from embryo transfer to newborn.

"You're going to be an aunt!" *What the hell*, Jen thought—just run with it. This was exciting progress.

"My sister, the mama. I'm so excited for you, doll."

If her heart rate had been high before the message, it was redlining now. So many things to do. So much to know. She was pacing the room, running down all the things she didn't have, didn't know, or hadn't done. Like a car seat—should she go get one? She hadn't finished decorating the baby's room, though Emily had helped her paint it, at least. Did she need to buy a new car? She might need to buy a new car. One with automatic braking and side-impact airbags, and—

"Jen? You still there?"

There was that huge exhale again. "Yeah. I got a little carried away in my mind. I have a lot of things to do. To get ready. Holy. Crap. This is happening!"

"Okay, let's take a breath. You have time. Why don't you schedule the appointment first, and then we can work on all the rest? I'll be right here with you. Promise."

"That's exactly what I needed you to say. Thanks, Mags."

"Of course. Now, get your ass on the phone and schedule this thing!"

When she hung up with her sister, she did as she was told—scheduled the transfer. As it turned out, the right time in her cycle was in two weeks.

She needed to see Emily.

Soon.

TWENTY-FIVE

From the side of a blistering hot two-lane highway in

Kona, Nathan Stapleton stood amongst a crowd of thousands, and looked for her. They were all there for the same reason: to find their person and cheer them on. To encourage their loved one to keep pedaling. It was impossible to find someone in the chaos of a mass-swim start, so he'd skipped it and positioned himself a mile into the bike course. There, he watched for that signature smile and hang-ten sign as she blew by him on her bike in pursuit of her dream. The field of bikers was huge, and they all seemed to be on red Specialized triathlon bikes, heads down, bodies folded as small as possible to minimize drag. When wearing a helmet, sunglasses, and skin-tight spandex, they all looked the same—and they all whirred by in a split second. It was futile—Liza could be any of the blurs whizzing past him—but he kept looking while redirecting his mind as it wandered off to the topic of *his* dream. This was Liza's moment, and his job was to be there for her with a cheer and encouragement. To be a source of energy to help propel her across what he knew was the hardest racecourse she'd ever faced.

As the early morning sun warmed his exposed skin—no reason for leather jackets or plaid button-ups here—it burned him up from the inside, its energy radiating beyond basic heat and moving into much deeper territory. The sun was a catalyst for the real burning issue, and it took a substantial amount of effort to push those thoughts down. He'd already thought about it plenty. Rehearsed what he'd say. How he'd say it. He'd wait until *after* the race. After she'd given her all.

It wasn't fair to blow up her world before such an important event.

His head buzzed with the clatter of cowbells and cheers of "You Got This!" and "Not much more!" (Who were they kidding? There were over 100 miles of biking left to go at that point.) Amidst a crowd of parents and spouses and siblings, alongside children and best friends, Nathan stood, the distinct aroma of Coppertone creating a coconut-infused ambiance. As the parade of strangers blew by, he cheered. He didn't have a sign or cowbell. Just his voice and hands, which he was quite sure would be blistered from clapping by the end of that day.

Hawaii looked like Google told him it would—cornflower blue sky meeting the azure sea. Vibrant greens and golds and pinks and oranges dotted the landscape of the parts of Kona he'd seen, a lush reminder that he wasn't in San Francisco anymore, the often grey of the city already in his memory. He'd chosen to stand close to the start, because Google also told him the race quickly turned into a barren wasteland of lava rock and not much else—he wondered how people willed themselves to bike for hours in those conditions. Maybe it was like performing in the heat—you ran on adrenaline and feedback. Maybe the feedback of the road under two wheels and seeing progress on the bike computer was like getting feedback from a cheering crowd.

The week before had plenty of time to replay itself as he stood, from getting to know Shellie on a deeper level to recording the demo to running into Jason on the street the night before he left. What were the odds? He was walking home late in the evening from finishing recording. Charles was going barhopping, but Nathan had an early flight out of SFO and needed to pack and come down from the fact that he'd just recorded a record. A three-song record, but a record, nonetheless.

Looking at his feet, he walked, replaying the tracks they'd recorded. They'd decided on "Shallow" as the cover. But was it good enough? Was anything ever good enough? Just as he'd promised himself to let it go and see what happened, just as he'd decided he'd given his best, and there was no shame in that, a hand tapped his shoulder.

He was standing at a stoplight, dutifully waiting for the walk sign—a rule follower to the core—when it happened. It was a light tap at first. Then, more determined. When he turned to tell whoever it was to leave him alone, his jaw dropped.

Jason, the bartender from Brazen, was almost unrecognizable in a pair of loose jeans and T-shirt, the ballcap on his normally coifed head embroidered with the SF logo of the city's baseball team. On the street, he was any other guy out for a walk. So different from his bar persona. So different from the hunk with the abs and bowtie.

But his eyes were the same: Gentle. And deep. The color of worn leather, with faint laugh lines that peeked out when he smiled.

After the shock of the impromptu run-in wore off and they'd bro-hugged—loose embrace, double hand tap on the back—Jason said they should go for a drink. Not as bartender/customer—as friends. He'd said he owed Nathan a going away drink; that he'd miss him and wanted to wish him well.

"That'd be great," Nathan agreed. After a full day of recording, of cutting and re-cutting the same songs, company would be a nice opportunity to get out of his head, he told himself.

In a tiny bar on Valencia Street, they tucked into a booth in the back, "Dust in the Wind" playing on the sound system, Jason's lips moving to the lyrics with no sound coming out as he looked a menu. He didn't need a bar menu—he was a walking bar menu—but he read it anyway.

Nathan found it adorable.

What happened next was unavoidable. And unforgettable. As much as he tried, the memory of that night in the bar was on a repeat loop in his head, so much so that his eyes sometimes lost focus as the highlight reel played deep in the recesses of his brain.

Now, back in real life, Nathan was in a sea of commotion, trying to find his girlfriend—and the man he was before. Before he'd agreed to drinks, before he'd stayed out way too late telling stories and laughing with someone he'd known for a mere minute in the scheme of his life.

But the thing was, that mere minute was—incredible.

Kona didn't care that he had a secret. The people around him didn't either. But Liza would.

# # #

Triathaliza.com—Your one stop source for tri gear reviews, news, and race reports

October 10
Posted by: Liza

Chasing the Dream—Ironman World Championships Race Report

This race report is twenty years in the making. Twenty long, sometimes exhilarating, sometimes devastating, always yearning, years.

Since the day I started racing triathlons, the Ironman World Championships has been on my racing bucket list. The gold standard of Ironman races, this jaunt in the water, along the shore, and through the lava fields of Kona has captured my imagination more than any other event. And it's eluded me. There were years I promised myself I'd quit racing—it's not healthy to be this obsessed, I told myself. It's not healthy to set yourself up for a goal that maybe you weren't meant to achieve, I thought. But just as fast as I'd swear off racing, something (or someone) would pull me back in. And this year, all that quitting and coming back—all the sacrifice and sweat—culminated in my first qualifying race at Ironman Coeur d'Alene.

The thing about Ironman is—no event is the same. No race is the same. No competitor field is the same. And, on any given day, even you're not the same.

Because of all the variables that come with racing three sports in one event, I learned long ago to plan for the worst and hope for the best.

I landed in Kona a few days before the race to get acclimated (as much as possible) to the heat and humidity. A Pacific Northwesterner, those are two weather patterns with which my body is not all that comfortable. Rain and grey, no problem. Sunshine and heat? Well, that might be a problem.

In the days leading up to the race, I practiced swimming in Kailua Bay, re-assembled and took my bike on a couple of practice spins and did some run course reconnaissance. Anytime I ship my bike, I make sure to test it thoroughly to make sure nothing has malfunctioned in the process. On her flight to Hawaii, my precious Specialized (I call her Lolita) endured a few minor injuries, and I was glad to find this out ahead of time. Big thanks to the Ironman mechanics who made quick work of replacing my bar-end shifters!

Before I get into the race report, I want to thank everyone for reading, commenting, and sending me notes of encouragement leading up to the race. Your words inspired me and propelled me!

With that, let's get to the reason you're here—the rundown of what happened out there.

SWIM—2.4 miles—1:15:35

When the alarm went off at 3 a.m. Saturday morning, I popped out of bed with the energy of a kid on Christmas morning! I'd just reunited with my boyfriend the night before after six weeks apart, which was a boost in and of itself. Not wanting to wake him, I tiptoed around the hotel room getting everything together that I'd sat out already—nutrition, wardrobe changes, special needs bag—downed a carbalicious breakfast of a whole wheat bagel and banana and sat for a moment with my coffee on the patio. Our room looked out on Kailua Bay, and while I couldn't totally see it in the still dark of night, I could feel the energy coming from the Bay. I could feel the hopes and dreams of my fellow competitors radiating through the pitch-black sky that was dotted with the high-powered lights of the start area. The air was electric with energy, and I took a few calming breaths before kissing Nathan goodbye, grabbing all my gear, and heading to the start.

Once tattooed with my number—867—I donned the timing bracelet around my ankle, dropped off my special needs bag (extra nutrition and some caffeine infused gels), and went to check my bike. A flat tire was not on my goals list for the day.

I've never seen so many nervous smiles in a start area as I did yesterday. Swim-cap clad athletes of all ages bounced around for no real reason—it wasn't cold—and smiled at each other. The smile says a lot about a person's mindset. I'm quite sure mine said, "I can't believe I'm here!" Because seriously—I couldn't believe I was there.

I watched in appreciation as the pros started, their compact arrowhead shape moving through the Bay as a unit, and eventually, the amateur women in my age group were called to queue, the voice over the loudspeaker deep and demanding. It was time. This was really happening. Each step down the black staircase to the turquoise water brought me that much closer to my dream. I was in a tunnel of noise but found a pocket of quiet inside my head. From the front left of the pack, I reminded myself something important: The race isn't won in the swim, but it sure as hell can be lost there. In other words, pace yourself.

Don't ever give me advice. I'm telling you this now. Because if I don't listen to my own advice, odds are, I won't listen to yours! I took off like a rocket-powered jet engine in the swim, the crystal-clear water surrounding my body enveloping me completely, save for the tiny bit of my swim-capped head that skimmed the surface. The hundreds of arms and legs kicking around me created the washing machine effect I'm used to, but I panicked, and my body acted independently of my brain as it sped up to get clear of the melee.

Once I'd turned around the sailboat marking the halfway point, I felt myself losing momentum. Each stroke was a little more difficult. Each breath, a little more labored. I couldn't find a draft that was going the right speed. I'd catch a pair of feet and lose them, unable to hang on. But I'd been here before, and I knew it was a matter of one stroke at a time. Swimming is just one of those things—it's easy to get in your head because water eliminates most of the noise around you. So, I felt back on my fallback—count to ten, repeat. Count to ten, repeat. Sight off the shore, adjust.

BIKE—112 MILES—5:44:45

Biking is the sport I love to hate. I enjoy it, but there's a limit to my competitiveness on two wheels. Biking 112 miles in a respectable, fast-enough time has always been my nemesis. Biking in 90-degree heat across lava fields with no trees and no shade? As my mama's brother says in his thick Italian accent, "Dimenticarlo." Translation: Forget about it.

After transitioning from swimming to biking, I searched for my rhythm. The pace where I'm working, but it's sustainable. For those who may think Hawaii is flat— it's not. The full course gains almost 6,000 feet, so this is where I felt I'd find my advantage. It's hard for me to sustain the watts required to compete with larger athletes on the flats, but when the road points up, the advantage tips in my favor. The course is an out and back, so as I pedaled and took in the scenery—what started as lush beach backdrop with greens and blues and palm trees changed to sandy-colored cliffs turned to what can only be described as the surface of the moon. Or what I imagine the moon might look like. Mounds of black lava rock filled the horizon, random wisps of dead grass the only vegetation. The changing landscape aside, my main view for what seemed like forever was a solid line of bikers dutifully staying outside of the draft zone of the rider in front of them. I imagine we looked like ants marching towards an uncertain destiny.

Of course, our destiny was known: Get to the top of the Hawi climb, turn around, and try not to be blown over by the crosswinds on the way back to town. I'd already planned to speed up on the climb, and as I approached the most dreaded section of the course, I kicked it into high gear. My plan was to climb fast, get it over with, and recover on the descent.

And what do you know? It worked!

The back half of the bike course is less memorable since I focused so much on the climb to the turnaround. After doing the course in reverse, I rolled back into the transition area with a growing smile and only a tiny stomachache from all the sports gels and bars it took to get through the bike ride.

Run—26.2 miles—3:48:03

To say that running a marathon is ever easy would be an overstatement of the grandest extreme. Willing one's body to run 26.2 miles when it really would be happy with five or 10 is an accomplishment any day of the week. Running a marathon when you've already been on the limit for seven (or more) hours is what Ironman is all about. For me.

It's the point when there's a growing blister on your left big toe and the only thing to do is keep running.

It's the point when the salt on your skin flakes off each time you wipe your forehead, a visible reminder to drink more electrolytes.

It's the point when your stomach says, "I'm not feeling so great," but you keep feeding it anyway.

At all these points, it's so tempting to quit. During all these moments, your brain demands your body to just stop. It would be so easy to stop the pain. All you have to do is—stop.

But I've never been able to stop. Which I suppose, is the point of this entire race report. Not stopping got me here. And not stopping got me through a hellaciously hot marathon when all I wanted to do was stop. I could feel the heat of the pavement through the soles of my running shoes with each step, the pressure on my left toe increasing with each mile—that damn blister determined to take me out. I could taste the gels sitting in my stomach, and somehow, slammed more down. At that point in the day, no sugar in would mean no energy out. So, I ate more gels. And like Forrest Gump, I just kept running.

I heard the crowd lining the finisher's chute way before I saw it. That arched sign that had captivated me—the line in the sand that said, "You did it," was finally in my view, twenty years after I started envisioning it. The wall of sound from people cheering on the side of the road propelled me to the line, and when my left foot hit the line and stopped the timer, the tears flowed like a waterfall.

It feels good to finish. But more importantly, it feels better to not give up.

If you're aiming for Kona, and you're struggling to qualify, trust me—don't give up. And if you've qualified for next year and are looking for words of wisdom, my advice is the same—don't give up. Kona is a race unlike any other, and I feel honored to have risen to her high bar.

If you stuck with me this far, Mahalo!

I don't know what my future will bring. If I'll try for Kona again. If I'll hang up my racing flats and call it a career. Or, if I'll branch out to something entirely new. And maybe that's the beauty of this entire story: The future is unwritten.

Here's to the future!

—LB

TWENTY-SIX

They sent her dos and don'ts to prepare for the embryo transfer. For such a monumental-feeling procedure, this list was short: Don't wear cosmetics on the day of the transfer, drink enough water to have a 2/3 full bladder when you arrive, no drugs or alcohol, and try to relax.

Try to relax? Yeah, right.

Jen had so much nervous energy coursing through her veins you'd have thoughts she was a world-class soccer player on the eve of a championship match. Or a scientist on the verge of a cure.

Alas, she was neither. She was a middle-aged woman who wanted a child with so much conviction that she'd punished her body for two years. When she'd decided she wasn't going to meet the right person in time, when she'd decided it was up to her to make her motherhood dream happen, Jen was at peace. She'd powered through the pills and procedures. She made going to doctor's appointments her top priority. And now, she was a week out from the transfer. Relaxing—even if it was prescribed—wasn't an option.

And now, in the penultimate days before her life might forever change, she'd met someone with promise. Emily hadn't run for the hills when she shared her motherhood dream. In fact, she'd done quite the opposite—offered an ear. She wanted to hear about Jen's journey; she shared her own motherhood stories.

Readying for their theatre date that evening, Jen had a familiar flutter in her stomach: the butterflies were taking flight. They'd been taking things slowly, getting to know each other. Learning the others' triggers and turn-ons, backstories and future dreams. They knew enough now, didn't they?

The old Jen would've jumped into bed much earlier without a hesitation.

She wasn't the old Jen. Mother-in-waiting Jen wasn't so hasty.

But there was something there. The voice in her head skipped over whispering, or even talking at a reasonable volume. The voice shouted, "it's time."

# # #

The feedback on her manuscript had been (mostly) positive—from both the editor and Jen. They'd both told her to keep going—keep channeling London's experience.

"What happens when they break up that draws them back together?" her editor, Darian, had asked. "What's compelling enough that can keep them together after it doesn't work the first time?" he wondered, while providing suggestions for tightening up some of the early pages to leave room for expanding the story around conflict.

"I'm loving the backstory," Jen had said. "And I can't wait to see what happens when you throw in a family."

That last comment was apropos, Emily thought as she walked up the steps to Jen's house, noting that life and literature were colliding before her eyes. "What *does* happen when you throw in a family?"

Jen told her the news already—she was going in for the embryo transfer in a week. And that information made everything really *real*. Saying you want a baby is one thing. Preparing to have a baby is another. But going in to transfer the embryo?

That shit is real.

With a head full of questions and a heart falling hard, Emily rang the doorbell. She'd worn a high waisted pantsuit for their theatre date—with pockets in the pants, a place for her hands—and had left her wavy brown hair natural, resting just on her shoulders. On a section of Jen's front stoop where others had stood before her, its worn floorboards creaking as she shifted, her mind ran away with possibilities. If they stayed together, would Jen and the baby move to her house in Greenlake? She didn't know. Could she raise another child in the house where she'd raised Angus? Again, who knew?

All she knew—all she understood—was that time with this woman was better than time away from her. That she made Emily laugh, and her penchant for books and interest in fashion were so in line with Emily's own interests it made everything *easy*. There wasn't friction—there wasn't walking on eggshells to avoid saying the wrong thing. She could be herself. How refreshing. She smiled when she remembered her hesitance to swipe on Jen's profile because she was Kate's ex, worried it couldn't work with shared history. She worried their working relationship would impact any chance at a romantic relationship. As it turned out, Kate hadn't been a part of the equation since that very first worry. And Jen had done as she said she would—put the editing and developmental feedback where it belonged—with the editor.

"Hey!" Jen greeted with a smile as she pushed open the storm door that covered her wooden front door. "Sorry about that—I was in the basement in numbers land. Lost track of time. Come in!"

She looked radiant that evening—she'd donned a fitted black dress with cap sleeves, and her straw-blonde hair was pulled back in a loose updo. She'd skipped the glasses—her trademark—but something else was different, too. Maybe it was hopefulness? Maybe relief?

"I want to show you something!" Jen enthused, pulling Emily by the hand to the bedroom they'd painted not long before. She'd decorated the room with a white crib that popped against the celadon walls, added a matching bright white dresser, and hung a few prints of zoo animals.

"It's adorable!" Emily said.

"It is! But look closer. At the prints."

"You didn't!"

"I couldn't resist. It'll be our little inside joke."

Among the zebras and hippos and giraffes, hung as if it belonged, was a print of an artist's interpretation of an alien, little antennae bouncing playfully on the top of its head.

"I love it," Emily said. "I feel honored to be included in the decorations. Angus doesn't want my decorating advice anymore. His idea of art is posters of basketball players and Ferraris."

"Oh, have I not shown you the art in my bedroom? Angus would love it!"

"You haven't—yet." Emily winked, and then beat herself up for a lame attempt to be suggestive.

"Oh, I will. Soon. But there's something I want to ask you first—" Jen said, leaning against the door frame, left leg crossing over right at the ankle.

"Okay?"

"It's about the transfer. I wondered if you'd come with me. To the appointment? I mean, I don't know how much there will be for you to do, I just thought—"

"Hey—" Emily stepped away from the alien art and toward Jen in the doorway, "you don't have to explain. I'd love to. Absolutely."

Just as she had in her spare bedroom before Angus's party, Emily stole a kiss that took her own breath away. She backed Jen into the door frame, took her face in her hands, and reassured her—it was going to be alright. She wasn't going anywhere.

"I have a wonderment, too," Emily said when they parted. "Can you show me this art in your room? I mean, I really don't care about basketball posters, but Ferraris—whew. Those get me going!"

"Oh, then you're going to really love this. I have so many Ferrari posters." Jen led the way to her room, which had no signs of posters. The bed was turned down and window blinds drawn. She'd lit some candles already, their warm cinnamon scent adding spice to the air.

"We're not going to make the show, huh?" Emily asked as she threw her blazer on an armchair in the corner.

"Most definitely not."

"It's okay. It's 'Cats,' I think I get the gist. It's cats doing cat things and singing about it. Sometimes I wonder about Eliott—I mean, was he high? Anyway, I have school tomorrow. Sunday night is a great night to just stay in and—"

"Em?"

"Hm?"

"Less talking. More kissing." Jen inched them toward the back of her room, where the bed she hadn't shared in ages waited, and made good on her request for more kissing.

As the moment they'd both thought about for so long arrived, and they landed in bed laughing, Emily realized this must be what *it* feels like. When you meet the person your body, mind, and soul feel at home with. When you've met your match.

# # #

When he'd told her, she stared at him. Like she didn't hear him at all. Like he hadn't said to her, "Liza, I love you. And, I have feelings for Jason." She looked in his steel blue eyes without emotion, and unlike Liza, didn't say anything at all.

"Babe, please—" Nathan begged. "Please, say something."

Finally, when they both had eyes full of tears and brows full of worry, she said one thing. "Okay."

They were on the beach in Kona, stretched out on lounge chairs, a pile of spent Corona bottles stacked on the ottoman between them. It was two days after her race, and the plan was to do nothing. No swimming, no biking, no running. Just hanging out in paradise and splurging on beer and poke. Waves crashed into the sandy shore, one after another, some gentle, some fierce. All, unrelenting. Which is how his secret felt inside of him. Each time Nathan redirected his thoughts, it snuck up on him and crashed, a mental reminder that he had to say something.

Maybe it was the beer. Maybe, the warm ocean air and tropical music playing at the resort behind them. Maybe the guy in the speedo who kept parading in front of him with abs that rivalled Jason's. Regardless of why, the moment arrived when he knew he had to come clean. So he did.

And all he got in response was a prolonged silence and then, "okay."

"So," Nathan searched, "obviously this impacts our relationship. I don't want it to, but it probably does."

"It does," she said, her eyes now fixed on the waves, blue sport sunglasses hiding how she felt, but the beer saying it all—the bottle that had been full just moments prior was empty. That was the thing about Coronas—the bottle was clear so you couldn't hide how much you'd drunk. "I love you, and I don't want to share you."

No discussion of open relationships. No, "maybe we could try a thruple." It wouldn't work for Liza—the sharing—and Nathan knew it. He also knew it was bad if she was slamming beers. "That's fair."

"And I also don't want to worry all the time. We've been down that road, and I know where it ends, for me. It's not pretty." By now, the tears were flowing, but she didn't look at him. Didn't remove the sunglasses and their imaginary shield. Probably because she couldn't.

"I know," he said. "And I couldn't live with myself for doing that to you. You deserve someone who can be with you 100%."

"So, what then? Are we breaking up?"

Wasn't that the hundred-thousand-dollar question? He'd wondered it himself. How would she take it? Would she want to stay together? Would she talk to him or just walk away? Now, he knew. "I guess so. I don't want to, so you know. But this isn't my decision alone. And I understand if it's too much for you—I'm so sorry, Liza. So, so sorry."

She waited a beat. And then another. Nathan shifted uncomfortably in his chair as Liza thought from behind the safety of her sunglasses. He couldn't see her eyes—didn't know what was coming next.

"Can I leave my stuff at your place for a while? Until I find somewhere to stay?" She'd asked, matter-of-fact.

And though he broke his own heart, he answered, matter-of-fact, "Of course."

As the waves rose and fell, so did Nathan's chest, his heart thumping as if he were performing, its pace faster than normal for someone lying in a beach chair. The sense of relief was enormous—he could breathe again. The sense of regret was even more so—he'd just lost the woman he'd wanted for as long as he could remember. Without fanfare. Without a fight. With a simple sentence, it was over.

Over what? A guy he barely knew? They hadn't slept together. They hadn't made promises or plans to see each other again. But there was something with Jason. It might catch fire like a cigarette thrown into a dry forest and burn up everything he thought he knew about himself. Or it might fizzle before it even sparked, causing him to throw away everything he'd told himself he'd always wanted—for nothing.

That was days prior, and his head played the scene on repeat: Telling her, wondering if it was a huge mistake, watching his elated girlfriend deflate in an instant. He'd ruined the afterglow of her race, their romantic relationship—and, probably, their friendship. With Liza's voice in his head, he sat cross-legged on the floor of his kitchen, the slate tiles cold on his butt, and stared at a pile of letters he should have opened years before. Until Liza found them, he'd stuff each new one in the drawer, slam it shut, and try to forget they were there. If he didn't care, he would've tossed them, each one a reminder of the family he didn't have trying to reach him.

But he'd saved them. Hell, he'd *moved* them. Several times.

On the flight back from Hawaii—a flight he hadn't intended to take alone, or so soon—he'd promised himself he'd open them. What could they possibly say that would hurt him now? His family hurt him so deeply already, there was nothing more they could say or do that would make it worse. Maybe, reading them would offer the closure he still needed. Or, maybe, there was an apology.

He'd stored them chronologically, but when Liza'd found them, they'd been shuffled. So, he dug through the pile until he located the first one—postmarked 21 years prior—tapped the contents to one side and ripped open the opposite edge with a swift motion.

At first, they were accusative. "Just come home and forget all this transsexual nonsense and we can go on like normal," an early letter signed by his mother said. "You're killing your mother with this," another, from his father reported.

As the years dragged on, the tone evolved. "Just wondering how you're doing. Love, Mom," read one birthday card. "Call if you want to talk," said a brief letter from his brother, Michael.

In the mid-2010s, the senders changed. What had been a mix of letters from both his parents, and occasionally, from his brother, became only letters from his father. The tone changed again, this time letting him know his mother wasn't well. She had ovarian cancer, but they were fighting it. The Stapletons were fighters, and she was entering chemo. She'd kick this thing, but she needed his prayers.

Years went by. His father's reports—which had intensified with the early diagnosis—waned. In one letter, he begged Nathan to put the grudge behind him and come home. The treatments weren't working—he needed to come home and say goodbye. He'd even addressed that one to Nathan Stapleton—not Natalie. He'd followed Nathan enough to realized he'd changed his name, bought a house, and who knows what else. And Nathan knew nothing of his family, outside of what he was learning through the letters. Over the years, friends had suggested he reach out to them. That he let bygones be, and make amends. "You only have one family," someone had said. "Yeah, and they abandoned me. When I was a kid," Nathan reiterated. It wasn't his amends to make. His anger ran deep, and his willingness to forget and forgive was nonexistent.

Had he made a mistake? They'd tried to reach him—and had apologized many times in print. The thing was, Nathan told himself, his hurt was too deep to patch with cards and letters. Too little, too late.

By the time he got to the last one—the one letting him know his mother died in the middle of the night just a few months prior—Nathan's head was between his knees and he sobbed like a little kid whose favorite dog had just died. Except, his mom had just died. No matter what she'd said to him, she was still his mother. She was still one-half of the reason he existed.

"Fucking cancer," he muttered, regretting the decision to read the letters. He'd told Liza no good would come of it when she'd asked why he hadn't read them, and this was validation of that assumption.

He needed to talk to someone. A few days before, that someone would've been Liza. But that wasn't an option. She was probably zooming around the Big Island of Hawaii on her bike cursing his name.

He wouldn't call Jason with this news—too much, too soon. His new bandmate Shellie would understand the most, but he wouldn't burden her with this amidst her own unfolding drama.

His fingers found the phone and he did something even he couldn't believe. When a husky voice on the other end answered on the third ring, there was only one thing to say. "Hi, Dad."

TWENTY-SEVEN

In the week-and-a-half she'd been in Montana, Kate had unpacked too many boxes to count, defended her reasons for putting things where she wanted against where her mother thought they should go, and leaned into a country life. She took the dogs on long afternoon walks without leashes and made hearty dinners. She relaxed on the back porch with a glass of wine and a fire in the fire pit each evening, her mom and dogs by her side. It was just as she'd hoped—except there was one thing missing. And that thing was a who. When she closed her eyes, Christine was there with her, and until that was true, she kept herself busy learning how to run the ranch.

Each day started with a ride around her property on Miles or Murphy, the geldings that came with the property. The third, Frank, only let the ranch hand ride him—she hadn't earned his trust yet. If she knew anything about horses, it was to not force a partnership that wasn't natural. Frank might come around; he might not. But the decision was entirely up to him.

From atop a horse, the world looked different, and yet, the same. The early morning sky was lazy as it awoke, its colors shape shifting as they turned a shade of blue so pure she didn't yet have a name for it. It went on forever, far beyond her ability to see, even with the horse-top advantage. The jagged mountains to her south were already wearing a shimmering layer of snow in mid-October, reminding her she wasn't in Seattle anymore. And the air was crisp and clean, no hint of smog, no lingering char from summer wildfires. She could *breathe* in that air.

Riding Murphy near the river early that Friday morning, her still-new leather cowboy boots lodged into the stirrups and with the reins in her left hand, Kate patted the dark brown fluff between his ears and thanked him for being such a good guide. When she pulled the reins to direct him, he obeyed, but mostly, she let him wander. He knew the ranch—where to find the best grass, the easiest route to water—so she let him lead. When the time came to head to the barn, she'd put her saddle away—a hand-me-down left by the previous owner that didn't quite fit—and give him a thorough brushing. There was comfort in this routine. Comfort in knowing there were things she needed to *do*, that someone depended on her. Sure, Parker would take care of them if she didn't—it was his job, after all—but she took pride in being hands on with the horses.

"You're a good friend, Murph," she said with another gentle pat to the top of his head, sure his reciprocal lean into her hand meant he thought she was a good friend, too. Young Kate wouldn't believe that she had not one, but three, horses to call her own. Funny how childhood dreams can sometimes happen in the most surprising ways.

"Hey, darlin'!" Glenda yelled from a rocking chair on the porch as Murphy trotted them back to the barn. "Your phone has been buzzing like crazy."

"Okay! Let me just get him settled and I'll come in," Kate yelled back, only just then realizing she'd left it behind that morning. Her phone was becoming less important as she detached from her old life. In the past, she'd look at the phone first thing in the morning and throughout the day when it summoned her with its demanding buzz. A month before, she wouldn't have dreamed of leaving the house without it stuffed in her back pocket. Now, mornings without screen time were natural. Her screen was the Big Sky just outside the door and her tweets came from birds singing in the trees that dotted the property.

Back in the house, a fresh pot of coffee dripped its way to completion thanks to Glenda. She could count on her mom for consistency—Glenda liked to read the paper and drink a pot of coffee every morning before wandering the land with her field guide, trying to identify native plants and flowers. Kate smiled and pulled out the pot, a few stray drops landing on the heating element with a hiss.

Kate's phone was face down on the kitchen island, and its screen came to life when she picked it up. She'd missed a call from Christine—awfully early for her, Kate thought. It was only 8 a.m. in Montana, and Seattle was an hour behind. There was a message from the local large animal vet confirming an appointment later that week to perform physicals on the horses. And a handful of texts from Liza, who was still in Hawaii and not sleeping—it was 4 a.m. in Kona. They'd been on marathon texts threads since Nathan told her he was attracted to a bartender he met in San Francisco. Most were circular, and most ended with Kate saying, "Just come to Montana," and Liza replying, "Maybe. I don't know."

When Christine told her about the forced leave of absence from the hospital, Kate expected her to head to Montana. It only made sense, she said. Leave it to Kate to lean on the logical.

"I want to give you some time with your mom, alone," Christine said. "And I need to go see my dad for a while."

"Okay, then when?" Kate pressed.

"I'm going to surprise you!" Christine said, her signature chuckle punctuating the thought. "But I will be there. Promise."

When they'd spoken the night before, as was their new routine—a nightly call replaced a goodnight kiss—she hadn't hinted about leaving Santa Barbara yet, but maybe that's what the call was about? Maybe she was on the way to Montana? Kate's heart hoped that's what it was about. Her mother was good company, but it wasn't the same.

The message only said to call her, and when Kate called, Christine's voicemail greeted her with instructions to leave a message.

"Tag, you're it. I love you," Kate said, adding sound effects to the message before disconnecting. "Who am I?" she asked herself aloud after she'd already hung up. Who was this person who made kissy noises into someone's voicemail and hoped with all their energy that the other person would do the same?

"You didn't hear that," she said to Dallas, who was sitting at her feet, thumping his black tail on the floor, big brown eyes begging her to take him out. "Okay, go get your brother and we can go play. Go!"

# # #

She hugged her dad and stepmom tightly before leaving late that morning, thanking them for their hospitality—and for the to-go box of homemade food for Sadie. "You've spoiled her!" Christine said as she hopped in the driver's side of her Jeep. "I'm never going to be as exciting."

"That's what grandparents do," Jim George said, his arm around his wife's shoulders, the smile on his face giving away his pride in winning over little Sadie. They'd spent the week going on walks on the beach and cuddling on the couch. He'd fed her his special dog stew with a spoon and she ate it up. Literally.

"I'll text you when I'm in San Diego. I love you both." Christine blew air kisses to her parents from behind the wheel, put the Jeep in reverse, and backed out of the drive with a purpose.

"Don't forget to check the tires!" Jim yelled after her when she was still in earshot. "We love you!"

"We are really lucky," Christine said to Sadie when she turned onto the residential street in front of her childhood home. "Your grandparents are incredible." Sadie couldn't agree more—her fluffy apricot tail wagged with great abandon as she watched from the back passenger side window, both paws propped on the door frame as her new favorite people faded out of sight. There went her gravy train.

The drive to San Diego was short in the trip's scheme, but not insignificant. She had almost four hours to prepare herself for the day she'd planned. With "Highway to the Danger Zone" blasting on repeat through the sound bar—one of Meg's favorites—she flew down I-5 South in search of peace.

When she rolled into the parking lot near the Torrey Pines Nature Preserve, Christine took a deep breath, turned to the passenger seat, and relaxed with the exhale. "You ready, babe?"

Meg didn't answer.

Christine let her legs slide to the ground from the driver's seat, a habit ingrained from years of leaving the SUV, her average height not quite enough to step down without a slide.

"Okay, Sade, let's get our picnic together and go to the beach!"

Sadie hopped out of the backseat when she heard the word *beach*, paws hitting the pavement with the softest thud. She only weighed 15 pounds—there wasn't a lot of impact.

With a backpack containing Meg's urn, a bottle of wine, one of water, Sadie's favorite dog biscuits, and two plastic cups, Christine tossed a floppy beach hat on her head, looped her pup into the leash tied around her waist and set off for Black's Beach. She'd timed her approach for low tide so they could take the most direct route down through the cliffs above the beach and pulled out her Tevas for the occasion.

Just stepping on the sandy trail took her back. Back to a time before grief. Before aloneness. Step after step, she and Sadie descended the trail between orange-brown cliffs, each distinct layer telling a story that happened long before humans, the roar of the ocean drawing them down, down, down, over loose rocks and firm ground, over rivulets of water and past tiny cacti tucked into the hill, until they ended up about a hundred yards from their destination: a secret cove.

The waves were active that day, and several surfers were out paddling, trying to catch and ride the perfect arch of saltwater under the light of a waning sun. She watched for a moment as a silhouette in a wetsuit paddled hard, hopped up on their board, took a brief ride, and fell back in again, completing the cycle. It must feel a bit like flying, Christine imagined.

When she'd watched enough, and with her dog on her heel, tongue out to take in the fresh air, she walked to the cove—their cove—and tossed out a blanket. "This looks good, huh Sade?"

Sadie didn't care. She was on the beach—her favorite thing, ever. Whatever her mom said was fine, as long as they didn't have to leave. She watched seagulls overhead and people running by and lunged for another small dog when it came too close.

The tartan blanket under them defined their space and added a layer of comfort, too. Meg had always brought a plaid blanket to Black's Beach. She never said why it had to be plaid; Christine never asked. With care, she pulled the urn out of the pack, placed it on the blanket, and asked Sadie to lie down.

With wine and water poured, they waited. The Farmer's Almanac told her sunset would be a half hour later. And they had until 9:15 before the tide rolled in. Plenty of time.

"Well, little girl, I know you never knew her, but your bonus mom was remarkable. We're here today to say goodbye, for good." She must've seemed a little off talking aloud to a dog, but she did it anyway, raising her red plastic cup to the sun as it dipped just below the horizon, her knees pulled tight to her chest to hold warmth. The blue sky inched its way towards lavender, its puffy cumulous clouds punctuation marks as the horizon became deep burnt orange with light yellow radiating through. "As the sun sets on this day, we say goodbye to one love and welcome a new one. Some lives are taken too soon, their work on earth left unfinished, but with immeasurable impact. I'll always love you, Meg, you can be sure of that. You opened my heart to what it means to love and be loved. And I know wherever you are, you're happy for me. I feel you saying it's time, and I thank you for honoring my needs, too. Knowing you, you're up there saying it's about damn time I figured this out. And it was the honor of my life, knowing you. Rest in peace, love."

Christine drank the Cabernet Sauvignon she'd packed in Meg's honor. This one had a fruity finish, not dry like so many cabs, and went well with the cheese and crackers she'd packed for the occasion. It wasn't a proper send off without their traditional picnic.

She and Sadie watched the sun set, donned headlamps, and hiked back out. She planned to take Meg on the boat the next day to complete their journey together. Just as the surfers had paddled, popped up, and balanced for a moment, only to fall back in the water, so goes life. Nothing's permanent. Everything has a time and place. Her time and place were becoming so clear: Her life had moved to Montana. She could get a job anywhere. Bozeman or Beaumont or Boca Raton. She didn't have to stay in Seattle, regardless of the suit.

The answer was so clear.

It had just taken her a while to understand the question.

# # #

"I think it's about time I head home, darlin'," Glenda Conrad announced from the foyer, her big black suitcase packed, heeling like an old bloodhound by her side, just waiting to be led. She'd acquired another as well—though smaller—and had filled it with mementos and gifts for her church friends. "I'm ready to see James and my grandbabies, and I think you're pretty well settled here. Not much more for me to do."

They hadn't talked about it, but this day was coming. Glenda bought a one-way ticket to Seattle to help with the move, saying she'd know when it was time to go home. Apparently, that time had arrived.

"Okay, Mom," Kate said, from the floor in her kitchen. She had the dishwasher pulled out from the counter and was kneeling next to it, troubleshooting a leak that had started the day before. "Are you going *now?*"

It sure looked like she was.

"Yes, ma'am. I'm on a 4:00 flight back to Knoxville. James says Tuesdays are a good day to fly, so I decided today is the day. I called a Lyft to pick me up." Glenda stood a little taller when she said, "Lyft," and straightened the navy-blue wool and suede overcoat she'd picked up at the Western Wear store. It would fit right in back home, she thought.

"Don't be silly! I'll drive you. Just give me 10 minutes to change and find the dogs and—" Kate was halfway to her bedroom, the bootcut jeans she'd been wearing for three days of ranch duties not appropriate for an airport run. She needed a fresh pair, a clean shirt, and probably, a hat to cover up her disheveled hair.

"I know you can drive me, Katie. But you've done enough, and I'm highly capable of getting there myself. Besides, you need to stay here."

"Why? I've already run the horses and mucked the stalls. Parker has everything else under control. The dishwasher can wait."

"Because I said so, is why." Glenda insisted. "Remember, a mama knows."

"Okay, what's going on? *What* do you know?"

"Oh, nothin'." Glenda dismissed the notion with a wave of her hand. "I just think you need to stay here and get comfortable in your surroundings. I've had such a wonderful time, dear. And I really loved getting to know Christine. That one's a keeper, so don't you blow it, okay?"

"I'm not going to blow it." Kate wiped her hands on the front of her jeans as she walked closer, the feeling of accomplishment from working with her hands—and not on a keyboard—filling her up. How did she ever sit at a desk all day?

"Good. You'd better not. Anyway, bring her home for Christmas, you promise?" Glenda hugged her daughter tight one last time, "I love you, Katie. Be good and enjoy your new life. You've earned it."

Why did it feel like she was saying goodbye forever?

Just then, a car horn sounded in the drive, it's clipped beep-beep the only loud noise they'd heard in days.

"It sounds like your driver's here. Let me at least take your bags out." Kate dragged Glenda's luggage onto the front porch, eyes cast down to channel her energy on the task and wondered, as she often did when the situation involved her mom's suitcases, *what the hell does she have in these?*

When she looked up, she didn't believe her eyes. In the driveway, right next to the new truck, was a dark blue Jeep. And out of that Jeep's window hung a fluffy apricot dog's head, tongue out and nose working overtime to take in the fresh air.

"Mom, is Christine your Lyft driver?" she asked over her shoulder, disbelief clouding her head. With dirt splattered jeans and blonde hair a mess, Kate stood and stared. Was it really her? Or some doppelgänger who picked up fares with their Sadie lookalike in tow?

"I decided a career change might be in order." Christine slid to the driveway, gravel crunching underfoot as she landed. She'd pushed her sunglasses into her hair, and her golden eyes said everything her words didn't—she was home. She'd pulled off a huge surprise, thanks to Glenda.

"And you knew?" Kate turned to her mom, who was now sitting in the front porch swing, sliding back and forth, a smile spread across her face.

"Mamas always know, darlin'."

"And you didn't tell me!" Kate turned back to look at Christine, who'd been a million miles away the day before and was now mere inches in front of her. "How? You didn't—I don't—"

"I promised I'd show up." Christine smiled before adding, "Are you going to kiss me, or what?"

"I most definitely am," Kate batted back the tears forming in her eyes as she pulled her love into her body, into an embrace so deep you'd think they'd been separated for two years, not two weeks. "God, I've missed you. I wasn't sure you wanted to come! If you'd have told me, I would've been presentable—"

"What are you talking about! You look great—like you work on a ranch. Anyway, I'm here now. And I'm not going anywhere. Except to drive your mom to the airport."

"What do you mean you're not going anywhere?"

"I mean, I'm not going anywhere. I want to be with you, and you're here. So, I'm here, too." Christine walked back to her Jeep, motioning with her hand for Kate to follow. That was big news. And she'd downplayed it.

"Are you saying you're *moving* here? You want to live with me? Here?" The engineer needed specifics.

"I am. Unless you don't want that?" Christine shut the passenger door, Sadie at Kate's leg in an instant.

"I want it! I'm stunned, but yes, I absolutely want you to stay." Kate petted Sadie, whose tail was flapping so hard it looked like she might take flight. It seemed Sadie missed her, too.

"Then, I'm staying. I have some things to take care of, but I realized I don't want a long-distance relationship, Kate. I love you and I want our life together to be *together*. There's no reason I need to be in Seattle. I can get a job anywhere. Probably. But there's a big reason I need to be in Montana—you. I had an aha moment and after that, I knew what I had to do. I'm sorry I didn't talk to you about it, I just—"

"Wow. Don't apologize," Kate said, breathless, her right hand finding her disheveled head of hair. How she wished she'd had time for that shower. "That's incredible. I'm shocked! And so happy!"

"Me, too!" Glenda said from the porch. "I love a good happy ending. Now you girls better get me to the airport so you can have this place to yourself."

"She knew?" Kate asked again before acknowledging her mom.

"Helped me plan the surprise."

# # #

Sunset that evening was her favorite. Not that it was particularly colorful or long-lasting. In fact, Kate couldn't even tell you when it went down. Her days on the ranch had revolved around sunrise and sunset since the moment she'd arrived—the daily bookends around her chores that reminded her life renewed itself each time the sun shone in the big Montana sky. That day, the sun set over new love, leaving a glow of optimism and the hope for tomorrow.

In the space between sunset and darkness, that place where you can still see figures and shapes, but it's getting harder and harder, they rocked. From the back porch, they watched as tall grass blew in the distance. As birds tucked into hidden nests for the evening. Pale-yellow light poured out of the barn, indicating Parker was still there, doing his final rounds for the day. At their feet, Dallas and Hunter were splayed across the deck, their eyes shut tight, and Sadie sat curled in her Mom's lap, a tiny snore escaping her snout now and then.

"I can't believe you pulled that off," Kate said, the red wine she'd been drinking near finished. She'd dreamed of this moment. Of ending the day on the porch with the love of her life, enjoying a glass of wine and talking about everything and nothing. She'd thought it would come with the inevitable time limit of long-distance relationships. The hurried weekends and rushed catch ups, the goodbyes that came faster than hellos. This was the first of what she hoped were many more nights just like it. "I had no idea. And my mom isn't known for keeping secrets. So, whatever you told her, it worked!"

"She was a brilliant partner in crime." Christine closed her eyes to revel in the moment she'd planned for weeks. "This place is amazing. I get it. Why you loved it and couldn't pass it up."

"Yeah, it is, isn't it? Sixty acres of paradise. When I bought it, I thought I was throwing it all away. Saying to hell with the city and dating and work and running away to the mountains where I could find peace."

"And?"

"And you kissed me when I told you. That was something I'd hoped for and dreamed about and was sure was never going to happen. But then, it did, and it rocked my whole world. I almost backed out so many times—I felt like I needed to stay. To see where things go with us. I've been waiting for you for so long—before I even knew I was—and as soon as I decided to leave the city, you found me."

"I'm glad you didn't back out! This is how it was supposed to be. You and me. Rocking chairs. Dogs so worn out they can't be bothered to move. It's perfect."

"It is," Kate agreed, and took Christine's hand in her own. Together they rocked and watched. The deck boards creaked. Crickets buzzed with their nightly songs. Tomorrow was waiting, with its logistics and chores and figuring out how to start a life together. But for that moment, that still moment in the almost quiet of dusk, fingers entwined and hearts full of joy, *it was*—perfect.

EPILOGUE

She walked into the coffee shop just as she had for four weeks—with her biking shoes clacking against the concrete floor, eyes shielded by sport sunglasses, arms bathed in sweat. And as she had— every day since he'd left—she smiled at the cute barista behind the bar and ordered a black Americano. Only this time, she didn't have to order.

"The usual?" Serenity asked, dark hair twirled and pinned to the top of her head with a ballpoint pen, the tank top she was wearing revealing sun-kissed arms slightly darker than that of her face, her smooth honey complexion flawless.

"Please," Liza Barrett smiled back, hopeful the false image was working. Hopeful the cute islander with dimples in both cheeks and tattoo sleeve on her left arm saw an active triathlete locked in a routine. Not a heartbroken fool who'd trusted someone when he told her she was the only one for him.

When Nathan told her, shock ran through system. Like she'd just dunked herself in a bathtub full of ice water after a hard workout, the pain was almost too much to handle. When he'd told her, she didn't know what to say, what to do.

But just as she experienced in her training ice baths, eventually, you get used to the pain and go numb. When she heard him—when she understood what he was saying—she found the numbness and let him go. There was no use fighting it. What she'd worried might happen had happened, and whether that was a self-fulfilling prophecy or just what was always going to happen, she couldn't change it.

When her only other wedding client for the rest of the year called it off two days later, she decided there was no reason to rush home. Why leave the tropical paradise of Kona for the dark, grey days of Seattle in November? No one in their right mind would do that. She might not've been totally in her right mind, but she found a room for rent with a local, moved all her belongings—one suitcase and her bike—into a 14th floor condo with a shared bathroom and a view of a parking lot. It wasn't forever, she told herself. And where did she have to go if she went back to Seattle? Nowhere. She was faced with having to move—again—with no notice. Her friend Gray had offered his guest room and roommate status, and she'd probably take it.

But what was the hurry? There wasn't one. The life she thought she lived had been upended faster than a rogue nail at the wrong time causes a flat bike tire. One day, she was reuniting with her lover—her partner. The next, she was confused and alone, starting over in more ways than one.

"Here you are," Serenity announced when Liza's coffee was ready, steam rising off the crisp white mug. She was already steaming milk for the next drink, but Liza lingered. Sipped. Tried to make eye contact. Breathed in the smell of the beans and felt the warmth of the cup on her hand. She liked how Serenity's Americanos were hot—but not boiling— you could drink it from the moment it was ready.

"Mm. You make the best coffee, thanks," Liza said, while willing herself to say something—anything—that didn't have to do with coffee. Her stop at the Java Joint was some of the only socializing she got each day—aside from texting with Kate. She needed to make it count.

"Aw, shucks," Serenity looked up, briefly. Her body was all business—moving cups and packing espresso into the machine's filter handle—but her smile said more. Her smile opened the door.

"Who says, 'shucks'?" Liza leaned into the mahogany counter that protected the fancy espresso machine from customers. The sun streamed in from tall windows and hit floor at just the right angle—standing in that spot made it appear as if she was standing in the light of a stage spotlight.

"Who wears spandex every day?"

Liza leaned some more. This was becoming borderline stalker-y. Serenity probably fought off customer advances all day—who hadn't had a crush on a barista at some point? She needed something witty to say, or to move on. Two choices. Pick one. "Touché. Listen, I wondered—"

"I'd love to."

"You'd love to, what?"

"Whatever you're going to ask. I'd love to."

What the hell?

"I was going to ask if you'd like to go for a hike sometime, but if you're saying yes to *anything*—"

"I'm saying yes." Serenity placed a lid on a paper cup and set it on the pickup bar. "Flat white for Kaeo. Kaeo!"

"Okay, well, then. It's a date," Liza said. "Um—I guess I need to get your number, then? So we can find a time?"

"Give me your hand." Serenity pulled the pin from her hair and let her shoulder-length locks fall. She scribbled her number on the back of Liza's hand, twisted her hair back up, and shoved the pen where it had started with the ease and efficiency of pressing a fresh shot of coffee.

"Is this really your number?"

"I guess you're going to have to find out."

Liza had to give her credit—Serenity was an expert volleyer. She hadn't served up anything that Serenity hadn't spiked back down. It was intriguing. And hot.

"I guess I am," Liza smiled—her signature All-American, I got this smile—and with a wave, walked away. Her bike cleats click-clacked as she walked toward the door, the intensity waning as she got farther from the bar. The smile didn't fade.

WHAT HAPPENED?!

Things were going so well for Nathan and Liza! Until they weren't.

For a behind-the-scenes look at the breakup, download this short first-person account told from both Nathan and Liza's points of view. It's free and easy to download on BookFunnel:

https://tinyurl.com/znrb3sh4

For sneak previews at new work, including first access to the final book in this series, join my mailing list at https://akrosewrites.com/free-stories.

GRATITUDE

Thank you for reading! If you liked *Long Distance Relationships* (or even if you didn't), I'd appreciate a quick review on Amazon so I know what you want to read from me in the future. Your feedback helps other readers find my work.

Have something you want to say to me directly?

Email me at akrosewrites@outlook.com

Want sneak peeks of future work, a list of what I'm reading, and other A.K.-happenings?

Just visit https://akrosewrites.com and read all about it!

THE VILLAGE PEOPLE

Raising a child and writing a book are similar—or so I've been told. They both take a village, and my "children" are much better for having input from my village.

A million thanks to the patient and generous friends who gave their time, feedback, expertise, and love to this book:

Sarah, who lets me ramble on endlessly about people I've made up. You calm my inner critic, provide a uniquely *you* perspective, and remarkably, don't gloat when I do exactly what you suggest after initially dismissing it. I love you big.

Heidi, somehow, you don't tire of my "what would you think if" questions! You've guided me to the path more times than I can remember with such grace. Thank you for always being there—in life, and in book writing.

Ellyn, amidst your own deadlines, you find time to read for me, and that means the world. Thank you for mind-melding with me about writing and life!

Ally, what more can I say than **thank you?!** Your attention to detail is beyond compare and your input made this a better book.

Cat, Jody, Kim, Hannah, Dean, and Mateo, your work-in-progress feedback was invaluable and is so appreciated. You all provided unique and important perspectives that helped shaped the story and characters. Thank you for keeping me on the rails, especially when I dangled precariously on the precipice of a major derailment!

OTHER STORIES BY A.K. ROSE

Novels

Short Term Relationships

Novellas

Learning to Love Again

Learning to Love Again 2

Short Stories

Laura and Mel Series Box Set

ABOUT THE AUTHOR

A.K. Rose lives and writes in Seattle.

When she's not writing for pleasure, Angela is a ghostwriter and occasional marketing project manager. She's the proud mama to a micro-mini double doodle (say that again?!). Incidentally, they have the same haircut.

If you'd like access to story previews, freebies, and more, sign up for A.K.'s monthly newsletter at https://akrosewrites.com/free-stories.

Printed in Great Britain
by Amazon

73520990R00190